PRAISE FOR *SEE HER RUN*

"Journalist Peggy Townsend's superb debut delivers an intense character study . . . Townsend's sophisticated plotting and affinity for character development elevate *See Her Run*."

—Associated Press

"Townsend's debut is driven by brisk plotting with bursts of stylish prose. Her eye for sharp character details makes her one to watch."

—*Kirkus Reviews*

"*See Her Run* is fast-paced with many surprising twists that make this a page-turner. When you think you know who the killer is, this book will prove you wrong, building up the mystery and leaving you on the edge of your seat until everything comes crashing down at the conclusion. *See Her Run* is truly a novel you will not want to miss."

—*RT Book Reviews* (Top Pick)

"An award-winning journalist herself, Townsend has created a nuanced young protagonist . . . This could be the beginning of an intriguing series."

—*Booklist*

"Aloa Snow, the appealing heroine of Townsend's gripping first novel and series launch . . . investigate[s] the apparent suicide of twenty-five-year-old adventure runner Hayley Poole . . . Aloa's pursuit of the story of Hayley's death plunges her into a world of murder and corporate intrigue. Readers will look forward to seeing more of plucky Aloa."

—*Publishers Weekly*

"If you're looking for a sweet little whodunit that could have been cribbed from *Murder She Wrote*, one that won't bother you with disturbing mental images of death, violence, and the darkness that lurks in the recesses of the human soul, look elsewhere. This ain't that."

—*GoodTimes Santa Cruz*

"Snow is a multi-faceted and intriguing character . . . Kudos to the author for providing a fresh and interesting protagonist."

—*Mystery Playground*

"With a flawed but relatable heroine and many twists, this book will grab readers' attention."

—*The Parkersburg News and Sentinel*

THE
THIN
EDGE

THE THIN EDGE

AN ALOA SNOW MYSTERY

PEGGY TOWNSEND

THOMAS & MERCER

Published by Thomas & Mercer, Seattle

www.apub.com

Amazon, the Amazon logo, and Thomas & Mercer are trademarks of Amazon.com, Inc., or its affiliates.

ISBN-13: 9781503903234
ISBN-10: 1503903230

Cover design by Shasti O'Leary Soudant

Printed in the United States of America

THE
THIN
EDGE

PROLOGUE

Aloa Snow stood on the headlands and looked out over the Pacific. Below her, waves thundered against a jawline of ragged rocks. The sky was the color of lead.

She shrugged out of the thick denim jacket she wore and laid it carefully on the dirt. Next, she took off her boots and placed them on the ground. Beyond her feet, the cliff fell seventy feet into the sea. The wind was hard and out of the north.

Fly, whispered the voice in her head.

Her body seemed loose and unconnected, as if gravity had lost its hold on her, and she hesitated for only a heartbeat before pulling the note from her shirt pocket and tucking it into her left boot, where the breeze wouldn't snatch it away.

"This is the most honest thing I'll do," the note read.

Behind her, the driver who had brought her here, a former dentist from Calcutta, backed his car out of the parking spot and left.

Aloa straightened, swaying slightly.

Fly, the voice whispered again.

She walked the few steps to the cliff's edge. An image of her father, long dead, floated into her memory. The water rushed in and then fled outward, beckoning her to follow.

She inhaled a long breath, spread her arms wide, and leaned.

DAY 1

Aloa leaned into the curve, her 1971 Honda CB-350 motorcycle humming with speed. A fog had slipped over the hills, spreading over the landscape, and her helmet visor speckled with moisture. It had been a good day.

She'd awakened that morning, made herself a cup of strong coffee, and climbed aboard the old machine. The bike had been a gift from a trio of aging anarchists known to the denizens of San Francisco's North Beach as the Brain Farm.

The three—an old war photographer called P-Mac who'd left whatever innocence and hope he'd possessed in the jungles of Southeast Asia, an ex–Black Panther turned college professor nicknamed Doc, and a gray-haired former monkeywrencher christened Tick for his supposed expertise with anything that had a tendency to go boom—had discovered the abandoned bike near Pier 39 last August. It had taken the men four hours and two stops at local watering holes to push the broken machine to Doc's apartment, where they'd spent two weeks bringing the old motorbike back to life with an assortment of salvaged and questionably acquired parts.

They'd presented the bike to Aloa as a celebration of their belief in the nobility of freeganism, and also to mark her first step back into the world of journalism with a series she'd written about the tangled murder of a young runner. The stories had not only appeared on the website of a newsmagazine called Novo but had also spurred a US House committee hearing into what had led to the runner's death. The three had then taken Aloa to a deserted parking lot and, over the course of two nights, taught her how to ride. Aloa had been instantly enchanted by the feisty machine and today had been a test of her skills.

She'd stopped once to watch a pod of surfers work a small but clean swell and later found a tiny café in the town of Pescadero that featured a fine guitarist and an even finer barista. She'd ordered a cup of coffee and a chicken pesto sandwich, which she ate with near-ravenous hunger, something which, as a recovering anorexic, she never took for granted.

Now she was headed home.

Outside Pacifica, the fog pressed more thickly against the ground and she slowed as the pavement grew slick. She wiped her gloved hand across her visor to clear it, felt the tiniest loss of control, and quickly put her hand back on the grip. Besides the rush of speed, the thing she liked most about riding was the absolute concentration that was required. There was no room for daydreaming, no room for thoughts to crowd in. On a bike, you simply were.

She took the long way back to her neighborhood and parked, the vibration of the old Honda echoing in her thighs. It was early, just after five o'clock, but a chill ran through her body and she thought a glass of wine was called for. She hooked her helmet over her arm and pushed her way into what was arguably the least trendy nightspot in the city, a hole-in-the-wall bar in North Beach named Justus.

"Omigod, did Amy Winehouse and Alice Cooper have a baby and not tell anybody about it?" called the linebacker-size man behind the bar. "Look at your hair and what have I told you about waterproof mascara, hon?"

Aloa rolled her eyes and slid onto a cracked leather stool, clunking her helmet onto the bar. "Speaking of Winehouse, how about a glass of red?"

"Here, make yourself presentable," said the bartender, wetting a napkin and pressing it into Aloa's hand. He poured a generous glass of pinot noir and pushed it in her direction.

She scrubbed the black streaks from beneath her eyes. "Thanks, Erik," she said as a middle-aged couple, dressed in matching fleece jackets and khaki pants, opened the door, glanced at the scattering of North Beach regulars—scruffy artists, down-on-their-luck musicians, divorced fathers—and quickly fled back onto the sidewalk.

"Tourists," Erik muttered and shook his head. "Why do they go places if they want everything to be the same as where they came from?"

A former Hollywood costume designer, Erik had left the glittery life of LA for the Bay Area after members of an unnamed Colombian drug cartel had threatened his husband, a slender chef named Guillermo, or Gully, as his spouse called him. The couple had come to San Francisco, found the failing saloon on one of North Beach's alleys, and used their savings to buy the liquor license and the aging building. They lived in a two-bedroom apartment above the bar and rented out a trio of third-floor studios to a revolving cast of writers, painters, and suddenly single men and women. "It's a living, which is a helluva lot better than the alternative," Erik always said. He pulled a mug of beer and slid it down the bar to a bleary-eyed regular.

"Something to eat, hon?" he asked Aloa.

"I'm good," she said.

He lifted his eyebrows. He was one of the few who knew about her slide into anorexia in college and her stubborn determination to beat back the demons that had reared their ugly heads a few more times in her life.

"Really," Aloa assured him. "I had a sandwich an hour ago."

He waited.

"Scout's honor," she said and lifted two fingers.

Erik leaned toward a narrow opening to the kitchen. "Gully, bring our biker chick a cup of your soup. She doesn't think she wants it but I'm 99.9 percent sure she does."

The face of a man twelve years Erik's junior appeared in the opening. He had dark hair, a fine nose, and brown eyes that missed little.

"Chica," he cried. "What brings you so early to this throat of the forest?"

"Neck of the woods, sweetie," Erik said.

"Whatever you say, *mi amor.*" Gully smiled.

Just as with his ability to meld multiple cuisines into remarkable offerings, Gully's fusion of English and Spanish sometimes resulted in extraordinary turns of phrase.

He nodded his head toward Aloa. "You have been on your machine?"

"I rode down the coast," Aloa told Gully. "Kind of needed a head-clearing. Novo wants me to do another piece, but I'm not sure."

"Writing is like food. You must not hurry," Gully said solemnly.

"Give them the old Harper Lee, darling. Let 'em wait," Erik agreed.

A few minutes later, Aloa was digging into a steaming cup of what Gully called Asian cioppino—shrimp, mussels, and halibut in an amazing ginger-lime broth—when she sensed another body slide onto the stool beside her.

"House red, and keep it coming," growled the familiar voice.

Aloa turned to the gray-ponytailed anarchist next to her. "Hey, Tick," she said.

"Ink," said the old man, lifting a grizzled chin in her direction.

The Brain Farm bestowed nicknames on the few people they liked. Aloa's was Ink for what they claimed ran through her blood after years of newspapering.

"What's up?" Aloa asked. "You look terrible."

"This." Tick fished a folded newspaper clipping out of his jacket pocket and slapped it on the bar as Erik slid a glass of red wine in front of him.

Aloa took the last spoonful of the seafood soup and smoothed out the rectangle of newsprint.

WIFE OF FBI HERO MURDERED, the headline declared.

Aloa frowned. "What's this?"

"Just read," Tick said and took a long pull from his glass.

According to the article, the forty-nine-year-old wife of a former FBI interrogator was found stabbed to death in their Potrero Hill home four days ago.

The newspaper described the ex-FBI man, Christian Davenport, as a hero for his role in wringing a confession from a suspect in the kidnapping of a wealthy CEO's daughter.

According to the article, the multilingual, Stanford-educated Davenport had gone on to pull admissions from a money manager who had swindled millions of dollars from his elderly clients, and from a shadowy computer programmer who was trying to sell secrets to the Russians in exchange for two Rolexes and $10,000 in cash. Four years ago, Davenport had been in a car crash that had left him paralyzed from the shoulders down and he retired from the bureau. His wife, Corrine, had been his chief caregiver.

Davenport, the story reported, had heard a knock at the door, voices, then his wife cry out. Lying helpless in bed, he had shouted his wife's name until, exhausted, he'd fallen asleep. Around 7:00 a.m., his assistant had showed up for his morning shift, saw the body, and called 911.

The article said the mayor had pledged a full investigation and that the FBI had issued a statement praising the interrogator and offering condolences for his loss. A police spokesman was quoted as saying the investigation was progressing but gave no more details.

Aloa turned to Tick, who had already drained his first glass of wine. "Interesting," she said, "but why did you want me to read this?"

Tick pushed his empty glass toward Erik and lifted an index finger for a refill. "Because the cops think my kid did it."

DAY 2

The sidewalk was gray with drizzle as Aloa left her North Beach home. The house was a wooden shotgun structure built by her paternal grandmother, Maja, and was now sandwiched between two monstrosities erected by a pair of millionaires from San Francisco's bumper crop of tech tycoons. But her home's stunning view of the Bay Bridge and its proximity to the landscaped Vallejo Street steps more than made up for its shadowed existence, and Aloa never forgot to mumble a quiet thanks to the woman who had spent her days styling hair and applying makeup in the basement of a local mortuary in order to pay for the simple house. Today was no different.

Aloa locked the front door and strode down the steep hill, her Timberland boots slapping the sidewalk with a percussive beat. She'd dressed that morning in jeans and a dark sweater, running her fingers through her short black hair. Her blue eyes were outlined in dark liner, and she checked the four silver hoops that pierced the upper cartilage in her right ear. Before she'd left, she'd slipped into the fine leather jacket she'd bought when she was working and living in LA and pulled on a startlingly pink watch cap against the cold. The cap had been bestowed on her by the Brain Farm, who'd unearthed it from the library's lost-and-found bin and thought it would be perfect for her. It wasn't, but she appreciated the gesture, and on a day when a cold marine layer pushed down on the city and temperatures hovered in the low forties, she was glad to have it.

She'd awakened at eight that morning, made a pot of French press coffee, and sat down at her computer. She'd done a little research and read through a series of articles about the murder, including a longer piece in the *Los Angeles Times*, where she'd worked until an error in judgment had caused her disgrace and resignation two years before. The article described the house where the crime occurred, gave more background on the victim's husband, said San Francisco police were questioning "a person of interest" in the case, and that the investigation was proceeding with "all available resources." Aloa knew that meant somebody important was leaning on the chief of police, who in turn was leaning on the acting head of the Homicide Detail in the Major Crimes Unit, which meant Lt. Rick Quinn would not be in the best of moods when she went to see him this morning. Of course, there wasn't much that was cheerful about facing a desk full of violence and murder every day.

She'd met Quinn five months earlier while working on her story about the runner's death. Quinn was six feet one with studious hazel eyes and just enough muscle to let you know he worked out but wasn't a fanatic about it. He also was married, she reminded herself as she headed toward the alleyway next to Justus where Erik and Gully allowed her to store her bike. Not that she was looking for a relationship at the moment. Chastity was just fine.

The CB-350 was cranky, a reaction to the wet and cold, but it finally started, the now-familiar rumble of its engine giving her the kind of happiness she couldn't explain to anybody who didn't own a motorcycle. She removed the plastic cover that protected the seat, stuffed the pink beanie into her leather daypack, slipped on her helmet—she liked the anonymity of the headgear—and took off.

Traffic was heavy and she threaded her way around cars and delivery trucks, admiring the palm trees that lined the Embarcadero and inhaling the scent of the ocean before turning inland toward Quinn's office. The ride, combined with a mission to figure out what was going on with

Tick's son, heightened her mood. She missed her days at the newspaper when her work made a difference, when she could right a wrong with a two-thousand-word story on the front page. She didn't know if Tick's son had been falsely accused or if he was guilty, but at least she could use her skills to help a friend. She parked the bike outside the Hall of Justice, removed her helmet, and spiked cold fingers through her hair. It would have to do.

Aloa gave her name to the receptionist, asked for Quinn, and proceeded to scan the press releases on the waiting room counter, including one about the arrest of a burglar who'd left his wallet and ID at the crime scene. Some crooks were so dumb it almost hurt to read about them. Finally, Quinn stuck his head through an open door and motioned her to follow him inside.

As Aloa trailed Quinn to his office, heads popped up from the tight warren of desks that was the department's homicide detail, then turned back to their work. The smell of burned coffee perfumed the air.

"It's been a while," Quinn said, settling behind his government-issue steel-and-fake-wood desk and gesturing Aloa toward a hard chair in front of it.

His desk was cluttered with folders, tilting stacks of paper, and a softball trophy with the head of a Ken doll mounted where the face of the player should have been. A photo of Quinn and his wife—which Aloa had noticed the first time she met the detective—was now missing, although a wedding ring still encircled his finger. A decorating decision or something more? She pushed the thought from her head and sat.

"I've been a little busy," Aloa said.

"So I've seen," he said. "Nice work on the series, by the way."

"Thanks. The scotch was good too."

Aloa had come home on the day her series about the runner's death had launched to find a bottle of Glenlivet and Quinn's business card on her porch.

Quinn shrugged.

"And nice job on that honeymoon murder," Aloa said.

The shooting deaths of a young couple on their honeymoon five weeks earlier had shaken the city—until detectives under Quinn's supervision discovered the killer was the bride's ex-boyfriend, who had followed the couple from their home in Modesto and gunned them down as they settled in for brunch on the first morning of their married life.

"Just doing my job," Quinn said.

"And the evidence is good?"

"We think so." Quinn leaned back in his chair, which gave a loud squeak. "But I'm guessing you didn't come here just to tell me how great I am."

Aloa smiled. "And everybody says what a lousy detective you are."

He shook his head. "So what's up?" he asked.

"I was wondering what you can tell me about the death of Corrine Davenport, the FBI interrogator's wife. One of your guys caught the case, right?"

Quinn gave a slight nod.

"The *Times* said you have a person of interest."

"So?"

"So I'm doing a little digging. To see if there's something there."

"Nothing's been released," Quinn said.

"I heard the guy you're talking to teaches poetry at a junior college," Aloa countered. Tick had given her the information about his son yesterday.

"Maybe," Quinn said.

"Is there any connection to the husband? Cases he worked on?"

"Not that we could find."

"And what about the Facebook guy?"

Quinn frowned.

"The one your victim blocked six weeks ago. The guy who was threatening her? I found it this morning while I was doing a little research on her."

Quinn leaned forward, his chair protesting with a high squeal.

"Apparently, he'd read a poem of hers in some magazine and decided she was a man-hater," Aloa said. "The comments were pretty nasty."

Quinn reached for a folder in front of him and flipped quickly through the pages.

"His name is Jeremy Green," Aloa said. "He lives an hour's drive from here."

After finding the ugly remarks, she'd traced them to an artist who'd started a group called Men4Meny, which asserted that men's rights were being stolen from them by a culture that gave women too much power. "He's got at least two restraining orders against him."

"Shit. How'd we—" Quinn began.

"You're welcome," Aloa said. "Now will you let me see the report?"

His eyes met hers. "You know I can't."

"I wouldn't say where I got it."

"It's an ongoing investigation."

Now came the tricky step in the always wary dance between reporters and police. "If I find anything interesting, I'll let you know."

He waited half a beat, rubbed his chin, and seemed to make a decision. "There's a press release. That's all I can give you," he said.

"Really?" Aloa said. "That's it?"

He stood, his chair giving another cry of protest.

"I've got an appointment. I have to leave," he said. "I trust you can see yourself out."

"I can," she said.

"Good." He grabbed his suit coat from a hook on the wall and left the room. Aloa watched him disappear, then got up and closed the door quietly behind him. She went back to the desk, dug her Moleskine notebook out of her pack, and reached for the folder Quinn had left behind.

She didn't have much time.

The photo of the victim clipped to one side of the folder made Aloa feel sick. Taken from one end of an otherwise serene-looking living room, the shot showed a woman lying on her side. She wore high heels and a pale-peach wrap dress that had fallen partially open to show an angry wound to her abdomen. It was a jagged cut that looked like the knife had gone in, then been jerked across her belly, causing part of her intestines to leak out. Another wound was on her neck and had spilled a river of blood down her throat and onto the floor. The woman's brown eyes were vacant, her lips pulled back in a Halloween-mask grimace. A dark trail behind her told of an attempt to claw her way across the hardwood floor after her injury. Aloa could only imagine how painful and frightening the woman's death must have been. She quickly folded back the cover with the awful photo and began to read.

The reports told a story that wasn't too different from what she'd unearthed so far. The wife had put her husband, Christian Davenport, to bed at 10:00 p.m., a ritual of lifting, turning, dressing, and catheter care that took thirty minutes. At 10:46 p.m. (Davenport had looked at the digital clock near his bed), the FBI interrogator heard a loud knock on the door. That was followed by a muffled male voice and his wife's reply, but he couldn't make out the words. He guessed the male was there for about five minutes when he'd heard his wife suddenly cry out, then a thump as if someone had fallen. He'd shouted his wife's name, heard rapid footsteps, and the front door slam. He'd cried for help for five hours until he'd fallen into an exhausted sleep, and was awakened by a scream from his assistant, who reported for work at 7:00 a.m. Davenport's time frame was corroborated by an elderly neighbor across the street, who'd said she'd seen a man knocking on the Davenports' front door about the same time.

Aloa stopped reading, printed the word QUESTIONS at the top of a new page, and began her list. "Neighbors not hear shouts?" "No way to phone for help?"

Someone like Davenport would certainly have had a voice-activated system for calling 911.

She read on.

Under questioning from the detective on the scene, Davenport said anyone significant he'd put in jail was either dead or still behind bars, and while there was a possibility he was the target, it didn't make sense that he would still be alive. He also said the violence of his wife's death pointed to something more personal.

Aloa had covered enough murder cases to agree.

Davenport had then asked if he and the detective could speak alone. The investigator had cleared the room, and Davenport had hesitated, seemed to gather his resolve, and finally told the detective that there might be another reason Corrine had been killed: two weeks before she died, Corrine had come to him and tearfully confessed to having an affair with the teacher of a poetry class she was taking.

According to the report, the wife had told her husband she'd been driven by the need for sex, for human touch. But that the guilt of what she'd been doing for the last six months had gotten to her, and she'd broken off the relationship with the teacher. The professor, however, had not taken the news well. Twice he'd followed her to her car, begging her to come back to him. She finally threatened to tell college administrators about the affair if he didn't leave her alone.

The cops had contacted the teacher, Burns Hamlin, who was Tick's son. He admitted there was a flirtation between him and the wife and there'd been a couple of meetings outside of class, but there'd been nothing physical, nothing even close to an affair. The wife, he said, must have imagined there was more between them. At that point, the detective had read him a number of texts from the wife's phone, which seemed to indicate more than a flirtation. Hamlin had called the texts poetic license and said the wife's increasing neediness had prompted

15

him—not her—to say they could no longer communicate outside of class. He insisted he was innocent but, unfortunately, did not have an alibi for the night Corrine Davenport had died.

Aloa jotted down Burns Hamlin's address—he'd apparently taken his stepfather's last name—and scanned through the evidence and the medical examiner's report. The wife was described as being of Asian heritage, five feet five, 126 pounds, with a tattoo of two skeletal fingers in a peace sign to the left of her pubic bone. The examiner listed her age as forty-nine years and four months, noted her muscle tone was consistent with a much younger woman, and described a penetrating wound to her abdomen, along with a second wound to her jugular, which had caused her to bleed out rather quickly. He estimated the assailant had been standing slightly behind Corrine Davenport when the first slicing wound was delivered. The second was made from the side of the victim, a lacerating wound from left to right.

The dead woman was found in a corner of the living room near the kitchen, her body facing north and her face turned toward the east. The weapon was consistent with a ten-inch boning knife, but it was nowhere to be found, and the fact she still wore her diamond wedding ring and an expensive watch seemed to rule out a home-invasion robbery. Her last meal had consisted of a soba noodle salad consumed four hours before she died.

There were no bloody footprints and few fingerprints besides that of the wife and her husband's assistant, Kyle Williams, age twenty-eight, who, according to his roommate, was at home when the killing happened.

Aloa made a few more notes, took one last look at the victim's photo, and set the folder carefully back in the middle of Quinn's desk where he had left it.

Aloa slipped the motorbike between two parked cars and looked up at the two-story Italianate row house located in the Mission District of San Francisco. It was set back on a sloping lot and painted a dark shade of gray, saved from resembling a skinny box by a three-sided cupola and decorative brackets that supported the eaves. A quick records search had showed Hamlin bought the house two years earlier for $1.6 million. *A junior college professor with Ivy League resources,* Aloa thought as she climbed the steps to the house's porch and knocked on Burns Hamlin's door.

The morning's cold fog seemed to have intensified, blurring the edges of buildings and swallowing pedestrians on the street twenty-five feet away. She watched a bundled jogger run past and saw a pigeon flutter onto a window ledge next door. She knocked again and this time heard a clump of footsteps.

"What?" demanded the man who answered the door. He was about six feet in height with serious eyes, a sensuous mouth, and a nose that took up a little too much of his face. His hair was fashionably shaggy, and he was dressed in black with dark Converse sneakers. A Burberry scarf was wrapped around his neck.

Aloa gave him what she hoped was a winning smile. "Hi, my name's Aloa Snow," she said. "I'm a journalist and a friend of your father."

The sun creases around the professor's eyes deepened. "That would be two reasons for me to ask you to leave," he said and began to close the door.

"Wait," Aloa said, taking a step forward. "I think you might want to hear what I have to say. I've found something. Something that might help you in your situation."

The door paused in its swing.

"There may be someone else. Another suspect," Aloa said. She waited.

The professor looked up and down the street. "Who is it?" he asked.

"Maybe we should take this inside." She cocked her head toward the neighboring house where an anxious yellow lab on a leash was tugging its female owner out the front door.

Hamlin made a sound somewhere between a sigh and a hiss. "All right. Come on, then," he said and turned, leaving Aloa standing on the front steps. So much for manners.

Aloa followed him up a flight of stairs into a high-ceilinged living room with a whitewashed brick fireplace and chocolate-colored hardwood floors. The view out the window was of a well-kept neighborhood lined with handsome trees. The view inside was of a bachelor pad, with a tan leather couch, a glass coffee table, and a decorating style somewhere between early flea market and late secondhand store.

The professor turned and folded his arms across his chest. "Well, who is it?" he said.

"Shall we sit?" Aloa asked, settling on the couch. It was a subtle message that she wasn't there to threaten him.

Hamlin remained standing. "This whole thing is a witch hunt, you know."

"That's what your dad said. Unfortunately, some of the evidence seems pretty hard to ignore."

Hamlin's eyes narrowed. "Those texts don't prove anything."

Unless your address is in the state of denial, Aloa thought. She'd skimmed the printout in Quinn's folder of the messages between the wife and her teacher. They were filled with declarations like, "I'm counting the minutes until I see you. Cloud Bar at 1," and "Your touch is the sun and the moon to me."

"Then you two weren't sleeping together?"

"No."

"It was just a flirtation?"

"That's right," Hamlin said as his phone rang. He snatched it from the table and examined the caller ID. "I've got to take this," he said and stomped from the room.

She heard a door close down the long hallway next to the open kitchen and pulled her Moleskine and a pen from her pack. She examined the room. A pile of books was stacked on a dusty treadmill, and a tumble of Chinese takeout boxes was on the kitchen counter. Not a cook, or an exerciser apparently. On the floor was a Persian rug (expensive) and above the fireplace was an oil painting done by a famous landscape artist (also expensive). Hamlin obviously had some source of extra income.

She turned to the mess of papers and books on the table in front of her and hesitated only a moment before she leaned forward and lifted the first piece of paper: a PG&E bill for $302. The place obviously needed some insulation. She glanced toward the hallway. Underneath the bill was a subscription notice for *The New Yorker* magazine and an appointment summary from an ear, nose, and throat doctor indicating Hamlin suffered from a dust allergy. The next sheet of paper was a $175 receipt for an Airbnb rental in Monterey for December 15 of last year. She noted the date and address in her Moleskine and lifted another page from the pile.

"Dear Burns," read the printed email from something called the *Midland Review* magazine. "Please review the attached page proof of your poem. Any changes should be made and mailed to our office before Jan. 30. And, again, congratulations on your selection for our March issue. Best, Pam."

"To See," read the title of the poem. Beside it was a scribbled note in red ink. "No! No!!!" it read. "'To Sea.' What's wrong with you?"

Aloa wondered if the professor's critique style extended to his students' papers.

She gave one more glance down the hallway and began to read. The poem described a cold ocean day, a clandestine swim between two lovers, and a reflection on the power of undertows. But what stopped Aloa was the next to last stanza of the piece.

She looked up at the sound of footsteps.

Hamlin was halfway down the hall. "What the hell are you doing?" he demanded.

"Reading your poem," Aloa said, keeping her voice even. "It's good."

"Leave my stuff alone."

"There's just one problem with it."

Hamlin stopped. Frowned.

"Maybe you can spot it too."

Aloa had grown up under the tutelage of her naturalist father, who had taught her how to see the details that told the stories of animals and birds. The upward turn of a mourning dove's head and the tensing of its body told a tale of a hawk on a determined hunt for her dinner. A flashing of colors on a male red-winged blackbird as he sang spoke of his confidence that this patch of marsh was his.

Aloa began to read: "I saw her then / cold, shaking / skeletal fingers / touching my lover's skin."

"So?" Hamlin said.

"So Corrine Davenport had a tattoo of skeleton fingers," Aloa said. "And on a place that I'm guessing only someone who'd been intimate with her would know about."

"Jesus," snapped Hamlin. "Give me that." He snatched the poem from her hand.

"Lying to me won't get you thrown in jail, Professor, but lying to the police will."

Hamlin's left eyelid twitched.

"Sit down, please," Aloa said. "Let's talk."

"Why should I?" Hamlin said.

"Because I might be able to help you."

It took fifteen more minutes of persuasion, but eventually parts of the story spilled out: the class field trip to a poetry reading, an invitation to his most promising student to get a glass of wine, talk of her self-publishing a chapbook, conversations about poetry and trips to Spain and Italy.

"She was sharp. One of the best writers I've had in a long time. And her body? Jesus Christ, she swam two miles a day. You could hardly believe she was almost fifty."

Aloa swallowed the urge to swat down his sexist and ageist comments.

"She told me her husband was disabled and that he couldn't satisfy her anymore. All those years without anything? No wonder she was kind of messed up." He looked down at his hands. The fingers were long and well shaped. *Just like Tick's,* Aloa thought. "But we both knew it wouldn't go anywhere. It was just sex. Then she said she was starting to fall in love with me. She wanted us to be exclusive. I told her I couldn't do that; I wouldn't do that. I told her I didn't love her, and I broke it off with her."

He'd already lied once about their relationship. Was this another one?

The wife, he said, had then threatened him, hinting that she would tell the administration he'd slept with a student unless he took her back.

"I'll bet that made you angry." Aloa watched him.

"Not enough to kill her."

"Did you ever say anything threatening to her? Or follow her?"

"Who said that?"

Aloa didn't answer. "What about an alibi for the night she died?"

The muscles in his jaw tightened. "What about the thing you said on my porch? That there was another suspect?"

"I found a guy on Facebook," Aloa said. "He wrote some threatening comments."

"There you go," Hamlin said triumphantly.

"Unfortunately, he doesn't fit the description of the man seen at the house right before Corrine Davenport died."

The police report said the neighbor had described the late-night caller as white. Jeremy Green was African American. Aloa had debated texting Quinn that fact after she'd read the police report, but figured he would find out soon enough.

21

Hamlin stood. "So you lied about there being someone else so you could get into my house?"

"Your dad asked me to see what I could find out. He's worried about you."

"Oh really?" Hamlin strode toward the front windows. "That selfish bastard suddenly cares about me?" His hands fisted, and he turned back toward Aloa. "When he professed his so-called concern, did he happen to mention how he walked out when I was five? Did he mention how Mom worked two jobs to keep a roof over our heads while he went off to fight the government and the banks and god knows who else? Did he mention he never wrote or called and missed every single one of my birthdays?"

Hamlin stabbed a finger toward the window as if Tick had suddenly materialized on the street below. "You tell that bastard to shove his sudden devotion up his wrinkly old ass."

"Listen, I don't know about what happened in your family," Aloa said, "and I'm not going to patronize you by saying I understand how you feel, but I can tell you this: Tick, your dad, thinks you're innocent."

Hamlin stared at her. "And how would he know that?"

"He said you were a good kid."

"Give me a break," Hamlin said, although Aloa thought she saw the faintest glimmer of pleasure in his eyes. "My father doesn't know a thing about me. He probably wants something. Money or absolution or maybe he wants to stick it to the man again by proving how the justice system sucks. You don't know him."

"I know he asked me to look into things."

Hamlin snorted. "And you're supposed to save me?"

"I'm going to see what I can find out."

"You know what I told you is off the record, right?"

"Sorry, but off-the-record isn't retroactive."

"You can't write about anything I said. I'll lose my job."

"Trust me. Unemployment is a whole lot better than prison."

"See, I knew it. You're here to do a hatchet job on me."

"All I want is the truth."

"All right then: Do you believe I'm innocent?" he demanded.

"I don't know yet."

He stomped away from the window and stood so he towered over her. "You're just like him: You come in here pretending to care but you don't. It doesn't matter who you hurt." He pointed toward the stairway. "You need to get out before I throw you out. And if you write anything about what I said, I'll sue you."

Aloa stood so she was toe to toe with him.

"Let me tell you two things, Professor Hamlin: If you're innocent, the best thing you can do for yourself is talk to someone like me. But if you're guilty, well then, I'd keep my mouth shut and call a lawyer."

"Go," Hamlin ordered.

Aloa picked up her daypack and stuffed the Moleskine inside. "And while you're at it, you also might want to think about rewriting that poem of yours."

Aloa wedged herself into a spot at the counter, the báhn mì—a toasted baguette filled with roast chicken, cucumber, pickled carrot, onion, radish, cilantro, and jalapeno pepper—warm in her hand.

She'd arrived at her favorite Tenderloin sandwich shop, hungry and pissed off at Tick's son, to find a long line of people trailing out the front door. But she knew the women behind the counter were efficient and even if they weren't, $4.25 for a sandwich that tasted of distant cultures was worth the wait. Ten minutes later she was shoulder to shoulder with a construction worker in a yellow safety vest and a hipster in a flannel shirt and taking her first bite of the sandwich. She nearly moaned with pleasure.

She was halfway through the meal, trying hard not to automatically calculate how many calories she was consuming, when her cell phone rang.

"Michael Collins" read the caller ID.

"Shit," she muttered.

Michael Collins was a software developer, tech genius, and the founder of Novo. He was also her first love and the man from whom the rest of her life had spooled out. She inhaled a breath and answered the call.

"Where are you?" came Michael's voice.

Around her were shouted orders, the hiss of grills, and the angry honk of horns from the street outside.

"In the Tenderloin, eating a sandwich and watching a guy in saggy pants piss on the back of a FedEx truck."

"You ever consider hanging out in a nicer neighborhood?"

"My people, Michael."

"I know. I know." She could hear the sigh in his voice.

Besides having no contact for years, what lay between them was the loss of Aloa's father, a high school biology teacher who'd brought home the teenaged Michael after the boy's father had shot his wife and youngest child, then turned the gun on himself. Michael had lived with them for three years, stealing his way into the hearts of both Aloa and her father. Then, on a warm spring night when he was eighteen and she was seventeen, he and Aloa had made love for the first—and last—time. He'd disappeared a few days later and, three months after that, her worried father had died of a heart attack, leaving Aloa with both a grief-filled heart and a secret she still carried.

"Is there something you need, Michael?" she asked. *Keep it short. Keep the past in its place.*

"Tick called."

"About his son?"

"Do you think it's a story?"

24

Aloa set down her sandwich. "I think it's too early to tell, but there may be something there."

"Enough to talk to Dean about?"

Dean Potter was the editor of Novo and the one who'd stood firmly by Aloa as her series about the runner unfolded.

"Maybe," Aloa said.

An aggrieved shout came from the FedEx driver who'd come out to discover the last dribbles of the liquid assault on his truck.

"Is that a 'yes' maybe or a 'leave me alone' maybe?" Michael asked.

She knew she was being too hard on him.

"I guess it's a 'yes' maybe."

"I'll tell you what. I'll give Dean a call and tell him you may have something and to send you a contract."

"Standard rate?" She would not let him pad the payment as he had tried to do the last time.

"Standard rate. I promise."

"I'll have to check with Tick first."

"Of course."

Both fell silent.

"Say, I'm in town," Michael said finally. "Maybe we could have dinner. I haven't seen you since the story."

An image of him standing barefoot in jeans in his beautiful house in the Marina rose unbidden in her mind.

"Another time," she said.

"Sure. OK." Disappointment and confusion tinged his words.

"I've got to go," she said. "I'll call Dean if I find something."

She clicked off the phone and took another bite of sandwich while, outside the window, a mother who couldn't have been more than seventeen walked by, kissing the forehead of a chubby toddler in her arms.

Aloa got up and threw the remains of her sandwich in the trash.

DAY 3

Aloa stared out the bay window of her house, a coffee mug cradled in her hands. The fog had refused to leave, painting the city a thick, pearlescent gray. Sounds were muffled, visibility reduced, and the cold kept people inside. It was as if the entire population had decided to retreat back to bed and pull the covers over itself.

The National Weather Service called it a rare tule fog, which could show up in the Central Valley of California in the winter but seldom extended to San Francisco. Plenty of poets and writers had celebrated the beauty of San Francisco's ethereal summer fog, but this wasn't soft or romantic. This was cold and thick with a feel of malevolence to it. Aloa's weather app predicted at least two more days of heavy fog and warned motorists to drive carefully.

Aloa drained her cup, wrapped her wool sweater more tightly over her chest, and went off to fry herself a couple of eggs. She ate them standing over the stove. No use wasting warmth in a house that leaked heat like a colander.

Quinn called as she stowed her breakfast dishes, asking if she'd known that the Facebook guy couldn't have been the late-night caller at the Davenports' house.

She told him she hadn't known until she'd read the report and he suggested she learn about this wonderful new thing called texting.

"I'll get right on it," she said.

She changed into jeans and a pullover sweater, topped it off with her leather jacket, then walked down the hill to Justus and piloted her motorcycle into the murk.

The house where Corrine Davenport met her death sat on a steep, wide street in the Potrero Hill neighborhood. The house was rectangular, two-storied, and looked as if it had been remodeled sometime in the early 2000s. The exterior was planked redwood with two giant picture windows on the second floor and a double ribbon of high windows on the first floor that let in light but allowed no view. The front door was painted blue with a short ramp up to the front porch for wheelchair access. On one side of the house were two residences that looked like they'd been built soon after the 1906 earthquake that had destroyed San Francisco, first with shaking, then with fire. In one of history's twists of fate, the city's fire chief was among the quake's first victims, killed when a brick chimney collapsed on him.

Hundreds of the displaced had fled toward the Potrero Hill neighborhood, which, thanks to a thick vein of serpentinite had survived the devastation. The refugees were working-class immigrants; they settled into a sprawling tent city, then gradually moved up the slope, rebuilding their houses and their lives.

If only these houses could talk, Aloa thought as she angled the motorbike into an open spot across the street.

My job would be a lot easier, she finished and smiled at her own small joke.

She knocked down the kickstand, tugged off her helmet, and looked up to see an old woman scowling out the window from the house behind her.

Aloa turned toward the Davenports' home. If it weren't for the fog, the woman—most likely the neighbor in the report—would have a good view of the murder house. She reminded herself to check the weather on the night Corrine Davenport was killed and hung her helmet over the bike's handlebars.

She crossed the street and gave two polite raps on the Davenports' front door. An old reporter at the *Oregonian*, where she'd worked in the early days, called these unannounced forays "knock and talks," which Aloa liked for the way it spoke of the working-class roots of her profession.

The door swung open a minute later to reveal a slender man in his late twenties with a tousle of dark blond hair and a slight overbite. His eyes were gray and hooded.

"Yes?"

Aloa smiled. "Hi. My name is Aloa Snow and I'm a reporter with Novo. I was wondering if I might speak with Mr. Davenport."

The man's gaze touched her face and slid away to a spot over her shoulder. "I don't think he wants to talk to reporters."

One of Aloa's earliest lessons as a reporter was to never piss off the gatekeeper. She smiled and held out a hand. "You must be Kyle, Mr. Davenport's assistant," she said.

The man gave an almost imperceptible nod but kept his hands by his sides.

"Well," Aloa said, dropping her arm, "I'd appreciate any help you could give me, Kyle." Another smile. "Maybe Mr. Davenport has changed his mind. Maybe he's a fan of Novo. You never know."

The gray-eyed man sighed. "Wait here," he said and closed the door.

Behind her came a low sound like a quick clatter of castanets, and Aloa turned. Sure enough, a crow was perched on a nearby fence. A crow's rattle, her father always said, was the bird's way of saying, "I'm curious about you but you make me a little nervous."

"Everything's fine. Nothing's going on," she said quietly to the bird. His answer was to flap away. "Suit yourself," she said as the door reopened.

"Follow me," Kyle said.

Aloa gave herself a mental high five and trailed the assistant into a high-ceilinged living room that looked like an ad from a decorating magazine. A low white couch was flanked by a pair of sculptural chairs in front of which sat a glass coffee table and a vase holding a single dark branch. A wide marble fireplace graced one wall while the other supported a free-floating staircase. *Stairs Christian Davenport could no longer use,* Aloa thought. She wondered if it bothered him to look at them every day.

Beyond the living room was a dining area and a modern-looking kitchen with warm gray cabinets and a backsplash of Mediterranean-blue tile. She calculated where Corrine's body had been found. There seemed to be no sign of what had happened.

She followed the assistant through a wide doorway, down a short hall, and turned right into what appeared to be an office-study.

"Wait here," Kyle said and disappeared through another door farther down the hallway, closing it behind him.

Aloa heard a murmur of voices and began a quick examination of the room. A pair of sliding glass doors on the back wall opened onto a verdant tropical garden surrounding a blue lap pool. In one corner, a single rough column of gray granite rose out of the green in a way that suggested the hard reality that sometimes lurked underneath beauty. A small wooden deck next to the pool provided a spot to sit and meditate. *Stunning,* Aloa thought.

The room itself was equally well thought out. The walls were paneled in exotic wood with floor-to-ceiling bookshelves covering one wall. Recessed lights shined warmly from the planked ceiling and an abstract painting in rich colors hung over a sleek desk with two Shaker-style chairs on either side of it.

Aloa moved to the bookcase. The Davenports' collection was admirable. She saw a few first editions and examined the curios displayed amid the books. She was pushing in a volume that protruded an inch from the otherwise perfect lineup of books when she heard a male voice.

"Thank god," said the voice. "That was bugging the hell out of me."

Aloa turned to see a man in his forties with a face that resembled a peregrine falcon, or maybe a red-tailed hawk. His eyes were dark brown and intense, his cheekbones high, his hair chestnut and almost shoulder-length. Broad shoulders spoke of an innate athleticism. A red scar on his throat told of a ventilator that he'd once needed in order to breathe.

"I couldn't help myself," Aloa said and stepped away from the bookcase.

His lips curved into a smile she couldn't quite read.

The man was dressed in loose black pants and a dark T-shirt, and was strapped into a motorized wheelchair so it made him look half man, half machine. One hand was covered in a black glove laced with metal and wires. He moved an index finger and the chair rolled to a spot next to the desk. A lift upward and the chair stopped. Kyle came into the room and stood near the door.

"I'm guessing you're here because you want to do a story about my wife's murder," Davenport said.

"I do," she answered.

He studied her in a way that made his resemblance to a falcon even stronger. "I don't really trust the media, you know. They want to believe they're objective, but most of them only see what they want to see."

"Then why'd you let me in?" Aloa asked.

He cocked his head slightly. "Maybe to take my mind off life."

"Or maybe you have something to say," Aloa said, not flinching from his gaze. "Maybe you want to put a little pressure on the investigation. Get things moving faster?"

She waited.

"Kyle, bring us some tea, would you?" said Davenport. "Let's try the Bancha Shizuoka."

The assistant shot a look at a spot somewhere near Aloa's feet and left.

"Bancha Shizuoka. It means 'third harvest,'" said Davenport. "It's grown in the Shizuoka Prefecture in Japan. Notes of the ocean and herbs. Beautiful terroir." He glanced out the window. "Perfect for a day like this."

From her years in journalism, Aloa had learned to never turn down an offer of food or drink from a source. It was a subconscious offer of trust on their part and a way of showing acceptance on hers. She'd drunk stale coffee, warm soda, and swallowed cake so sweet it made her teeth hurt as a way to open up the people she'd interviewed.

"It sounds wonderful," she said.

"Have a seat," Davenport said. "I hate talking to people's belt buckles."

"Sure," Aloa said and lowered herself into one of the Shaker chairs.

"So why is Novo interested in my wife's murder?"

"The editor said that when a hero's wife dies, it's news. We all want to believe that if we do good, we'll be rewarded."

Davenport seemed to weigh her answer.

"I get it. The broken champion and all that," he said. "Fair enough."

His eyes caught and held hers for a moment. Then: "So how about we get your first questions out of the way? 'What the hell happened to that poor guy and how can he live like that?'"

"That's not what—" Aloa began, but Davenport continued.

"Come on, everybody wants to know but they're too afraid to ask," he said. "So here's the tragic story." Another smile. "I've been like this for four years. Since December 18, about five o'clock in the morning. I was coming back from an assignment in South Korea. A long week, a bad flight, and I was wiped out. I got picked up and fell asleep in the car. The next thing I knew I was waking up in the ICU and wondering what the hell happened. The docs wouldn't say, but a nurse took pity and told me a garbage truck had come through an intersection not far from here and slammed into the passenger side of the car I was riding in. The car flipped and skidded into a light pole. The first hit broke my pelvis. The second damaged my spinal cord. C4. I spent a year in rehab and all I got for it was a thumb, a forefinger, and a bit of a shoulder shrug."

Aloa couldn't help it. Her gaze went to his ungloved hand. It was so still, it looked almost like a movie prop.

"The docs said it was a miracle I got that much. I told them the only miracle I needed was for a lightning bolt or some guy with a high-powered rifle to put me out of my misery." He winked at her. "They didn't like that. They wanted me to fall all over myself and thank them for saving me. But I asked them: saving me for what?"

He looked over as Kyle came into the room and set a tray with a teapot and two ceramic cups on the desk. Kyle decanted the tea, set one cup on the desk near Aloa, and put the other on a tray attached to a metal stand. He lifted the tray and turned it so it was level with Davenport's chin. He slipped a bamboo straw into the cup and put it near Davenport's mouth.

Davenport drew in a sip of tea. "A little too hot, but close enough," he told Kyle. "Try yours," he said to Aloa.

The tea was earthy and smooth, with a faint hint of the sea, as Davenport had described.

"It's wonderful," she said.

"I thought you'd like it. And so for the second question: How do I live like this? The answer is: barely." His glance went toward Kyle, who had moved to stand next to him. "You might think I feel nothing, but parts of my body buzz the way your foot does after it falls asleep. It's like living with a hive of bees inside you. Plus my organs don't work like they used to and there are muscles spasms and pressure sores, and the occasional nasty infection, and you also have to have somebody like Kyle here scratch your nose and shave your face and wipe your ass. I'll tell you, you learn humility real fast."

"It must be hard," Aloa said.

"It is what it is, as they say." Davenport took another sip of tea. "At first I was mad as hell, but after a while you stop wondering 'what if': What if I'd stopped to get a cup of coffee? What if the customs line had moved more slowly so the garbage truck had gone through the intersection thirty seconds before I got there?" His glance went out the door into the fog-cloaked garden. "As much as we want to control life, we can't. Every small decision ripples outward and changes our path."

His gaze traveled back to Aloa. "Even the night Corrine died, when that prick came and stabbed her, it was one little thing. One little thing that was the difference between her living and dying."

She watched his jaw work.

"I heard her scream," Davenport said, "and I shouted for the phone to dial 9-1-1, but we'd decided to watch a movie and Corrine had muted the speaker on my virtual assistant because it kept interrupting when the TV was on."

Aloa had heard about that problem.

"And, for whatever reason—whatever stupid reason—Corrine forgot to unmute the thing when she put me to bed. All I could do while she bled to death was lie there and yell for help." Davenport's lips went tight. "Like, I said, one little thing, man . . ."

He looked away and Aloa could see his eyes shimmering with sudden emotion. "A goddamned baby would have been more help than me."

Kyle put a hand on Davenport's shoulder. "It's all right."

"No, it's not. Corrine's dead." Davenport closed his eyes, causing a tear to zigzag down his cheek. "I should have been able to protect her. I should have stopped what happened." He pressed his lips together. "Wipe my face, will you?"

Kyle grabbed a tissue and blotted Davenport's face. He turned to Aloa. "It's not good for him to get upset. If his blood pressure gets too high, it's hard to bring it back down."

"My blood pressure is just fine, Kyle," Davenport said, although Aloa noticed his breathing had turned shallow and quick.

"He needs his pills," Kyle said.

Davenport's brow furrowed in what looked like a spasm of pain.

"You should go," Kyle said.

Aloa stood. "May I come back?" she asked.

"Probably not," Kyle said, bending down to fish through a pouch on the back of Davenport's wheelchair.

"Here's my card, just in case," Aloa said and set it on the tray.

"I wouldn't hold my breath," Kyle said. He stood and picked up a water bottle. "Now go."

Aloa hesitated only a second, then left. On her way out she couldn't help glancing into the other room, which was filled with shelves of medical supplies, a large-screen TV, some kind of complicated lift, and a wide hospital bed.

From behind her came Kyle's voice. "I said go."

She moved into the living room, glanced behind her, and crouched down at the spot where she calculated Corrine's body had been found. Close up, she could see a small nick and a faint rust-red stain in the bamboo flooring. She pivoted on her heels and saw a baseboard covered in a layer of dust, a low scrape on the wall, and a black scuff mark on the doorframe that led into Davenport's office-study. Small imperfections that stood out in what appeared to be a room worthy of a magazine shoot.

She stood and let herself out.

Back home, Aloa changed into her running clothes and headed out the front door into the cold miasma. Her feet took her down Sansome Street to Green, where a plaque marked the building where Philo

Farnsworth and a lab crew that included his wife, Pem, had transmitted the first television image.

The building was two-story and industrial looking, situated on a short, tree-lined street. Above it, expensive homes perched on a steep hillside.

Aloa imagined the excitement that must have coursed through the young inventor when he saw his invention spring to life. The success, however, had been trailed by lawsuits and a descent into bankruptcy, followed by the inventor's slide into a deep depression.

Did he and his wife ever imagine what would flow from that one moment? Aloa wondered, her mind going to Christian Davenport and what he'd said about small decisions leading to consequences we couldn't imagine. She picked up the pace.

At the Embarcadero, she turned and headed for Rincon Point, doing quick sprints to build lung capacity, then jogging to recover. By the time she got home she was wet with sweat and starting to chill. She took a hot shower, running a washcloth over her small breasts, her rib cage, her belly with its hint of roundness. She shoved down the urge to count the calories she'd consumed so far today. That was the trouble with an eating disorder. A drunk could stay out of a bar. An anorexic couldn't avoid the world of food around her.

She toweled off, changed into sweats, and made herself a piece of avocado toast. Back at her desk—a scratched dining room table her grandmother had purchased on layaway sometime in the 1950s—she fired up her laptop and did a more thorough search for background on Christian Davenport.

According to magazine stories she found, Davenport had grown up in Colorado Springs, the son of a mining company accountant and an elementary school teacher. He was something of a golden boy who won the state singles championship in tennis, was class valedictorian, and got a scholarship to Stanford where he majored in international relations and linguistics. He spoke Arabic, French, and Japanese. Despite job offers to work in Washington, DC, he'd surprised everyone by enlisting in the army, where he served as an interrogator at a detention center in Afghanistan. His best-known break was of a young Pakistani who gave away the location of a house where a Taliban operative lived with his two wives when he wasn't out teaching recruits how to blow up innocent people.

"Once you put a knife on the table, you can't take it away," Davenport said in answer to whether threats or violence had had a role in that interrogation. "The best intel comes from the details, the stuff they think doesn't matter."

One tour of duty in Afghanistan had morphed into a job with the FBI and his most famous case: the kidnapping of a wealthy CEO's four-year-old daughter from her parents' sprawling house in Los Altos. According to the article, while questioning one of the family's two housekeepers, Davenport had noticed that whenever he'd ask the maid details about the little girl, she'd reach for the small pearl hanging from a delicate gold chain around her neck. From the gardener he learned the jewelry had come from the housekeeper's new boyfriend, and Davenport had followed the clue to the housekeeper's cousin, who'd given up the boyfriend's name. Davenport had then tracked the boyfriend to an auto shop where the guy worked until a week before the girl's disappearance, then to a wife and two kids the housekeeper hadn't known about.

When the maid learned the truth about her boyfriend, she'd confessed, saying her beau had convinced her she was being exploited by the family because they didn't pay her overtime when they took her to their weekend house in Lake Tahoe.

"He said they owed me," she insisted.

Aloa leaned back in her chair. *Davenport was good,* she thought, *and to have it all taken away?* She knew a little of how that felt. But losing the ability to walk and move and turn a book page was way beyond losing a career.

She was skimming Corrine Davenport's LinkedIn profile when there was a pounding at the door followed by a shout: "Open up, will ya. It's colder than a banker's heart out here."

Aloa sighed and stood, opening the door to find three bundled figures on her porch.

"What's up?" she asked as the Brain Farm pushed past her.

"We're here to get the skinny, the scoop," said P-Mac, blowing onto fingers that had once wielded a camera like a weapon and were now bent and swollen with arthritis. He had sharp blue eyes and a slightly hooked nose. An old ski cap hid his silver crew cut.

"Yeah, when you didn't show at Justus, we came here," said Doc.

"And we brought you something," Tick said, shoving a box of cabernet into Aloa's hands.

"Yeah, we're regular Martha Stewarts," P-Mac said when Aloa rolled her eyes.

Tick took off his porkpie hat and slapped it against his thigh. His thin gray ponytail was wet from the fog. "Christ, it's like a meat locker in here," he said.

"I could make coffee," offered Aloa.

"We don't have time. We're old. Remember?" Tick said.

All the men knew her elaborate ritual of making French press coffee: bean grinding, water heating, steeping, and pressing.

"Just pour us the cab," said Doc, lowering his six-foot-five frame onto the couch, while P-Mac settled himself with a groan into Aloa's grandmother's favorite chair, a fat overstuffed thing that had once been the color of burgundy but had faded now to a cheap rosé.

Tick circled the desk and sat in front of her computer. "What do we have here?" he asked.

"Research on the vic and her husband," Aloa called over her shoulder as she headed into the kitchen.

She came back and passed out three tumblers of the red wine.

"You talk to my son?" Tick asked.

"I did."

"And?" he asked, lifting his glass in a small salute to his comrades, then taking a long pull.

"He threw me out," Aloa said.

"Sonofabuck," Tick said.

"But not before he admitted to sleeping with the wife," Aloa said. "He told the cops they didn't have sex."

"And now the idea that he killed her because she threatened to report him is going to be a lot harder to shake," Doc finished.

Tick's lips went tight.

Aloa gave the men a quick rundown of what she'd learned so far: the late-night caller, the texts, the male voice right before Corrine Davenport was murdered, Burns Hamlin's denials.

"Sounds like he just bought himself a ticket on the express bus to San Quentin," said P-Mac of Tick's son.

"Is there any good news?" Tick said.

"It's still early," Aloa said.

Tick held out his glass. "How about a refill?"

She fetched the box and topped off their glasses.

"What was he like?" Tick asked.

Aloa knew he meant his son. "Intelligent and a little full of himself, but with an undercurrent of insecurity, I think. Lives in an expensive house in the Mission."

"I'd bet my hat Mr. Moneybags, his stepfather, bought it for him," Tick said.

"'Money buys lands, and wives are sold by fate.' Willie Shakespeare," Doc muttered.

"What the hell does that mean?" P-Mac said.

"Basically, that you can't buy love," Doc said.

"Oh yeah?" Tick said. "Try telling that to my ex-wife." He looked at Aloa. "Speaking of buying love, did the boy say anything about me?"

Aloa hesitated. "He pretty much said you abandoned him."

Tick got up from her desk chair. "If you call getting arrested twice for violating a restraining order 'abandoning him,' then yeah, I guess I did."

"A restraining order?"

"His mother got one after I had the nerve to show up at her and her new husband's snooty New York apartment with a birthday present for the boy." Tick shook his head. "What's the matter with a seven-year-old having a full set of Dylan studio albums 1964 to 69?"

"Nothing," P-Mac said vigorously.

"It wasn't my fault I had to climb the fire escape. The doorman wouldn't let me in. 'Orders,' he said. So maybe I broke one of their windows when I tried to open it. Maybe I got a little loud." He flung out his arms. "What would you do if somebody wouldn't let you see your own flesh and blood?"

"Exactly," Doc said.

"Twice I tried to see him. Twice she called the cops. She returned my letters, hung up the phone when I called. She turned him against me, said I was a bad influence," Tick finished.

"A bad influence is a husband who makes his living off the backs of the proletariat," Doc said and threw back the rest of his wine.

"Yeah, and look how the boy turned out. Accused of murder," P-Mac said.

"You watch it," Tick said. "That's my kid you're talking about."

"Sorry, man," P-Mac said.

Tick walked to Aloa's front window and stared out into the fog. The sky was darkening. The mist had swallowed the city whole. "I know I wasn't the best dad. I know I should have fought harder for him." He swallowed the last of his wine and shoved his hand in the pocket of his faded jeans. "You know, you spend your whole life running toward something, but it's only when you look back that you see what you missed." His shoulders sagged. "I can't make up for leaving him, but I'd like to try. I'd like him to know his old man loved him. Not the way I should have loved him, but the best somebody like me could."

He turned back toward Aloa. "You've got to help him, Ink," he said.

Aloa had just brushed her teeth and changed into her pajamas—thick socks, a pair of flannel boxers, and a Foo Fighters T-shirt from college—when a text alert chimed from her phone. She debated ignoring it, but years of late-night calls from editors and sources made it a hard habit to break. She picked up her phone.

If you want to talk tomorrow, I'm available, the text read. C. Davenport.

Aloa glanced at the time—11:10 p.m.—and called him back. Obviously, he was still awake.

"It's Aloa Snow. I got your text," she said when Davenport answered.

"I didn't mean to wake you."

"I wasn't asleep."

"A night owl?"

"Something like that." She didn't tell him of the insomnia that made semiregular appearances in her life.

"I used to sleep eight hours; now I'm lucky if I get five," he said. He paused. "I looked you up. That series you did for Novo on the runner was good."

"Thanks."

"What happened before that? You know, at the *Times*? You got fired for making up a source?"

She could hear the sound of slide guitar and violin playing softly in the background and mentally cataloged the fact Davenport liked country-western music.

"I resigned," she said, then, realizing that sounded petulant, added, "but only because they were going to fire me. My mom had cancer. The chemotherapy drugs she took were destroying her heart. I needed to get up to see her but first I had to file this story I'd been working on. About a bunch of nail salon workers who were being exploited. I swallowed a couple of bennies, pulled an all-nighter, and got on a plane. Long story short, I used interviews with three people to make up the nail salon worker I used in the piece. They were all immigrants, all making less than minimum wage, and working six days a week. I figured what I wrote was close to the truth. That's not an excuse, just the reason. I knew better."

"And you paid the price."

"Still am."

"Tell me about it. The mistake that keeps on giving, right?"

Aloa moved into the living room and got her Moleskine. "Do you mind if I ask a few questions while I've got you on the line?"

"If you don't mind me asking a couple first."

"Sure." She settled onto the red leather couch she'd hauled up from LA—one of the few reminders of her life there—and pulled a throw over her shoulders.

"Who'd you talk to first, me or the professor?" Davenport asked.

"The professor. I wanted to get a feel for him."

"What did he tell you?"

Aloa plucked at a thread in the throw. "Sorry. I don't discuss one source with another."

"That's right. First rule: keep 'em in the dark."

"Is that from interrogators' school or something?"

"It's what they taught us. But so you know, we don't call ourselves interrogators. We prefer collectors. Collectors of human intelligence. Just like you."

She waited.

"We both look for inconsistencies, details, places where people are vulnerable. Anybody can get someone to talk, but not everybody can get somebody to tell the truth, right?"

Aloa thought of Burns Hamlin saying Corrine Davenport was falling in love with him and had wanted a commitment, and compared it to the trail of blood in the photo that showed Corrine had tried to crawl to her husband as she was dying. Who did she really love?

"So one of the things I noticed was that your wife was dressed up on the night she died. Why was that?" Aloa asked.

"Fair question, but I've got one more thing to ask. A little test I'd like you to take."

"I stopped taking tests in college."

"Can you humor me?"

Aloa looked out the window. Fog pressed against the glass. "All right."

"Name ten things you saw in my office."

"Really?"

"Please."

"Why?"

"Let's just say I don't want to waste my time if you're not as good as I think you are."

Clever, Aloa thought. "OK. I'll give it a shot."

Aloa closed her eyes. It was her naturalist father, not journalism, who had taught her to notice details, inconsistencies.

"First, a book. 'Aoi No You' or something like that."

"The book you pushed in. *Aoi No Ue*. It's a Muromachi-period Japanese Noh play. Good."

"A full set of Hemingway in chronological order. A bird's nest. Hummingbird, I think." She moved her mind's eye along the bookshelves. "A baseball signed by Tim Lincecum. A gold medal from the FBI."

"They give that to all the quadriplegics."

"A photo of you with an older couple who I think may be your parents. There was a slight resemblance."

"Yes."

43

"Some kind of long pipe. *Treasure Island*, first edition, I think."

"Correct."

"Also, there were no rugs on the floor and your left shoe was untied."

"OK."

"And on your desk there was a small statue. Clay. A woman with a necklace, wearing what looked like a graduation cap," she finished.

"A *haniwa*," Davenport said.

"I don't know what that is."

"In the old days in Japan, when an important man or woman died, their servants would be buried up to their waists around their master's tomb. They'd be left there without food or water, moaning and crying until they died of thirst or exposure. Or the wild dogs ate them."

A shiver ran down Aloa's spine.

"According to the stories, the practice was finally stopped by Emperor Suinin after his brother died and he saw the horrible suffering of his servants. When one of his wives, Empress Hibasu, died, Suinin hired one hundred potters to make clay figures and bury them instead. The figures were called *haniwa*."

He paused. "It's also the answer to your question."

Aloa sat up a little straighter. "I don't understand."

She heard the music go down and the sound of another voice in the background.

"All right, Kyle," Davenport said. Then to her: "I'm sorry, but Kyle's here with my pills and he won't go away until I take them. I'll explain more tomorrow. Why don't you stop by?"

"What time is best?"

"Around eleven? After my therapist comes and we pretend I didn't wish I was dead too."

DAY 4

Aloa, bundled in sweatpants and her wool sweater, took a long pull of coffee and looked out her front window into the gloom. The fog dripped water from the eaves and shrouded the neighborhood so the apartment building across the street was only a dark outline in the gray. It was cold and miserable and she closed her eyes for a moment, feeling the grit underneath her lids.

She hadn't slept well last night.

Images of humans planted in the ground like flowers had haunted her dreams and she'd awakened at 7:00 a.m. feeling unsettled.

She scrambled some eggs, cleaned up the kitchen, made her bed, and straightened the towels in the bathroom. She liked putting things in their places. It was partly why she became a journalist. To make order out of chaos. To make the puzzle pieces fit. It was also the seed of her eating disorder. Control suited her.

Now she sat at her computer, skimming the day's news. A robber had been shot dead by a ten-year-old in Arkansas; a movie star had behaved badly at a fancy restaurant in LA; and, in her own city, weather watchers were labeling the stubborn marine layer "Fogpocalypse."

According to the story on her screen, three people had died in a thirty-car pileup on the 101 when visibility had suddenly dropped to less than twenty feet. Then, a tourist had stepped into the path of a Mercedes sedan, neither seeing the other until it was too late, and an old woman with asthma had died trying to take a bus to the hospital for treatment.

Aloa debated getting up and putting on gloves against the chill in her house, but instead she clicked through her newsfeed and stopped at one of her favorite columnists, who recalled another time when the city's fog had spawned disaster.

According to the writer, it was 1950 when a pea-souper like this one had descended just beyond the Golden Gate Bridge, causing the WWII cargo ship the SS *Mary Luckenbach* to collide with the *Benevolence*, a US Navy hospital ship, and tear a big hole in the *Benevolence's* side. The *Benevolence* sank to the bottom in twenty-five minutes, forcing most of its 509 passengers—nurses, corpsmen, shipyard workers—to jump into the frigid ocean, where they floated and clung to debris until rescuers arrived. Twenty-three died.

The fog could be beautiful, the columnist wrote. It rolled over the headlands and slipped through the cables of the Golden Gate Bridge like it sought to fill the blank spaces in the city's heart. But it also could be deadly, a killer with lethal gray tentacles, and that was its form now.

"Perhaps the lesson is that the beauty that brought us all here can turn on us if we aren't careful," the columnist concluded.

Aloa thought of the overpriced houses next door and had to agree.

A separate article quoted meteorologists saying the winds they'd expected to disperse the fog hadn't materialized and that the deadly murk might get worse. Officials urged people to take mass transit to work, noting an inversion layer also was trapping pollution and causing a decline in air quality.

At 10:30 a.m., Aloa stood and stretched, and went to change her clothes and put on some mascara. By 10:45 a.m., she was at Justus firing up the motorbike, which coughed and sputtered in protest. She heard a shout and looked up to see Erik leaning out the window of the second-floor apartment he shared with Gully.

"A little less choke, and a whisper of throttle, honey," he called.

Aloa was one of the few who knew Erik had been a certified mechanic before he'd turned to costume design, and so she did what he suggested.

"Thanks," she called as the motorcycle rumbled to life.

"And not to be too picky, hon," Erik said, "but unless you're training to be a ninja, that outfit is a death wish just waiting to come true."

Aloa looked down at her black leather jacket and boots, the dark jeans, the chrome-and-black motorcycle that would disappear like a ghost in the gray that had swallowed the city.

"I don't really have anything else," she said.

"Just a sec, sweetie," Erik said, returning to drop a knot of bright-yellow scarf into Aloa's hands. The fabric was studded with scores of tiny round mirrors.

"I got this from a handsome young boy in India. Put it around your neck," Erik said. "It's better than nothing."

Aloa untied the bundle and wrapped the long, gaudy covering around her throat. "I look like a mutant wasp."

"A living and breathing mutant wasp," Erik corrected. "Now buzz off, little bee. And stop by tonight. Gully just left for the docks. A load of fresh crab came in."

Aloa gave him a thumbs-up.

Aloa was careful as she steered the motorcycle through the city to Christian Davenport's house. Pedestrians seemed to come out of nowhere. Familiar places suddenly appeared foreign. She parked the bike in the same spot as before and couldn't help the quick exhale of relief that came from having arrived in one piece. She walked across the street, knocked on Davenport's door, and waited for it to open.

"Oh, it's you," Kyle said and pursed his lips as if he'd bitten into something rotten.

"It sure is," she said and smiled.

If passive aggressive was what he wanted, that's what he would get.

"Mr. Davenport asked me to stop by," she said. "I'm sure he told you." Another smile.

"Of course he did." Kyle sniffed in a way that made Aloa pretty certain Davenport hadn't.

He opened the door and Aloa trailed him into the study, where she found Davenport dressed again in loose dark pants and a black T-shirt. This time, however, his brown hair was pulled into a topknot.

Davenport looked up. "Ah, the intrepid reporter has returned."

He turned to his assistant. "Make that two cups of matcha instead of one, Kyle." Then to Aloa: "Matcha is a kind of powdered green tea. The veins of the leaves are removed and what's left is ground between millstones until it's superfine, then it's beaten into a foam. I think you'll like it." He inclined his head toward one of the chairs. "Have a seat."

Kyle returned a minute later with a tray containing two cups with strainers and a pale-blue teapot.

Aloa watched as Kyle poured hot water over the tea, removed the strainers, then began whisking the liquid into a bright-green froth. He worked with deliberateness, as if he'd spent time practicing the steps.

"You know a lot about tea," Aloa said to Davenport as Kyle handed her a cup. As before, he set Davenport's cup on the tray and inserted a bamboo straw.

"I lived in Japan for six months," Davenport said. "Take a sip. Tell me what you think."

Aloa did what he asked. The tea gave off scents of berries and dark chocolate. Its taste was rich. "This is good," she said.

"I'm glad you like it." Then: "You can leave us alone, Kyle. I'll be fine."

"I don't mind," Kyle began.

"Take a break, Kyle," Davenport said a little more forcefully.

Aloa watched the assistant leave.

"Poor guy," Davenport said. "He gets like this every time the thera-pist comes. She tells me how other quads are living these wonderful lives and Kyle then thinks it's his duty to help me have whatever amazing life those other crips are having. The last time she was here, he tried to get me to go tandem skydiving. I'd tell the counselor and her happy quadriplegics to go to hell, except I need her in order to keep my health benefits."

Aloa let her gaze travel to the *haniwa*. Now that she knew what it was, the little statue seemed slightly ominous.

"Don't worry, we'll get to your question," Davenport said.

He didn't miss a thing.

"But before we do," he continued, "I'd like us to agree on a few rules. No recording of our conversation, no photos, and if I want some-thing off the record, I want you to put down your pen so I know you understand."

"Fine," she said.

He was a control freak. Just like her.

"The only reason I'm talking to you is because I want this case to stay on the front burner. If the police know Novo's interested, if they know someone's watching, they can't slack off. I want that bastard behind bars. I want him to suffer."

"You know it's not my job to convict someone," Aloa said.

"You're right, but it *is* your job to be a watchdog."

Aloa had to agree.

"Now, for your question about why Corrine was dressed the way she was." Davenport took a sip of tea from the bamboo straw. "My acci-dent basically turned my wife into what the *haniwa* represents: a servant buried around this tomb of a body I've got. She gave up everything for me. Her job, her friends. She fed me, gave me baths, and listened to me rage."

"What about Kyle?"

"He came later. Those first few years, Corrine wouldn't let anybody help her. She came from a family that prided itself on sacrifice, on loyalty, and on a virtue the Japanese call *gaman*. It means endurance or patience, but if you take that a step further, it means you're supposed to suffer quietly through trouble, not fight it."

"Tell me about her."

"Well." Davenport looked out the window to the garden where Kyle, now bundled in a down jacket, was standing with his hands stuffed in the pockets of his jeans.

"She was smart. Number ten in her law class. She was on the swim team in college. She majored in economics, even though she would have preferred to study creative writing. Her parents put her up to that. They were immigrants, descended from an old *daimyo* family in Japan. 'Daimyo' is what they called feudal lords back in the day. Her parents' lives were all about achievement and honor. Corrine had a lot of that drilled into her. It was one of the things that attracted me: that integrity and depth and loyalty. You don't see that much these days. But she was also beautiful and kind. There's a photo of her on the second shelf over there."

Aloa stood and carried her teacup over to the picture. It showed a woman with chin-length black hair and a slender body standing in front of the Eiffel Tower. She wore ballet flats and a summer dress that reminded Aloa of Audrey Hepburn. She couldn't help but remember the way Corrine Davenport had looked in her death photo.

Aloa turned. "If loyalty and honor were drilled into her, why would she have an affair?"

"That's an excellent question," Davenport said, "and the honest answer is that I drove her to it."

Aloa frowned.

"This might be when you want to take notes."

Aloa came back to her chair, set down her cup, and pulled out her notebook.

According to Davenport, it had taken him more than two years to convince his wife to hire Kyle, then another four or five months to get her to leave the house for something besides grocery shopping and pharmacy runs. One evening, he'd urged her to go to a poetry event at Books Inc., where one of her favorite poets was reading. It turned out Burns Hamlin also was on the program. When she came back, she described the reading to Davenport and the look on her face—one of excitement and passion—made him press her to do more than simply go to readings. She signed up for Burns Hamlin's class and was soon spending her free time either writing or going to gatherings with other students. One day, Davenport saw her leave for class in beautiful slacks and high-heeled boots, trailing the scent of her favorite perfume, Chanel N°5. He told himself it was good to see her taking care of herself again. Soon, she was spending more time away from home, asking Kyle to work extra hours and, sometimes, when Davenport asked her about the class, she'd touch a finger to her lips as she described the afternoon's lecture.

"I knew they were sleeping together even before the day she came home from class and I smelled sex on her," Davenport said. "It broke my heart, but I didn't say anything. She deserved what I couldn't give her: the chance to feel like a woman again, to be touched." He looked into the distance, then back at Aloa. "That's the trouble with being a collector. We can read people's weaknesses. We can see their guilt whether we want to or not. It's like a bad movie you can't turn off."

"So she didn't fall in love with Hamlin?" Aloa asked.

Davenport shook his head. "I'm pretty sure the affair was just physical for her. I couldn't have handled it if it was more." He paused. "But I think Hamlin had fallen in love with her. When she came and confessed the affair, she said she'd broken it off with Hamlin and that he'd gotten angry. He'd frightened her, she said. Once, she'd come home to find him parked across the street from our house. She said he wouldn't leave her alone and when she threatened to report him to the college administrators, he said he'd tell me about the affair."

A much different story than the one Burns Hamlin had told.

"That's why she confessed. He had her against a wall."

"So on the night she died . . ."

"I think she was going to tell the professor that I knew about the affair and to leave us alone or we'd file a formal complaint with the college. She didn't talk about the meeting specifically, but I could tell something was up that night. That's why she wore the dress. She called it her suit of armor, her closing-argument dress. My guess is she wanted to confront Hamlin at our house to make the point I knew about the affair and he didn't have any leverage to get her to come back."

"She was an assistant district attorney, right?" Aloa asked.

"Yes. For nine years."

"Was it possible somebody she prosecuted came back to kill her?"

"I doubt it. Corrine was incredibly smart, but she didn't have the teeth for big cases. Mostly she prosecuted drunk drivers and low-level drug dealers. A few months in county jail isn't exactly a motive for murder."

"Could you identify the voice you heard on the night Corrine died?"

"I'm sure it was him. Corrine closed the bedroom door when she left so I couldn't hear what they were saying. But it had to be him. He was jealous and he killed her."

"How do you know he was jealous?" Aloa began but he was already turning the chair.

"Come on, I'll show you."

She followed him into the white room with the wide hospital bed and the complicated lift. Underneath the scent of disinfectant were the odors of illness and bodily functions: sweat, digestion, elimination. Eau de hospital.

Aloa remembered her own mother, once so put-together, lying diapered in a hospital bed, wailing for more pain medication. She shook the memory away.

Davenport stopped in front of the TV screen. "I found this. After she died," he said. He moved his gloved finger. Suddenly, Garth Brooks poured from hidden speakers.

"Dammit," he muttered and shut down the music, only to have the curtains over the sliding glass doors begin to close.

"Sorry," he said, "I'm still getting used to this remote-control glove. Kyle rigged it up for me."

Finally, the TV sprang to life with a video featuring Burns Hamlin onstage at a poetry conference. He was dressed in black and wore the same Burberry scarf she'd seen him wearing two days before.

Davenport fast-forwarded to a few minutes in and Aloa watched as Hamlin paced the stage, telling a story about nearly starving after a bear destroyed his food cache while he was living in backcountry Alaska writing *Eternal Light*, the poetry book that had given him a degree of success.

Davenport fast-forwarded the video again. "OK. Watch what happens when this guy in the audience asks him why he didn't just call for a supply plane. The guy says he used to live in Alaska. It's a valid point."

Aloa watched Hamlin say "good question" and explain how bad weather had interfered with his satellite phone and his nearest neighbor was ten miles away over rough terrain. Davenport stopped the video and rewound it a few seconds. "OK, now watch Hamlin's face when he says 'good question.' See how his lips are tight? That's a microexpression, a brief but intense flash of emotion. He's angry at the question, which is a sign he's probably lying about almost starving. Most of us don't realize our faces and bodies are telling the world things we don't want it to know.

"Now watch this." Davenport fast-forwarded the video to a spot where a woman asked Hamlin how he dealt with criticism, like the critic who said reading his book was like being bitten by a thousand mosquitoes while a bear chewed his head.

"See how he touches his throat just before he answers?" Davenport asked. "That's violence there. He wants to strangle her for bringing up something that puts him in a bad light. He's got some real issues with self-esteem and with women, I think."

"Can you really rely on facial expressions and body tics for such important clues?" Aloa asked.

"If you're trained in it, then yes. One time, I interviewed this programmer who kept insisting he had no connection with a hacker group called Sandsnake and when I asked about one of its members, a guy called AnthillPhil, he said he'd never heard of the guy. But in the middle of his denial, he touched the side of his nose. His subconscious was saying his story stunk and I knew I had him. Eventually, we linked the guy to Sandsnake. Real interrogation is about seeing details."

Aloa thought of the skeleton fingers that marked Corrine Davenport's lower belly.

"Speaking of details, your wife had an interesting tattoo. Did it mean anything?"

"You're good," Davenport said. "You could have been an agent."

"Thanks, but I don't do well with bureaucracies," Aloa said.

"Neither do I," he said. "But to answer your question, the tattoo was based on customs in the old houses of pleasure in Japan. If a courtesan and customer fell in love, and if the customer couldn't buy the courtesan's contract and free her, they would give each other tokens of their undying love. They would write pledges of loyalty, cut off a lock of hair, get a tattoo, pull out a fingernail, or cut off a finger. Corrine's tattoo was the symbolic version of cutting off a finger. She wanted to show me her eternal love and loyalty. I was against it. I told her I would probably die long before she did and that she should remarry."

"She got it after your accident?"

"She did."

A discreet knock came and Kyle stuck his head inside the room. "Sorry to interrupt, Christian, but your lawyer is on the phone. He says he finally got a settlement offer from the garbage company and that it's good news, but he wants to run it by you before he goes any further."

Davenport pressed his lips together. "I guess I need to take the call."

"It's important," Kyle said.

"Kyle, will you show Aloa out? And give her the stuff we found." He nodded at Aloa. "I think you'll find it interesting."

At the front door, Kyle put a manila envelope into her hands. "Be careful with him," he said in a low voice. "Christian's not as strong as he pretends to be."

Back home, Aloa heated up a can of tomato soup, noticed the amount of salt on the label, and calculated how much water weight she'd gain. She almost dumped it down the sink, except she knew that's exactly what her disease wanted. *Screw you,* she told her illness and added a pat of butter to the soup, although she fished it out a few seconds later and set it aside.

She washed up the few dishes she'd used and retired to her desk. The manila envelope Davenport had given her sat unopened. She shook out its contents. The first set of papers turned out to be a printout of the texts between Hamlin and Davenport's wife.

Aloa had skimmed the texts at Quinn's office, but now she read each one more carefully.

From Burns: When will U get here? I'm waiting.

Corrine: Sooner than soon. I can still feel UR touch.

Burns: I would be with U all night if I could.

A few weeks later, from Corrine: I've laid out my heart for you. Be gentle.

A plea for understanding, Aloa thought.

Burns: Your heart is safe with me, sweet one.

Four months later, again from Corrine: I can't meet. C has a fever.

Burns: Can't Kyle take care of him?

Corrine: I sent the little prick home.

Corrine, later: I know what you're doing.

Burns: I'll see you. In class.

Aloa wasn't sure whether to believe Hamlin's or Corrine's version of the relationship. It was clear, however, the affair had unraveled—and also that Corrine had disliked Kyle. Was there something there?

She turned to the last page and saw a final text from Corrine, which was sent the morning of the day she died. The gray sea and the long black land. Shall we?

There was no reply.

She stared at the text for a few minutes and turned to her laptop, typing in the words and wondering if the police had done the same. The sentence was a quote from the poem "Meeting at Night" by Robert Browning. It was about a suitor who traveled across land and sea to rendezvous with his secret lover one night.

An invitation for Hamlin to meet her?

If so, the guilt meter had just swung strongly in the professor's direction.

She pressed her lips together and sketched out a quick timeline of the affair based on the texts, made a note in her Moleskine about Corrine's dislike of Kyle, and added the Browning quote to the list of questions she had for Hamlin.

She turned to the next document: a full transcription of the interview with the Davenports' neighbor, who said the late-night caller had knocked once and that the door had opened quickly. Almost as if whoever was in the Davenports' house had been expecting the visitor, the neighbor said. She didn't see the caller leave (her cat had chosen that moment to throw up on the rug) but she described the visitor as about six feet in height and medium build, wearing a black hoodie pulled over his head, blue jeans, and dark canvas shoes.

A description that could fit Hamlin—and thousands of other males in the city.

The caller also was white (the neighbor saw his hand when he knocked on the door), and if the caller had arrived by car, he hadn't parked it on their street, she said. The rest of the interview was about how sorry she felt for poor Mr. Davenport and how it wasn't safe to live anywhere these days.

Aloa set the report aside and wondered how Davenport had gotten the documents. She guessed he still had connections in the FBI, people who would want to help him, but it was unusual for a local jurisdiction to provide reports to the bureau unless the FBI was asked to get involved in the case. She made a note to dig further.

The next sheet of paper made her set down her pen. The police had gotten a warrant for Hamlin's cell phone locations for the three days surrounding Corrine Davenport's death. While the locations were only general, they cast another dark shadow on Hamlin's claims of innocence. According to the report, Hamlin had been in Corrine's neighborhood on the night she died.

The news about Hamlin sent Aloa back to her bedroom, where she yanked on her running clothes, pulled on the pink watch cap and an old sweatshirt, and strode out the front door. She headed to the Embarcadero, where she let her frustration with Hamlin's arrogance and lack of transparency dissolve with a series of wind sprints. The last text from Corrine and the cell phone records didn't prove he was the killer, but it certainly gave her doubts about his innocence. *Patience,* she told herself.

Forty-five minutes later, finally calm, she headed for home, slipping into her favorite market for a loaf of bread, a couple of avocados, and two fat oranges. She stopped in front of a cluttered hardware store with a display of space heaters in the window and went inside, using her phone to buy one of the electric warmers. If she had to fight her way through this case, at least she would do it at a pleasant temperature.

Back home, she set up the heater by her desk, put away the groceries, and stood in the shower until she thawed out. Half an hour later, she was pushing her way through the front door of Justus.

The place was noisy with people escaping the cold and gray.

In one corner, a tired-looking man in his early forties sat nursing a beer, a skinny, one-eyed cat curled on his lap. Baxter, the stray Gully had adopted after it had been tossed out of a car at six weeks of age, had a way of locating those most in need of comfort and giving them the gift of his soothing purrs. As she closed the door behind her, Aloa wondered about the tired man's story.

Across the room, the Brain Farm, armed with glasses of house red, were hunched over a table, stabbing fingers at a scattering of papers and books. When Doc looked up and saw her, the whole crew began shoving everything onto their laps and into worn satchels.

What the hell were they up to?

Aloa waded through the crowd to the bar, catching Erik's eye.

She looked up at the chalkboard menu. "A glass of red and whatever Singapore crab pasta is," she called as Erik hustled whiskeys and beer.

"You won't be sorry," he said, turning to shout her order through the pass-through window into the kitchen.

Guillermo popped suddenly into view. "You have survived the cat's foot," he cried.

Aloa frowned.

"I was reading Carl Sandburg to him this morning," Erik explained, "his poem about fog." Then to Gully: "It's 'little cat feet,' my love."

"*Pues*," said Gully, "the kitten did her no harm." He gave Aloa one of his beautiful smiles. "I hope you will like today's special. It is a crab that has its claws in both Italy and Asia." And with that, he disappeared.

"How can you not love that man?" Erik said as he poured Aloa a glass of pinot noir and two men at the end of the bar shouted orders for Irish coffees.

"He's pretty great," Aloa agreed.

She took her wine and pushed her way over to the Brain Farm. "What were you guys looking at when I came in?" she asked.

"Nothing," P-Mac said. "Just planning a little jaunt. A getaway."

Doc elbowed him in the ribs.

"So what's new with the case, Ink?" Tick asked hurriedly, throwing a glare in P-Mac's direction.

"Well, I had a chance to take a long look at the texts between your son and the victim," Aloa said.

"And?" Tick asked.

"And they don't prove what happened one way or the other."

She gave them a brief rundown.

"Then Burns could be telling the truth," Tick said.

"He could be," Aloa said slowly. "There's one big problem for him, though."

The Brain Farm leaned in.

"The cops are pretty sure he was in the area on the night of the murder."

Doc snapped his fingers. "Those bastards got his cell phone records."

"I didn't say that," Aloa started, but the gray-hairs were already in full outrage mode.

"Privacy means nothing to Uncle Satan," P-Mac cried. "I'm telling you, it's time to make our move, Tick."

"I agree," Doc said.

"What move?" Aloa asked.

"It's time to get the kid out of here," P-Mac said and pulled a stack of papers from his lap, on top of which lay a half-open map of Mexico.

"Oh, no, no," Aloa said.

"Why not?" Tick said. "You're a fool if you rely on the justice system. Just look at all the innocent people rotting in jail. We're no different than some Third World dictatorship. We pretend we have rules, but it's all about money and power. I say it's better to get the hell out of Dodge."

"Yeah," Doc agreed. "Look at the Central Park Five. Five kids, all of color, coerced to confess to the rape of a white woman—a rape, it turned out later, some other guy committed."

The men nodded vigorously.

"The cops will take running away as a sign of guilt," Aloa said.

"It's not against the law to take a vacation," P-Mac said.

"Lots of people go to Puerto Vallarta this time of year," Tick said in a voice that was anything but innocent.

"Who says he'll even go with you?" Aloa asked.

"We'll tell him about the cell phone records," Tick said.

Aloa groaned. "Listen. Before you do anything, I have an idea. Something that might help show he wasn't the guy who knocked on the door the night the wife was killed." The thought had come to Aloa when she'd seen the tired man with the cat on his lap.

"What is it?" the men demanded.

"I need to look into it first," she said.

Now it was the men's turn to groan.

"I also want to check out the cases the wife prosecuted. Davenport said she did low-level stuff, but that doesn't rule out that somebody was crazy or angry enough to want revenge. It's way too early to be pulling a Butch Cassidy and Sundance Kid."

"Bolivia," said Tick. "Now there's an idea."

"Please, Tick," Aloa said and put her hand over his. "Before you go running off somewhere, let me see what I can find. Let me do what I do. You know nothing's simple, and if the cops were going to arrest Burns just because he was in the area when Corrine died, they would have done it already. You have to trust me."

60

His faded blue eyes searched Aloa's face.

"You got some ideas?" he asked.

"I do."

He took a slug of wine. "All right," he said.

"That's my guy," said Aloa and leaned over and kissed his rough cheek.

"One Singapore crab pasta," Erik interrupted, setting a steaming plate of handmade pasta topped with arugula and fresh crab in chili sauce in front of Aloa. Her brain automatically cataloged the calories—1,500 for the entire plate, 500 if she only ate part of it—and she shoved the thought away.

"Everything good here?" Erik asked, seeing the serious faces and the map on the table.

P-Mac flipped the map facedown. "Just doing some vacation planning."

Aloa looked hard at the men. "But then you decided not to go, didn't you?"

Only Doc nodded.

DAY 5

Aloa piloted her motorcycle toward Burns Hamlin's house, her eyes and brain on high alert. Thick fog pushed against the ground, wrapping around buildings and making pedestrians on the sidewalk look like apparitions. Halfway there, a delivery truck pulled out from a side street in front of her. She swerved, missing the truck's bumper by inches. It took a few minutes for her heart to stop pounding.

This morning's headlines had chronicled four more deaths from the fog. A produce truck had crashed into a car on the Golden Gate Bridge, claiming another life, and a pair of asthmatics without health insurance had come to the hospital too late to be saved. The body of a frail seventy-two-year-old Vietnam vet had been found on Ocean Beach, dead of exposure.

Aloa had read the article over a cup of coffee. It described how the vet, then a twenty-two-year-old in the special forces, had survived firefights and ambushes only to have accidentally been shot in the head by a fellow soldier. He'd come home suffering from severe headaches and bouts of paranoia and, after a few years, had ended up on the streets.

He died huddled near a driftwood log, dressed only in a T-shirt and a pair of ragged camouflage pants.

A casualty of war that would never be counted, Aloa thought.

Muggings in the city also had spiked, the perpetrators disappearing into the murk before their victims could get a good look at them. It was as if the world had been wrapped in some horror-movie version of cotton candy: gray, thickly spun, and deadly.

She parked the motorcycle near Hamlin's house, took off her helmet, and ran her fingers through her hair. The ride here had been gnarly, but the real hard work lay ahead: talking her way back into Burns Hamlin's house.

She'd checked his course schedule last night and planned her arrival so that if he wouldn't open his door, she could at least nab him an hour later when he had to leave for class. Her pitch to him would have to be quick.

She knocked, pulled up the collar of her leather jacket against the chill, and waited.

"I don't want to talk to you," came Hamlin's voice from the other side of the door.

"I'm sure you don't, but you might be interested in this."

"What?" Hamlin demanded.

"I ran into Esther Sterling the other day and she said she's looking for a new poetry collection. Sea-based poems," Aloa called through the door. Esther Sterling was a celebrated UC Berkeley professor and novelist who'd married a multimillionaire and started her own indie publishing house. Aloa had taken Esther's class her senior year and been befriended by the silver-haired teacher, who'd recognized her own eating issues in her student. They met for coffee a couple of times a year to talk about what was going on in their lives and, at their last gathering a few weeks earlier, Esther had mentioned her plans. Aloa was pretty sure her professor wouldn't mind having her name used in the pursuit of justice. Besides, Hamlin wasn't a bad poet.

The door cracked open. "You know Esther Sterling?"

"We're friends."

"My agent has been trying to get hold of her for months."

The door swung open wider.

"I could give her your name," Aloa said. Then, quickly, "I also read the witness statement from the neighbor who saw someone at the Davenports' front door that night, and I think there's a way to clear you."

"You think I'm going to fall for that again?" he said.

The door began to close but Aloa quickly shoved her Timberland into the space, thanking her father again for the sturdy footwear.

"No. This is good," she said. "Something the cops didn't see. Give me five minutes." She waited. "I'll call Esther after we talk."

The pressure on her boot eased but Hamlin's frown didn't.

"Show me your closet," Aloa said.

"What the hell?"

"Please?"

"This is ridiculous," Hamlin said but he led Aloa upstairs, down the hall, and into a good-sized room with an unmade king-size bed, a nightstand brimming with books, an antique bureau cluttered with socks and papers, and a window with a view of the house's small backyard.

The tired man at Justus had been dressed head to toe in black, which had sparked Aloa's memory, and she opened Hamlin's closet to see exactly what she'd hoped to find. Everything in it was black: shirts, pants, sports coats, and jackets.

"Do you own any blue jeans?" Aloa asked.

"God no. I'm not some soccer dad," Hamlin said.

"The guy at the door that night wore blue jeans," Aloa said.

"See, I told you," Hamlin said. "I'm innocent."

"It's a start," Aloa said. "Unfortunately, you've still got problems. There's a text from Corrine that appears to ask you to meet her on the night she died." She recited the line of poetry to him.

"Browning," he said and frowned, "but I never saw a text like that."

"Then why were you in Corrine Davenport's neighborhood around the time she was stabbed?" She wouldn't put it past Tick to get in touch with Hamlin and tell him about the cell phone trace, and she wanted to get the professor's reaction before he had time to prepare.

"Jee-zus, what?" Hamlin said.

"Your cell phone," Aloa said. "It puts you near her house."

His gaze darted to the antique bureau and back. "Maybe I just like to walk. It's not a crime to exercise at night."

Aloa followed his glance to a framed photo of a gawky teenaged boy with horn-rimmed glasses, dark hair, and an oversize nose that was almost an exact replica of Hamlin's.

Did Tick know he had a grandson?

"What's your son's name?" she asked.

"None of your business."

"That's Coit Tower in the background. Does he live here?"

"Christ, you're nosy."

"Side effect of the business. Do you see him often? He's a good-looking kid."

Something shifted in Hamlin's eyes. "I see him on Tuesdays," he said quietly.

Corrine Davenport died on a Tuesday.

"Were you with him the night of Corrine's death?"

Hamlin rubbed a hand over his face. "You can't tell anybody."

"Tell me how I can get ahold of your son," Aloa pressed.

Hamlin sank onto the edge of the bed. "This has to be off the record. You can't write about this or tell the cops."

"This isn't a game," Aloa said.

"Off the record or not?"

Perhaps she could change his mind later. "All right," she said.

According to Hamlin, when he was twenty-two and living in New York, he'd met a woman and they'd moved in together. Things had been good. She'd worked in the kitchen of an important chef while he worked toward his MFA at Columbia. They spent their free time reading and eating and going to plays. She was intense and mercurial, which offset his tendency to fall into routine. A year later, she'd broken up with him after an argument, but they'd gotten back together after a month. She told him she was pregnant, and when she delivered a healthy baby boy, he'd cried. A year later, she'd discovered he'd slept with one of her friends during the period they'd been apart and accused him of cheating on her.

Couldn't you have kept it in your pants for four weeks? Aloa thought.

The lover had taken a $20,000 painting he'd bought for her, spray-painted "B. Hamlin is a cheater" on the wall of his apartment building, and moved out.

Hamlin, torn apart by the loss of his son but not the boy's mother, had sued and won partial custody of his then two-year-old boy. His ex-lover, however, had later found a bulldog of a lawyer who persuaded a judge that Hamlin had failed to properly care for the boy. The attorney recounted how Hamlin had taken the boy with him on a visit to his new girlfriend on Cape Cod, forgetting both his son's medication and the fact the child was allergic to cats, of which his girlfriend had three.

"I took him to the ER. Everything turned out OK," Hamlin had explained.

But the judge had disagreed and his ex-lover had moved without leaving a forwarding address. Hamlin, however, had hired a private investigator who found the boy and his ex three years later, living with a fisherman near Dillingham, Alaska—hence, the stay that inspired *Eternal Light*.

Hamlin had arrived in Dillingham and knocked on her door, demanding to see his son. The fisherman's answer had been to give Hamlin two black eyes and a broken nose.

Hamlin had retreated inland, rented a cabin, and tried to get a judge there to allow him shared custody of his son. The attempt failed: the former lover claimed Hamlin was drunk when he came to their house, and since the judge wasn't a fan of outsiders coming to his state to escape court judgments in the lower forty-eight, the ruling went against him.

Six months later, the boy's mother broke up with the fisherman, left Alaska, and was gone for seven years. Finally, the investigator discovered the boy and his ex living in San Francisco under another name, and Hamlin, who was then back in New York, moved west.

This time, however, he tried a different tack. He found the boy's school and waited outside, eventually handing the boy the only photo he had of his short-lived family—one taken at the hospital after the boy was born.

"Unlike my own father, I wanted a relationship with my son," he said.

Aloa decided it wasn't her place to tell him what Tick had said about why he hadn't seen his son.

Hamlin, meanwhile, said he'd given the boy a cell phone he'd bought in his own name and told the boy if he wanted to talk, to call him and they could go get pizza or tacos or something. He asked the boy not to tell his mother.

The boy had called, they'd had Mexican food, and the meeting had turned into a standing date for Taco Tuesdays while the boy's mother worked as a cook at some tourist restaurant on Fisherman's Wharf. The boy was smart, Hamlin told her, but, like a lot of smart kids, was the target of bullies. Hamlin had taught him how to fight and the boy had proudly been suspended for landing a punch to the throat of his biggest tormentor—although his mother was not quite as overjoyed.

"He's an amazing kid, my whole world," Hamlin said.

Aloa's mind raced ahead. "So on the night Corrine Davenport died, a Tuesday, you'd had dinner with your son."

"Yes. We ate and he went home to study, and I went to a bar down the street to have a beer. Corrine had threatened to report me, and if I lost my job I'd lose my trust fund, thanks to a lovely stipulation my stepfather included. Before I can get the seven million dollars he promised, I need to have a 'real job' for at least five years," he said, making air quotes. "His lawyer makes me send W-2 forms. I've got three more years to go."

Again, Aloa wondered why Hamlin couldn't keep it in his pants.

He told Aloa he drank two Stellas at a table by himself. Around 9:30 p.m., he'd gotten a call from his son. A girl he liked had just texted to tell him she didn't want to eat lunch with him anymore. The boy was heartbroken.

"His mother was still at work so I walked over to meet him and we talked. I left around ten forty-five, I think."

"So you never went to Corrine's house?"

"No."

"And does your son live nearby?"

"Not too far away. I walked home."

"So your son is your alibi," Aloa said.

Hamlin stood. "He's not part of this."

"You'd rather go to jail?"

"I'm not going to jail. I'm innocent."

Aloa had met people who'd stubbornly insisted on their innocence, only to be caught later in a lie. But, for some reason, she believed Hamlin. Maybe it was the look in his eyes when he talked about his hunt for the boy and about his son's pain that night.

"Do you have a credit card receipt from the restaurant or the bar?"

"I always pay cash."

"How about if you tell me names of these places? Maybe somebody will recognize you."

"I don't want you snooping around, period. If my ex somehow finds out I've been anywhere near her neighborhood—for any reason—she might leave again. The last time she disappeared with the boy, they ended up in Thailand. It's a screwed-up situation, I know. But it's all I've got. My lawyer says there isn't much hope of getting custody. Not after all this time."

"If you're in prison, you won't see him either."

"At least I'll know where he is." Hamlin looked at his hands, then up at Aloa. "I know I was wrong for sleeping with a student, but I didn't kill her. Please. Find out who did it. Figure out who was there that night. It wasn't me, I swear."

She thought of her own father and how he'd been torn from her, and how she still felt the ache of that loss.

Hamlin's voice cracked. "I can't lose my son."

"I'll see what I can do," she said.

Aloa thought Hamlin was being a bit too paranoid about his ex and, besides, she knew she could be discreet. Thanks to Hamlin's slip of the tongue, she found two Mexican restaurants within a three-mile radius of Corrine Davenport's home and visited both, asking the managers if they'd seen a tall man wearing a plaid scarf who came in regularly for Taco Tuesdays.

At the second restaurant, the manager said he'd seen a guy like that and that he usually came with a teenage boy. He couldn't be sure, however, whether or not they'd been there on that particular Tuesday. And, no, he didn't know the boy's name—or the man's name for that matter.

Aloa found the bar a few doors away. The bartender, who had an Irish accent as thick as a peat bog, said he always worked Tuesday nights but didn't remember Hamlin. "I'm not just sitting around staring at my customers, now am I?" he said.

Aloa supposed she could wait outside the Mexican restaurant the following Tuesday, which was six days away, or she could hang around every public school in the area looking for a boy who matched the photo, but the kid could have been enrolled in a private school, which would add a dozen more locations to the mix. She would leave surveillance as a last resort.

On the way home, she stopped at her favorite grocery and bought a chicken to roast and the makings for a green salad. Then, she settled in at her desk, the space heater baking the lower half of her body but leaving her torso to freeze.

What sadist designed these things?

She spent an hour searching online for a custody lawsuit involving Hamlin, but if it existed, it had been sealed. After, she took a wild stab and looked for stories about female chefs in the city but none of them worked at Fisherman's Wharf. Frustrated, she closed the lid on her laptop and went into the kitchen and drank a large glass of water. While she was there, she scrubbed the sink and swept the floor until her irritation eased.

She was into her third hour at her computer when she found something interesting. A search of Corrine Davenport's name and title as assistant district attorney had brought Aloa to a prison-rights website and the story of a twenty-nine-year-old defendant named Pablo Ruiz. Ruiz had been sentenced to four years in state prison for selling a half pound of heroin to an undercover agent near his son's elementary school. Corrine Davenport had been the prosecutor.

According to the article, Ruiz, who had no prior criminal record, had claimed that he only sold the drugs because he needed the money to pay for his wife's stomach-cancer treatments.

Aloa sat straighter in her chair. Could the fact Corrine Davenport had been stabbed in the abdomen be a symbolic payback?

The writer chronicled how Ruiz had fallen apart in prison when he learned his wife had died and their two children had been put into foster care. Advocates said the only reason Ruiz had been given a maximum sentence was because the district attorney was being pressured to get tough on heroin dealers in the city and the judge's son had died of a drug overdose eight months before.

It was the perfect confluence of overzealous prosecution and lack of sympathy for the terrible choices faced by the poor when they got sick, activists said.

Aloa did a quick search on a prison inmate site and found three Pablo Ruizes, but none of them were the right age. She glanced at the clock and dialed her friend Steve Porter, a computer whiz who worked for the State Department and owed her a lifetime of favors for clearing his name in a murder investigation.

"How's it hanging, girl?" Steve bellowed.

A forty-year-old white guy who graduated from Harvard, he talked like a street tough from the wrong side of the tracks.

"In case you didn't notice, I've got nothing to hang, Steve," she said.

"True that," he said. "So what's the refresh?"

Sometimes she thought she needed a Steve Porter translation app.

"I'm working on another article."

"Fives to you."

She frowned. "And I need to find out where a guy who was in prison for selling heroin might be."

"No prob. Give me the deets."

It took Porter only four minutes to come up with the answer. Pablo Ruiz had been paroled from Folsom Prison back to San Francisco four months before Corrine's death.

"Looks like he had some trouble inside," Porter said. "Six months in the SHU, the Special Housing Unit, for trying to light another inmate on fire. Got caught with a shiv too." He made a clicking sound with his tongue. "If you're looking for him you'd best be careful. You know what solitary does to a dude."

Aloa knew. While doing a story on a man who'd been released from prison after DNA tests had overturned his rape conviction, she'd read the testimony of a professor of psychology named Craig Haney. Haney compared solitary confinement to a long form of social death. Most of those who went into those silent, windowless cells came out so psychologically damaged they could never fit into the world again.

Aloa asked for the name and phone number of Ruiz's parole officer and thanked Porter.

"Ain't nothin', girl," he said. "And I'm going to email you a photo of the dude. Got to be wary, you know."

Ruiz's parole officer was brusque when Aloa called. Ruiz, he said, had been paroled to a halfway house in the city and hadn't lasted a month before he rabbited, and if she knew where in the hell Ruiz was she'd better tell him.

She told him she was on the hunt, too, and broke the connection.

She got up, preheated the oven, and pulled the chicken from the refrigerator. She fired up a little early Madonna as background music and stuffed a few pats of butter under the chicken skin. She rubbed the skin with olive oil, salt, and garlic, and put it in the oven to roast while she tossed a salad. She thought about what she'd accomplished so far and poured herself a glass of wine. She was still a long way from finding the answers she needed, but at least she had a new path to follow.

DAY 6

Cold and fog still pressed down on the city. San Franciscans who accepted the gentle summer fog as a fact of life were growing unnerved by the frigid miasma that seemed to weigh them down. The dark clouds were suffocating and mean, as if they were determined to bring the too-pretty city to its knees.

The mayor had announced the opening of warming shelters, and a suicide hotline reported calls had increased by 50 percent. The same columnist who had written about the shipwreck in the fog now told a story about the time the US military used San Francisco's fog as part of a germ warfare test.

Aloa made herself a slice of avocado toast, poured some coffee, and sat down in front of her computer to read. According to the columnist, in 1950 a navy ship had spent six days spraying what was believed to be harmless bacteria into the fog over San Francisco as a way to test the susceptibility of a big city to a germ warfare attack. The experiment was a success. Monitors showed hundreds of thousands of unsuspecting residents had been exposed to the germs. But the microorganisms may not have been as harmless as was thought. Right after the spraying, eleven people landed in the hospital with urinary tract infections caused by a rare bacterium—the same one that had been sprayed.

Aloa couldn't help looking out her front window into the grayness and wondering what lurked out there.

She told herself to stop imagining what wasn't there and shook away thoughts of germs in the mist. She got up, washed her few dishes, and slipped into jeans and a thick sweater before heading out the door.

Twenty minutes later, she parked the bike and climbed cracked steps to the halfway house where Ruiz had been paroled. The manager of the house, a man with a bulldog face and a long scar that bisected his top lip, told Aloa it wasn't his job to track down parole violators, and besides, Ruiz had been nothing but trouble.

He had harassed other residents, refused the chores he'd been assigned, and had missed two mandatory meetings.

"Good riddance to bad seed," the manager said.

Aloa let herself outside and was considering her next move when a skinny woman slipped out the door behind her.

"I know where he is," the woman hissed, plucking at Aloa's sleeve. "For twenty dollars I can show you."

The whites of the woman's eyes had yellowed, and beneath the open coat she wore was a bloated belly on a too-thin frame.

"Where is he?" Aloa asked.

"In the Jungle," the woman whispered.

The Jungle was a homeless encampment under the 101 freeway where more than a hundred of the city's most vulnerable citizens had created a small village for themselves. They were the sick, the unemployed, the just plain unlucky. More than half had substance abuse problems or mental illness. Many had both. Overdoses, fights, and stabbings occurred with regular frequency, and for a moment Aloa considered calling Rick Quinn and asking if she could buy him a cup of coffee in exchange for a little backup. But she knew the arrival of a police officer at the encampment would send everybody running for cover. This woman in front of her, now picking at her lips with nervous fingers, would be a much better guide. She'd just have to try to outrun whatever trouble came her way.

"I'll pay you when we get there," Aloa said.

Twenty minutes later, the woman pointed toward a section of the encampment under the sweep of highway. "He's in there. Over by that big pillar," the woman said. "Ask for Elvis. He knows where to find Pablo."

The place looked like it had been dreamed up for an apocalyptic movie. Packed-dirt paths led through a maze of tents, tarps, and graying sheets of plywood. Shopping carts—overflowing with mildewed sleeping bags, broken chairs, and discarded rugs—were parked in front of makeshift huts. Trash piled along the edges of the place and shattered glass lay scattered on the ground.

After Aloa had left the newspaper and when she thought she might lose her grandmother's house, she sometimes considered what it would be like to not have a home. She imagined herself as a vagabond, traveling the country with only a sleeping bag and a car, working a series of mindless jobs and having her freedom. Part of her thought it wouldn't be a bad way to live. But what was in front of her wasn't freedom. This was being so tied up in the chains of poverty and illness that you couldn't move.

Aloa took a breath and walked in.

Eyes followed her from beneath piles of dirty blankets. A man in saggy jeans and a faded Raiders jersey waved his arms and shouted at one of the freeway support pillars in the center of the space. "God will judge you and find you wanting," he cried. "He will send you into the fires of hell." His gaze caught Aloa's and he pivoted, pointing a finger at her. "Only God can pull you from eternal punishment. Only God's grace can lift you up. Ask for forgiveness, sinner, and you will be saved."

Aloa hurried on.

If only forgiveness were that easy, she thought, remembering the looks in the newsroom as she boxed up her desk and the faces of her so-called friends who turned away as she walked past. She'd broken not only the trust of the newspaper's readers, but also of her fellow journalists. Reporters did not forget when one of their own betrayed them. And they didn't forgive easily either. Even with the series she'd done for Novo, redemption was a long way off. If it was there at all.

She passed a tattooed man working on a bicycle and a man so covered in sores he looked as if he were a leper. "Spare change, sister?" he asked.

The place smelled of rot and overflowing sewer. The noise of cars above created a never-ending roar. Ahead of her, a toddler dug in the dirt with a teaspoon as a tired-looking young woman with a headful of dark braids watched. Aloa's heart cracked and she wished she'd thought to bring sandwiches and coffee. She smiled at the young mother but the woman wouldn't meet her eyes.

What was her story?

A little farther in, Aloa approached two guys in stained clothes seated next to a wood-and-canvas hut. They were warming their hands over a hibachi.

"Welcome to Shackteau Saint Shithole," said one of the men. "What can we do you for?"

"Do you know where I can find a guy named Elvis?" Aloa asked.

"I told you, Ronnie, fine ladies never come looking for us," said the second man, shaking his head in fake regret.

"That's because you scare 'em off with the way you're smellin'," said the man who apparently was named Ronnie. "Lucky for me, I got sinus problems." He thumbed toward a plywood-and-tarp lean-to a short distance away. "That's Elvis's place over there."

The other man leaned forward. "But be careful," he said, "he might bite."

The two men rocked back with laughter and Aloa moved on, hoping it was a joke.

She stopped in front of the makeshift shelter. "Elvis? Are you in there, Elvis?" she called.

She heard a rustle of tarp and a phlegmy cough. "Who's askin'?" said a voice.

She took a step back just in case. "My name's Aloa. I'm looking for Pablo. Pablo Ruiz."

The face of a grizzled and toothless man poked out from the hut—the biting threat was a joke after all. "I got first dibs," he said.

"Sorry. I don't understand," she said.

Elvis cocked his head toward a blue tent next door. "Pablo lives there, and if he ain't back by tomorrow the place is mine. Them's the rules. You can't be jumpin' ahead."

"I just want to speak with Mr. Ruiz," Aloa said.

"Well, he's gone," Elvis said.

"Do you know where he went?"

"I guess a Jackson could jog my memory," the toothless man said.

Aloa pulled a twenty from her jacket pocket. She was starting to feel like an ATM machine.

"Last I saw him was about two weeks back. He was going to a recovery meeting over there at that old yellow storefront on Cesar Chavez. Then nothing until about six days ago. He come back, middle of the night; didn't see him, but heard him rustling around and saw a light in his place."

"Can I look through his tent?"

"Sure, but don't take nothin'," Elvis warned.

Aloa crouched in front of the nylon shelter and unzipped the door. Inside was the facsimile of a tiny and tidy home: a neatly made cot, a faded rug, a camping stove, and a framed photo of a smiling family. A cardboard box held a stack of papers. Aloa reached out a hand and pulled it toward her. "People vs. Pablo Ruiz" read a superior court document. Clipped to that was a printout of the story Aloa had seen, along with a photocopied picture of Corrine Davenport.

Davenport's face was circled in red ink.

Aloa took photos of the interior of the tent and a shot of Corrine Davenport's altered photograph with her phone.

Maybe she'd found something.

She stood as a man pushing a big-screen TV in a shopping cart shoved past. "'Scuse me," he said.

Elvis was now sitting on an overturned milk crate, a grimy sleeping bag wrapped around his shoulders. He looked to be in his late sixties, but Aloa guessed he was younger. Life on the streets would do that to you.

"Do you know when Mr. Ruiz is coming back?" she asked him.

"Say, you got a cigarette on you?"

Aloa shook her head.

Elvis made a sucking sound with his lips. "He's gone a week, I get his place. I woulda had it a lot earlier but ol' Pablo jumped me to it. Billy used ta live there, but he disappeared and the next thing I knows, Pablo took over and I sure as heck weren't going to mess with him. He a crazy dude. Just outta the joint. He threwed down a knife in front of this girl, Star, who offered to blow him for a speedball."

Elvis leaned in and Aloa could smell his stale breath. "Then her, that Star, well, she up and disappeared too," Elvis said. "Just like Billy. Lotta people been disappearing around here lately." Elvis rocked back on his crate.

"Disappeared?"

"Poof," Elvis said.

Aloa's brain clicked. "Are you saying maybe Mr. Ruiz killed them?"

"Ain't nothing impossible in this place."

Her mind raced. Not only did the documents in Ruiz's tent point to his apparent interest in Corrine Davenport, but now there was also a possible connection to two missing people.

She asked for the address of the recovery meeting and got the full name of the missing Billy (Elvis didn't know Star's real name) along with a request to return with a pack of Camel Lights.

Aloa was sitting in a coffee shop nursing a black coffee with a crowd of other chilled San Franciscans when Rick Quinn returned the call she'd made after she'd left the Jungle.

"Are you going to tell me why you're asking about a guy we found dead in a duffel bag, one William Lisowski?" he asked.

"Oh crap," she said. "How'd he die?"

"First, you tell me how you know the guy."

Aloa paused. "His name came up."

"Are we going to play this game?"

Aloa knew she'd get nowhere with Quinn if she didn't lay at least some of her cards on the table. "I was at the Jungle, looking for this drug dealer Corrine Davenport put away, and somebody mentioned him."

Quinn swore. "What the hell were you doing in the Jungle? That place isn't safe."

"Nothing happened," Aloa said defensively.

"This time," Quinn warned.

"Can you spare me the lecture and just answer my question about how Billy, Mr. Lisowski, died?"

"The coroner says it looks like somebody shot him in the forehead with a bolt gun. Then they slit his throat. His skull had a dent a half-inch deep. That's not something you see every day."

Aloa shuddered. *Poor Billy.*

"Where'd they find him?"

"On Howard Street." He gave her the address.

Aloa waited. "Are you going to tell me more?"

"Not if you're going to be wandering around homeless camps."

"I wasn't wandering. I was looking for a suspect who might have wanted Corrine Davenport dead."

Quinn sighed. "Listen. We already checked that out. There were no threats made against the victim. The only person who had it out for her was the professor."

"But what if he's the wrong guy?" she pressed.

"You got something I should know about?"

Aloa thought of her promise to Hamlin. "Not yet, but I'm working on it."

"Well, work on it somewhere besides the Jungle."

"Yes, boss."

Quinn paused. "And if you find something different, you'll let me know. Right?"

"Say pretty please."

Quinn hung up.

It took Aloa a half hour of searching on her phone before she found information about Billy's death from a street blogger who went by the name MistaNews. Apparently, the death was the second murder of a homeless person in the new year, a fact that hadn't made it into the regular news. Billy, who'd had two convictions for opioid sales, had been seen peddling his wares on a street corner controlled by MS-13, a violent international ring of criminals that engaged in drug smuggling, human trafficking, and money laundering. His body had been discovered by another homeless guy who'd opened the duffel bag thinking he might find something good to sell, only to discover Billy dead and curled in a fetal position—bound hand and foot with barbed wire.

Aloa stood near the address on Howard Street, getting a feel for where Billy's body had been found. It was a trick she'd learned from an ex-lover, an LA homicide detective she'd dated until his darkness had threatened to overrun her.

A crime scene will tell you stories, her ex had said, but only if you have patience.

Often, he would order everyone from the room, then sit and silently contemplate everything in front of him. On one murder case, he'd spotted a bloody thumbprint on a picture frame. The print was later connected to the killer. Another time, he'd noticed part of a navy-blue button that had slipped between the wall-to-wall carpet and the baseboard. It turned out to belong on a shirt the victim's ex-husband owned.

Aloa's father had taught her something similar. If you walk into a meadow or a forest without stopping, you'll never see what the environment is really like, he'd said. Birds will scatter, insects will fall silent, and animals will freeze in their tracks. But stop and sit and the world will gradually reveal itself again. You'll see the butterfly alight on a flower, you'll notice animal tracks and hear the call of birds.

Aloa leaned against a pale masonry wall, observing what was around her. A clump of people huddled under a bus stop shelter, their arms laden with grocery bags, shuffling from one foot to the other in an attempt to stay warm. A bored attendant sat on a folding chair at the entrance to a parking lot. A nearby bar advertised happy hour from four to six every day but Saturday. It was a busy place.

She guessed Billy's corpse had been dumped in the early morning hours when the bar had emptied and traffic was lighter, and that it had taken two people to bring the body here. Either that or someone who was very strong. Prison strong? She wondered.

She caught sight of an advertisement for the California lottery on a distant billboard. **GOOD FORTUNE FOR ALL** read the ad, which certainly hadn't been true for Billy. His life had been hard, his death gruesome. Nobody deserved that.

She was just crossing the street to take in the view from another angle when her cell phone rang.

She saw the caller ID and answered.

"I was wondering if you might stop by the house," Davenport said in a voice that sounded tired and used up. "Kyle found something I'd like you to see."

"Sure," she said. "Give me twenty minutes."

"That's fine," he said.

Now she was in Davenport's study once again, sipping a tea that Davenport had called Gyokuro Tamahomare, which, he said, was one of the most sought-after teas in Japan. Its name meant something like prestigious pearl of dew and its taste was intense and velvety. The kind of tea that could almost change her mind about being a coffee drinker. Aloa took a sip, then another.

Davenport had been quiet as Kyle prepared the tea and now asked his assistant to fetch the information they'd discovered.

Aloa heard Kyle's footsteps going up the stairs. "Does Kyle live here?"

"He moved in after Corrine died." Davenport sighed. His eyes were glassy and feverish.

"Are you feeling all right?" Aloa asked.

"Just having a bad day," Davenport said.

He looked toward the living room where flames crackled in the marble fireplace. "Last night I thought I saw her," he said softly. "She was right there. Just standing. Her hair was down and she was wearing that dress, the one she wore when she died. She turned and smiled, and I called for her to come, but then I saw she didn't have feet. She floated away."

The hairs on the back of Aloa's neck tingled.

"Do you believe in ghosts, Aloa?" he asked quietly.

"I guess I've seen enough things I can't explain to not rule out the possibility of ghosts."

"I think ghosts are our regrets. What we didn't say or do before someone died," Davenport said. "I think we all have them. Even you."

Aloa thought of her secret and also of her unthinking words to her father before he'd gone on his last run. He'd asked her to take out the trash and she'd rolled her eyes. *Yeah, whatever,* she'd said.

Her fingers shook slightly and she wondered how much caffeine was in the tea she was drinking. She set the cup aside.

"My regret," said Davenport, "is that I didn't die, that Corrine suffered so much because of me. Remember *gaman*, the virtue of endurance?"

"I do."

"She was the definition of it." His gaze went to Corrine's picture on the shelf and came back. "There was this prisoner in Afghanistan, a guy about my age, who claimed he was a farmer. He wouldn't break no matter what I did. I tried talking about his family. I tried telling him how his comrades had abandoned him and that he should look out for himself now so he could go back to his village. I offered him cigarettes. I offered him a nicer cell. And you know what happened?"

Aloa shook her head.

"After a couple of months, one of the guards found him dead. He didn't hang himself with his clothes or his bedsheets like some of the others. The guy just willed himself to die." Davenport inhaled a long breath and looked toward the photo of his wife at the Eiffel Tower.

"After my accident, I tried to do what that guy did. Every night I would lie in bed and try to make my heart stop beating. I did it for hours, but I didn't have whatever he had, and so I kept on living. Do you know what it's like to want death but not be able to have it?"

Aloa shook her head.

"It's worse than any torture you can think of. I begged Corrine to help kill me but she wouldn't and neither would Kyle. I even asked my old lieutenant, Tim Everson, when he stopped by. But he told me it was more courageous for a warrior to continue to fight than to kill himself. I told him being a coward was fine with me, but he wouldn't do it."

The room suddenly felt close and too warm. Aloa slipped out of her jacket. She could hear Kyle coming down the hallway.

"The only reason I have now for living is to make sure Burns Hamlin suffers for what he did," Davenport said. "I want him to hurt. I want him to hurt every single minute of every damned day. I want that sonofabitch to pay." His nostrils flared. "I want him to rot in prison, the same way I'm rotting in this chair. To see how it feels to be caged up."

Luckily Kyle came into the room and Aloa was spared from answering.

"Here you go, Ms. Snow," he said, handing her another manila envelope.

She looked at Davenport. "What's in here?" she asked, but he turned his head away.

"It's a complaint filed against Hamlin when he was an undergrad at a private college in New York," Kyle said quietly. "A classmate claimed he'd stalked her and that she was afraid for her life. The info is all there. Plus, there's an interview with Mrs. Davenport's old boss, who said she'd never been threatened by anyone she'd prosecuted, and two years' worth of medical records for Hamlin. He was seeing a psychiatrist and had a prescription for Xanax."

"How'd you get this stuff?" Aloa asked. She knew the records, especially medical reports, weren't public.

Kyle looked down at his shoes and cleared his throat. "It's not hard to find things, plus Christian still has friends."

"The FBI?"

Kyle cleared his throat again. "You should go."

Aloa glanced again at Davenport and knew she would get no answers from him.

"I'll check back later," she said.

Aloa piloted the Honda motorcycle south through the fog to a spot where land met bay. She needed to clear her head of thoughts of ghosts and a man who'd willed himself dead, and nature was the perfect cleanser.

She parked the bike behind a row of old shipping containers that had been transformed into clandestine businesses—an auto detailer, a welding shop—and ducked through a chained gate toward an expanse of salt marsh unvisited by tourists and yuppies. The fog had lifted slightly and she sat on a graying log, tugging her watch cap more tightly over her ears and tucking her hands into the sleeves of her jacket.

The air was scented with salt and tidal mud. The soil was dark and dotted with clumps of tall grass. She spotted a great blue heron on the hunt and stilled. The bird moved through the shallows with the grace and patience of a tai chi master, stepping one slender leg forward, pausing midstride, and finally setting its foot back into the water. It waited long seconds before taking another slow-motion step. Then another.

Aloa knew she didn't have the heron's patience when it came to the hunt, but she had its persistence. She'd never had a problem spending hours, days, and weeks following the twisting trail to truth. Even when the path led her to a dead end, she simply turned around and tried another way. Dogged obsession was the only redeeming quality of needing to be in control. She thought about this case. Was she on the right path or had she wandered astray?

She watched the heron as the cold seeped through her jacket. She wound Erik's yellow scarf more tightly around her neck and thought she wouldn't leave until the bird either found its prey or flew away. Ten minutes later, the heron finally struck, its sharp bill thrusting lightning-fast into the water and coming up with a small silvery fish.

Aloa stood.

"There you go," she said.

Aloa was chilled but clearheaded as she left the shoreline. She sent the faithful old Honda along side roads in an attempt to avoid as much traffic as she could. A short time later, she was at the old yellow storefront where Ruiz had supposedly attended his recovery meetings. The front windows of the shop were covered in butcher paper, but a small sign taped inside the window listed the schedule for meetings and the name of the program: **HOPE RECOVERY SYSTEMS**.

Could you conjure hope when none was there?

She tried the door. It opened to a fluorescent-lit space filled with two dozen folding chairs and a restroom, where a man in jeans and a plaid shirt was bent over a toilet with a plunger in his hands.

"Meeting doesn't start for another thirty minutes," he said, not looking up.

"Actually, I'm trying to find someone," Aloa said. She waited for him to turn in her direction, then approached him with what she called her church-lady smile: warm with a touch of innocence. She held up her phone. "Would you happen to know this man?"

The man set down the plunger and studied the photo of Ruiz that Steve Porter had emailed. Aloa saw recognition in the man's eyes along with something that told her that, like the manager of the halfway house, he wasn't a member of Pablo Ruiz's fan club.

"'Fraid I can't help," he said.

"You haven't seen this guy?"

"Not saying one way or the other. Anyway, I'm not supposed to talk about what goes on here," he said.

Aloa did a quick calculation. "You must like your job."

The man looked at the overflowing toilet and clucked his tongue. "Thirteen bucks an hour for opening and closing, making coffee, security, plunging toilets, and cleaning up puke. They've got me working six a.m. to eight p.m., but then they tell me I got to take a four-hour break when there ain't any meetings. There ain't no way to get another job for four hours, so I'm stuck. Unless I want to work night shift at a bar, which has its own problems. I guess a guy with a felony record can't be choosy, but this ain't exactly my ideal career choice, if you get what I mean."

"Thirteen bucks an hour, huh? That's tough in this town." Aloa gave him a sympathetic look and dug her wallet out of her pack. "How about sixty bucks and you tell me what you can? It's all I've got."

At this rate, her whole paycheck would be used up by bribes.

The man considered her for only a few seconds before he walked across the room and locked the front door.

The story he told made her path to the truth seem even more twisted.

Apparently, Ruiz had been banned from meetings about the same time Elvis had last seen him. According to the toilet-plunger guy, who would identify himself only as Ace, when Ruiz first showed up, he'd hardly said anything, but as the days passed, he became aggressive. After a while, he started talking about how he'd deserved to go to prison for the sin of promoting addiction because drug use was a defilement of the pure bodies given to us by the creator. Addicts, Ruiz said, should be locked up in work camps instead of being allowed to roam the streets, and dealers should be executed for how many lives they destroyed and how many people died of overdoses. Finally, he'd told a woman who'd confessed to a relapse after she'd been sexually assaulted by her boyfriend that she deserved to be raped.

"That's when they tossed him out," Ace said. "My guess is he was using again too. Heroin or oxy, probably."

"Do you know where he went?"

"I heard a rumor," he said.

Aloa waited.

"There's some church out there, some church that pushes the same things your friend Ruiz was talking about. I overheard one of the clients telling our facilitator about it later. Church of the Sacrificial Lamb, I think it was called. He might have gone there. Guys like him find religion and think it's going to save them, but it won't, you know. It's got to come from inside you. You have to be sick and tired of the life."

Aloa knew the truth of that.

"Do you know where the church is?" she asked.

Ace shook his head. "The guy said it was near Irish Hill, but I've never heard of any place called that."

Something tickled Aloa's brain. She gave the man her last three twenties and went outside.

Daylight was fading by the time Aloa arrived at the remnants of the place once named Irish Hill. After meeting Ace, she'd stopped at a Starbucks and searched on her phone for a place with that name, and found a mention of the neighborhood on a history website. Sitting atop a high knoll near the water in the late 1800s, Irish Hill had once been filled with rough shanties and ramshackle boardinghouses packed with immigrants from the old country. The men worked in nearby foundries and mills, and when the whistle called an end to their labor, they'd climb the two hundred and fifty wooden steps to their homes to share stories and smokes and maybe a few drinks. Every Saturday, bare-knuckle fighters would square off in front of Mike Boyes's saloon. Afterward, the crowd would celebrate by retiring inside the bar to plunk down their nickels for pints of steam beer.

According to the site, when World War I broke out, the homes were demolished and the hill was excavated to allow the expansion of the Bethlehem Steel factory, then leveled during the Second World War. Now it was just a small, sad hump of dirt sprouting clumps of pampas grass and fennel.

Aloa sat astride her rumbling bike, looked at the fenced-in mound, and sighed. She'd walked the area but hadn't seen anything that even faintly resembled a church. She put the CB-350 in gear and began to cruise, winding her way through a maze of abandoned brick-and-metal factory buildings that hugged the waterfront nearby.

Jagged shards of broken glass edged window frames. Weeds sprouted through pavement. A dog barked somewhere in the distance. Even without the fog, the place would have been spooky. Aloa thought about Davenport's story of his wife's ghost floating through the living room and again felt the hairs on the back of her neck rise.

She rounded a corner and saw a man and woman leaning against a parked car. A light shined from a window above them. *Did people actually live here?* Another turn led her parallel to a long building made out of rusting sheets of corrugated metal and surrounded by a dilapidated chain-link fence. Aloa stopped the bike, imagining the building's walls echoing with the clatter of tools and machinery, the workers inside laboring long hours to build what they hoped would be a better life for themselves and their families. Now all that remained was ruin.

She told herself to stop making up stories about empty buildings, put the bike in gear, and began to pull away when her eyes caught movement. She turned the bike slightly and spotted a puppy with matted chocolate-brown fur hobbling across the road as fast as it could, one front paw held gingerly above the ground.

Aloa stopped the bike and considered for only a few moments before she shut down the engine and took off her helmet.

"Hey there, boy," she called in her most trustworthy voice. "Let me see what's wrong. Can you stop? Will you sit?"

The dog looked over its shoulder at her and, as if it understood, sat, its tail thumping the ground. Aloa guessed it was about a year old.

"That's a good boy," Aloa crooned, moving slowly in the dog's direction. But when she came within a few feet of the pup, it gave a panicked bark and darted away, slipping through a hole in the fence.

"Dammit," Aloa said.

She shrugged out of her daypack and scrambled through the fence. There was no way she was leaving an injured animal out there.

A spotlight on a corner of the old factory shined dimly through the fog and she saw the little dog hop-limping toward the abandoned building. She knelt and opened her pack. Chasing it would do no good.

"Hey, boy, I've got something for you, boy," she called, digging into one of the pockets for the sample packet of almond butter a way-too-perky vendor had shoved into her hand when she'd stopped at the store to buy her dinner makings.

She tore open the packet with her teeth and smeared some of the goo on her finger. She whistled softly. "Here, boy. Come on, boy. I've got something for you."

The pup stopped and sniffed the air.

"That's right. Come and get it," Aloa called.

She waited as the pup edged toward her in a crouch, then snatched it up when it got close. She held the little dog tight against her chest as it struggled, throwing its head and thrashing its paws.

"It's OK. It's OK," Aloa murmured even as she wondered how much damage was being done to her leather jacket.

She held her cashew-buttered finger in front of the pup's snout until hunger overcame fear and she felt its rough tongue against her skin. She waited for the pup to calm before lifting its paw to discover a piece of wire protruding from the dog's foot.

"Ouch," Aloa said in sympathy.

She squeezed the pup tight under her arm as the animal began to struggle again. Tucking her phone under her chin for better light, she began to ease out the offending wire from the pup's paw, all the while murmuring about its bravery and good manners.

She had just pulled the piece of wire free when the animal's good behavior failed him and he nipped her hand.

"Ow," she said, falling backward as the pup sprinted away, disappearing around a corner of the building.

"You're welcome," she muttered, standing and brushing dirt from the seat of her jeans. She plucked her phone from the ground where it had fallen, examined the bite mark (it hadn't broken the skin), and saw a trail of bright-red drops where the pup had fled. She sighed and followed the crimson trail around the corner until she came to a partially open door. What was that saying about no good deed going unpunished?

Her boot crunched on broken glass as she pushed into the abandoned building. The place was dark and cavernous, lit faintly through its high windows by the spotlight outside. Aloa flicked on her phone's flashlight once again. The dusty concrete floor was littered with hulks of rusting machinery, fallen beams, and the empty shell of an ancient truck. She picked her way carefully around the debris, following the trail of blood droplets along a path that ran down the middle of the old factory and thinking once she got the dog's wound cleaned properly she would see if she could find it a good home.

At the far side of the building, she came to a wall, bisected by a hallway lined with doors. She guessed this was where the factory's offices had been located. The blood droplets were getting farther apart, which meant the bleeding was already slowing, but she could see another crimson spot ahead of her. She stepped into the hallway and opened her mouth to call for the pup when the words died on her lips.

Halfway down the hallway a sliver of light fell across the floor.

She stopped and heard a murmur of voices.

"What the hell?" she muttered.

A normal person would have turned around and come back to look for the dog the next day, but curiosity was both Aloa's Achilles' heel and the reason she had won so many awards as a journalist.

She switched off the flashlight app and crept forward. She passed one door, then two more until she was about five feet from the narrow beam of light.

"In the Lamb's name," said a man's voice.

"In the Lamb's name," a chorus echoed.

From down the hall, the pup gave a sharp bark and whoever or whatever was behind the door fell silent.

Some friend you are, Aloa thought, mentally scolding the dog.

Footsteps approached and Aloa pressed her back against the wall. She was about 99.9 percent sure she was trespassing—but then, whoever was behind the door was too.

She held her breath as the footsteps stopped, then moved away, the scratchy notes of a violin rising and a dozen or so voices beginning to sing: "Our bodies, our temples. Our destroyer, our savior."

Aloa edged closer to the door.

"Hoist your mighty sword. Seek those who sin," the voices sang.

Aloa used her finger to push the door open a few centimeters and put her eye to the narrow crack. What she saw made her breath catch.

Inside the rectangular room, dozens of candles burned around an inverted wooden cross with a crude metal symbol—a triangle superimposed over a circle—nailed to it. About twenty people, led by what looked like a priest in a scarlet robe and hood, circled the cross. The worshippers sported an assortment of clothes in shades of red, and each wore a crimson hood over their head and carried a tall wooden staff.

"We follow your word," they sang as they circled the cross. "We die so that we may live."

Aloa watched, transfixed.

The violin's tune grew more intense and the marchers' voices rose. "Help us in our fight. Give us strength. Give us courage. Cleanse the world. Cleanse our hearts."

The violin squealed its final notes.

"Justice for all," the hooded marchers cried and banged their staffs against the concrete floor. The sound was like cannon fire.

Silence dropped.

Finally, the robed and hooded priest broke the quiet. "Remember those who have died in your name," he called.

Aloa heard a mumble of words from the tiny congregation.

"Now go and live in purity," the priest said.

"Live in purity," the worshippers answered.

Aloa watched for only a second as the worshippers broke out of the circle.

Time to get out of there.

DAY 7

Aloa woke up at eight in a tangle of sheets and blankets. She'd gone to bed at 11:00 p.m., but images of hooded marchers and floating ghosts had haunted her thoughts, making sleep impossible. At 1:00 a.m., she'd debated going for a ride to calm her thoughts, but decided foggy and dark was a bad combination and got out her cello instead. She'd taken up the instrument in junior high, loving its tone, the way the notes vibrated from the instrument through her body. She'd been accepted to a prestigious summer music program, considered applying to Julliard and to the New England Conservatory of Music, but then her dad had died and her plans fell apart. Until the Honda arrived in her life, her cello had been the best antidote to the intermittent insomnia that plagued her. She turned on the space heater and played until her mind cleared.

Now, she climbed from her bed, donned sweatpants and her wool sweater, and made coffee. She swallowed a full mug in a few gulps, cut up an orange, and spread butter on a piece of toast.

She went to her front window. The fog still held the city in its hard gray embrace.

At her desk, the space heater blasting and another mug of coffee beside her, Aloa jotted notes from the strange ceremony she'd witnessed last night. Was that the church the Hope Recovery Systems worker had talked about? If so, could Pablo Ruiz have been one of the hooded worshippers?

She searched for information about the Church of the Sacrificial Lamb but was frustrated to find nothing. She drank a glass of water and turned to the envelope Kyle had given her. Davenport's hatred for Burns Hamlin made the information suspect, but she also couldn't ignore it.

She dialed the number for the former classmate Hamlin had been accused of stalking, a woman named Camille Walker, who lived in a suburb outside Boston.

According to Aloa's research, Camille had two children and was now a psychologist working with battered women. She answered on the third ring.

Camille was guarded but honest as she answered Aloa's questions. Even in only a few minutes of conversation, Aloa liked her.

"I met Burns in my Brit Lit class, British Literature, and he asked me out," Camille said. "I liked him, thought he was cute. But after a couple of months he started to feel too needy, a little controlling. He'd be waiting outside my classes, showing up every morning with coffee, hanging around my dorm room, wanting to know where I was all the time. I told him it would be better if we were just friends. He cried."

Maybe Hamlin's arrogance was an act to cover up insecurity.

"After that, he started writing me poems and sending me flowers," Camille said. "I'd see him sitting on a bench outside the library while I studied."

"Stalking you?"

"Not exactly. Just always there. I told him to stop and the next day I found this beautiful silver bracelet in a box outside my room with a note begging me to take him back. I returned the bracelet and told him he needed to leave me alone, but I saw him outside the library again the next day. My roommate said I should report him so I went to the dean of student affairs. I told her Burns was following me around and I was afraid."

"Were you?" Aloa asked.

"More like creeped out," Camille said. "But my roommate told me that telling them I was afraid was the only way to get the administration to do something."

In the background Aloa could hear a door slam and the sound of running footsteps, an explosion of giggles.

"My kids are home. It was a mini-day at school," Camille said.

"So did they? Did the administration do anything?" Aloa asked, knowing she didn't have much time.

"They did an investigation and even scheduled a suspension hearing, but two days before it was supposed to happen, a lawyer showed up at my door. He had a check that would pay off all my student loans with twenty thousand dollars left over. He told me he represented the Hamlin family, and that the check was mine if I would drop the case and transfer to another college. I had close to thirty thousand dollars in student loans."

"You took the money."

"Wouldn't you?"

"Mom!" came a shouted voice.

"I've got to go," Camille said.

"One last question," Aloa said. "Did you ever think Burns might hurt you? Did he seem capable of violence?"

Camille considered the questions. "He was insecure and used to getting his own way but, no, I never felt like he would hurt me. Still, in my line of work, I've seen how behaviors like his could escalate. I'm sorry, but I've got to go."

Aloa thanked Camille and hung up. The woman's account didn't prove Hamlin was violent one way or another, but it did seem to show he had a fraught relationship with women. As for Hamlin's visits to a psychiatrist and a prescription for Xanax, there could be any number of reasons for his anxiety.

She called Tick to tell him what she had learned so far but got no answer, which wasn't unusual. All three of the old anarchists mostly kept their phones turned off in order to thwart what they believed was widespread government surveillance. She left him a message to call her and considered her next move.

Forty-five minutes later, she was standing inside the room where the weird ceremony had occurred the night before. A rough wood table was pushed against one wall and there were small blocks of wood nailed into the wall every few yards. Drips of wax indicated the tiny shelves had been used to hold candles. There appeared to be no electricity or running water and the floor had been swept clean.

She turned in a circle, imagining the thumps of staffs and the strange violin. What kind of church was it?

She searched the rest of the building, whistling for the pup. She went outside and did the same, but there was no sign of the animal. She left a pie tin of kibble beside the building. At least she'd found no more blood.

Back on her Honda, she wended her way through the gloom. Maybe it was wishful thinking, but the fog seemed to be lifting. She could see the hazy outline of the Financial District and a hint of the Bay Bridge. *The city had suffered enough,* she thought. A total of twenty-two fog-related deaths, a spike in crime, and an 80 percent increase in liquor sales. The worst of it was a man who'd accidentally backed his car over his daughter in the murk, and after she was pronounced dead, he'd gone home and shot himself.

It was like a dystopian movie, people cloaked in a grayness that distorted their vision, their lives, and their thoughts. Is that what she was facing? A view of the truth that was obstructed by lies?

She parked her bike at the top of Davenport's street. Time for some knock-and-talks with his neighbors.

"She'd be there every morning, swimming lap after lap in that pool," Devon Resnick said.

Resnick was a college student living with her parents in the house next door to the Davenports. She sported dyed blue-black hair and was dressed in an outfit that walked the line between bohemian and 1960s hippie. She and Aloa were standing on her front porch.

"It didn't matter if it was raining or cold or whatever. She was out there," Resnick said. "My bedroom is in the back. I could see her. It was weird. Like she was punishing herself or something."

"Punishing herself?"

"You know, like for screwing up her husband's life. Like because she was the one driving when the garbage truck hit them," Resnick said.

Aloa nodded as if it were a fact she already knew but inside she was thinking, *What the hell? Why hadn't Davenport mentioned that?*

"Yeah, she quit her job and everything because I think she felt terrible. She was kind of his slave, you know. Even before he got hurt. I'd see them in the backyard and she'd be bringing him a drink and taking away his tie and jacket and bringing him snacks and he wouldn't even look at her. He'd be talking on the phone or reading papers or something. She always looked tired and kind of sad. I wouldn't put up with that if it were me."

She pulled her phone from the pocket of her bell-bottomed jeans. "Sorry. I gotta go. I've got class," she said and disappeared into the house.

Aloa looked next door. Maybe it wasn't loyalty that had kept Corrine by Christian's side.

She was standing by her motorcycle after visiting the old woman who'd seen the late-night caller—a visit that included a vile cup of reheated coffee and repeated claims that "I know what I saw"—when Kyle approached, his hands shoved in the pockets of a down jacket.

"What are you doing here?" he demanded.

"Talking to the neighbors, seeing if anybody saw or heard anything unusual on the night Corrine died."

"And?"

Aloa decided it would be worthwhile to see his reaction. "One of them said Corrine was the one driving when Christian got hurt."

"That has nothing to do with anything," Kyle said. His gaze flitted like a sparrow from Aloa's face to the neighbor's house and then to her feet.

"Maybe not, but it helps me get a better picture of her," Aloa said. "I think if you'd been the cause of your husband's paralysis, it would put a strain on you, on your marriage."

"You don't know anything," Kyle said. "He forgave her."

"But did she forgive herself?" Aloa asked. "Maybe it wasn't only sex she wanted with Burns Hamlin. Maybe she wanted to be with someone who wasn't a constant reminder of her guilt. Maybe she was tired of always feeling like she had to make up for something."

"That's not true," Kyle said.

Aloa knew remorse was its own circle of hell.

"What if she fell in love with Hamlin? Even if she hadn't planned to?" Aloa pressed. "Christian said he couldn't handle it if Corrine fell in love. Maybe he found out and that's why he's pushing the case so hard with Hamlin?"

"No," Kyle said.

"There could be some other reason, you know. Some other person who wanted her dead. You can't just accuse the easiest suspect."

"Hamlin did it," Kyle insisted. "Everything adds up. He was jealous and angry. What about the stuff we gave you? About him stalking that woman?"

"It didn't prove anything one way or the other."

"Christian won't be happy."

"Tell him I said this: a collector has to consider all information, not just the facts he or she wants."

It was as if the fog was punishing the city for having a glimmer of hope. The slight clearing earlier in the day had been replaced by a thicker veil of gray that trapped smoke and car exhaust and made Aloa's eyes sting. She thought of the Jungle's residents who, unlike those who were being advised to stay indoors, were unable to escape the polluted chill. She drove to a chain drugstore, where she cleaned out its inventory of warm socks, grabbed some toys from the specialty aisle, and bought a $50 Target gift card. After, she paid for a dozen premade sandwiches at Safeway and threw a pack of Camel Lights into her purchases.

She found a little-used wool coat in her closet and filled a string bag with toys from the drugstore: three coloring books, a teddy bear with a T-shirt that read I wuv you, and a small plastic pail and shovel. She'd lashed the string bag to her pack, then stuffed the gift card in the coat pocket and folded it into her pack.

At the encampment, she handed out her offerings, stopping by the young mother's tent. Again, the young mother was outside, sitting in a broken beach chair. Aloa greeted her, handed her two sandwiches, and pulled out her gifts.

"I saw you in here yesterday," the woman said. "I guess you're feeling that good old liberal-white-people guilt, huh?"

Aloa knew there was a kernel of truth in the insult. Despite the city's progressive bent, there'd been no real solution to the problems of homelessness and rampant drug use on the streets.

"Maybe a little," Aloa said. "But I saw your daughter and thought she might like a few things to play with."

"You got kids?"

The hollow spot opened again in Aloa's stomach.

"No, but one of my friends had a brother that age when I met him. He loved coloring books."

She didn't tell her how Michael's little brother had been coloring at the kitchen table when his father put a bullet into the boy's chest, then turned the weapon on himself.

"Is it all right if I give the toys to her?" Aloa asked.

"Sure," the woman said.

Aloa squatted down and set the string bag in front of the little girl. The child's hair was pulled into two puffballs, one on either side of her head. She wore blue fleece pajamas and a faded pink jacket.

"Mine?" asked the little girl and pointed.

Aloa smiled. "Yes, these are for you," she said and opened the bag.

The girl tugged out the shovel and the pail.

"I saw she liked to dig," Aloa said.

"I think she's going to be an architect or something," said the young woman. "Her name's Destiny."

"I'm Aloa." She held out her hand.

"Keisha," the woman said.

"She's beautiful," Aloa said.

The woman sighed. "Don't I know it."

"How long have you been here, Keisha?"

The woman's gaze went to the dirt, then to the tumble of tents and huts around her. "Here, about six months. Before that, Destiny and I had a place, but I got into a little bit of trouble, you know, and my man left. Couldn't keep up with the rent. Me and her are on a waiting list."

"For an apartment?" Aloa knew the wait for affordable housing in the city stretched into years.

"Yep," Keisha said.

"There are programs," Aloa said.

The woman watched as her daughter dug into the dirt. "Too many rules," she said.

Aloa knew, most likely, that the rules Keisha talked about were no-drug regulations. But Destiny seemed well cared for.

"I thought you might like this too." Aloa pulled the coat out of her daypack. "It's wool so it should keep you warm."

Keisha took the coat in her hands, which were calloused and nail-bitten, and shook it open. "Oh my," she said. Sudden tears pooled. "I used to have a coat just like this. My granny gave it to me. It was a red one."

She pulled the coat to her chest and wiped her eyes with the back of one hand.

"I loved my grandmother too," Aloa said. "She always said you learn from your failure, not your success."

"My granny said something pretty close. Whenever something bad would happen, she'd tell me our greatest glory comes from the ability to stand up every time we fall." Her voice cracked and she dug the heels of her hands into her eyes.

Aloa let her have a minute.

Keisha sniffled. "I don't know why I'm crying. It doesn't do a bit of good in here."

"Sometimes it helps to let it out," said Aloa, although she hated to cry.

"Yeah." Keisha wiped her eyes. "'Cept it makes you look all raggedy and pitiful."

Aloa smiled. "There's a gift card in the pocket of the coat. In case Destiny needs anything." She dug a business card out of her pocket and handed it to Keisha. "I hope you get to the top of that list soon," she said. "But in case you don't, you call me if you or Destiny need anything: food, bus fare, even more coloring books." She gestured at the card. "That's my cell number. Call anytime."

"Thanks," Keisha said. "Maybe you aren't so white after all."

The men with the hibachi were gone, but Aloa saw the pillar preacher who'd called her out on her sin. He was asleep on the ground, his arms folded over his chest, his head supported by a small chunk of concrete. She set a pair of clean socks by his shoulder and moved on.

"Hey, Elvis," she said when she got to his lean-to.

"Over here," said a voice from the tent that had once been Billy's. "Come on in."

Aloa squatted in front of the tent and pulled up the long zipper. Elvis was hunched on Pablo's cot, a camp stove in front of him on the ground.

"You got my cigs?" Elvis asked.

"Sure do. Some socks too."

"Come and set. I'm making hot cocoa."

Aloa hesitated, then crawled inside, sitting cross-legged on the dirt-stained rug. She handed Elvis her offerings.

"An angel from God," Elvis said, taking the cigarettes with fingers blackened with grime, "and them socks are real nice too. When I worked for the post office back in North Carolina, I always said a good sock equals a long career. Course, then things got messed up. Weren't no sock could save that."

He sucked in his lips and tore open the package of Camels. He knocked out a cigarette, lit it with the flame from the camp stove, and took a long inhale.

"Christ on a cross, that's good."

Aloa remembered her first cigarette. It was her freshman year in the backyard of a girlfriend's house and included a forty-ounce bottle of malt liquor shoplifted from a gas station convenience store. The combination of nicotine and sugar made her so sick she'd vowed never to smoke—or drink malt liquor—again.

"Found some milk in the dumpster this morning. Only a week past the pull date," Elvis said and reached under the cot, pulling out a box of cocoa mix and a quart of milk. A plastic baggie filled with an assortment of pills tumbled out with the cocoa and Elvis shoved it back with the heel of his shoe.

Aloa knew better than to say anything.

"Yup, my boy used to love hot cocoa," Elvis said, the cigarette bobbing in the corner of his mouth. "Fourteen years old, and he'd still sit down with his old man for a cup." He pulled over a cardboard box and dug out a small pan, pouring half the milk into it and setting it on the flame. "Them were good times. Sometimes you don't know it until it's gone, eh?"

He inhaled, held the smoke, and blew a plume out the side of his mouth, pulling a chipped mug and a tablespoon from the box where he'd gotten the pan.

"I'd offer you some but I only got one cup."

"It's fine," she said.

"Sep, that was my boy's name. For Septimus, his grandfather. Great kid. Not much for schoolwork but he played third base like nobody's business. Good-looking kid too. Not like me. Took after the wife."

Elvis tore open a corner of the hot cocoa packet and poured its contents into the cup.

"About April his freshman year, Sep started complaining about his leg hurting. The coach told him it was a pulled muscle and to ice it and give it a few stretches. Only it kept on hurting."

He lifted the pan and swirled the milk so it didn't scald.

"Finally, come June, we took him to the doctor. Turns out he had something called an osteosarcoma. They took his leg. Right at the hip. We thought we had it but lo and behold, the thing comes back. After that, it's hospitals and chemo and all kinds of nasty stuff. Sep said he could beat it. So did the docs."

Elvis dipped a grimy finger into the milk to test the heat. "Just right," he said and pulled the pan from the flame, balancing his cigarette on the edge of the cot. "The secret's in the stirring."

He poured the milk slowly into the mug, stirring hard while he did it. Bubbles rose in the mixture, the spoon clanking against the side of the cup.

"Turns out Sep was wrong and so was the doctors. We lost him the next June and, God's honest truth, it kinda broke me." He licked the spoon and watched steam rise from the mug. "I tried to work but I couldn't and I started drinking and after a year of it, Jess, that's my wife, told me to move out. Then it was whiskey and crystal and oxy and horse. Whatever. Didn't matter none. I kept moving but the pain—well, the pain kept following me and now here I am."

He set the spoon on the ground, picked up the mug, and retrieved his cigarette.

"I can still do my route in my head, though. A hundred and thirty-four houses."

He took a gulp of the cocoa.

"I wish I still had that job. I wish Sep didn't die. I wish I wasn't such a weak old man who couldn't do nothing to save his kid or his wife."

His eyes glistened and he took a long inhale of the cigarette. "I don't know why I told you that, except you got the face of a listener."

"Thanks," Aloa said quietly and left him alone with his memories for a few moments. "So Pablo didn't come back?" she asked finally.

"Nope," he said, "and speaking of that, you know that girl I told you about, that Star? The one who wanted the speedball?"

"I remember."

"They found her body, just like Billy. Put in a bag and stuffed into the branches of a tree. Yup, somewheres over on Pacific. Kinda near Chinatown, I think, but I really ain't sure. Two days ago. Nasty business."

Aloa thought of what she knew about Billy's murder and her stomach gave a lurch.

Elvis took another gulp of cocoa, followed by a pull from the Camel. "Ain't really safe here. I was thinking about movin', but now I got this place, and besides, where else would I go?"

"Have you ever heard of something called the Church of the Sacrificial Lamb?" Aloa asked.

"Don't sound too friendly."

"I don't think it is."

From outside the tent came a loud whistle, which caused Elvis to stab out his cigarette and set the cocoa aside.

"Sorry, I got me some business," he said, suddenly gruff. "Best you get out of here."

"Go on," he said when Aloa hesitated.

As Aloa crawled from the tent, she noticed a dark-haired man with sunken cheeks and black eyes standing across the path from her. He wore faded jeans, a black jacket, and a pair of run-down cowboy boots embossed with an image of a coiled snake.

She could feel his eyes on her as she left.

Another dead body, a missing felon, and a weird church? She didn't know yet if there was any connection to Corrine Davenport's killing, but Ruiz was the only lead she had. Her gut told her that Burns Hamlin had told the truth about being with his son on the night of the murder, but gut feelings weren't a defense you could use in court. Finding the real killer was.

She rode the Honda to Pacific, parked the bike, and began to walk. She came to a place where a row of trees punctuated the sidewalk and stopped. She didn't know if this was the exact spot where Star's body had been found, but she hunkered down, her back against the wall of an apartment building, and studied the area.

The street was fairly quiet. A handful of pedestrians hurried past. They wore down jackets and expensive shoes and walked with the kind of purpose that signaled they had somewhere important to go. Either that or they wandered like sleepwalkers, staring at their phones. She wondered if that was the reason the duffel with Star's body had been stuffed in the crook of a tree. Did the killer know that Star's body would remain there for a while because most people didn't bother to look up anymore?

She considered calling Quinn to ask the exact location of the body dump, but knew he would only tell her how insane she was for going back to the homeless camp—and maybe she was. But when a story led you someplace, you followed.

She saw a man in coveralls painting the outside of a building down the block and pushed herself away from the wall. She walked down the slight slope of the street, told him she was a reporter, and asked if he knew about a body being found nearby.

"Sure," he said and pointed. "Right near that intersection there. I couldn't believe it when the boss told me. Now I'm always looking up. You just don't think about stuff like that."

Aloa thanked the man and went to the spot.

She looked up into the row of trees, their branches low and welcoming, then examined the ground beneath them. A trio of rust-red drops dotted the sidewalk under one of them. Blood. She studied the Y-shaped branches.

Unlike the place where Billy had been found, it seemed like the killer or killers had wanted to put a little time between them and the body being discovered. She leaned against the wall of a nearby house and contemplated the area. Why here? Was there a connection between this place and the location of Billy's body?

She closed her eyes, letting her mind run free. Nothing.

She shoved away from the building just as a text alert chimed from her phone.

Back in SF. Buy U lunch?

It was Michael.
Working. Next time, she thumbed.

110

The dots pulsed.

I get the feeling you're avoiding me.

Just busy.

Dinner, then? Your favorite spot in the Tenderloin?

Aloa knew she should meet Michael and lay everything out for him, but what good would it do? It would only stir up the past and make her feel worse about what she'd lost so many years ago; what he'd lost without even knowing it.

Maybe another time, she typed. Hot into Tick's story. Will keep you posted.

No pulsing dots.

She watched the screen for a long moment and shoved her phone into the pocket of her jacket. One of these days, she would have to tell him.

DAY 8

She was at Justus and knocking on the front door at 10:00 a.m. She saw Gully's head pop up in the pass-through behind the bar and a few seconds later, Erik was opening the front door.

"Hair of the dog, sweetie?" Erik said.

"Do I look that bad?"

"Besides the uncombed hair and lack of makeup, no. But that sweater looks like something the cat coughed up."

Aloa tugged the old sweater tighter over her chest. "I need to ask a favor."

"At your service, darling. Come on in." He locked the door behind her. "Gully, we've got company."

Gully's voice came from the kitchen. "Have you eat your breakfast because Erik say I must make a something for the sad man above. I could make for you also. I am thinking a beautiful poached egg with salad greens. A mustard shallot vinaigrette to give it the bite of an angel."

"No thanks, but it sounds wonderful," Aloa said.

"One of our tenants, he's having a hard time," Erik explained. "You know me. I see a little chick in need and I have to take it under my wing. I'm just an old mother hen."

"With a handsome set of feathers," Aloa said and touched his arm.

Erik smiled. "Thanks, but I would say yes to your favor even if you didn't tell me how good-looking I am."

"I was wondering if you might have time to sew something for me."

"Oh sweetie, of course. I thought you'd never ask." Erik took a step back from her. "I'm picturing a wool cape. Maybe a plaid mini underneath. Black tights. Your boots. Fabulous."

"Actually, I need a hood." It was item No. 4 on her to-do list for the day.

"A hood? Is there a kinky Big Bad Wolf in your life I don't know about?" He winked.

She hated to lie to Erik, but she knew if she told him the truth, he'd worry himself sick. "It's for a party. The theme is comic book villains."

Erik lifted an eyebrow. "That's not much of a costume."

"I'm going low-rent," Aloa said.

"At least let me make you a cape."

"It's fine. Really."

He grabbed a napkin and pen from the bar and shoved it in her direction. "Well, show me this hood you're talking about."

Aloa sketched the design. "It's not exactly red, but more crimson."

"Fabric?"

"I think it was cotton."

"You think it was cotton?"

"I mean that's what I want. Cotton. A heavy cotton." She'd almost blown it.

"And who do you know that throws a comic book party?" Erik asked.

"An old reporter friend. It's her birthday. She got in touch after the runner story."

He studied her. "You're not in trouble, are you?"

"No." At least she could be honest about that.

"And you just want a hood?"

"That's all."

"Well, I'll do what you want," he said, "but I'm still going to make you that minidress. You'd look fabulous in it."

"I haven't worn a dress in years," Aloa said.

"Well, it's time you start, hon," Erik said. "Legs are the show horses of the body. You've got to let them run free."

"*Mi amor*," Gully interrupted from the kitchen. "Will you tell the sad friend above that it is time to break his fast?"

"I'll go up as soon as I let our friend out."

"Until later, *chica*," Gully called.

Erik walked Aloa to the door. "I'll have your so-called costume ready in a few hours." He put a beefy hand on her shoulder. "And, whatever it is that you're really doing, I hope you'll be careful, sweetie."

"I'll do my best," Aloa said.

Back at her house, she put a line through item No. 4 on her to-do list and concentrated on No. 1: Kyle Williams.

Yesterday's meeting had made her wonder about his connection to his boss. He seemed a little too protective, a little too defensive. Like the way an anxious dog growls and barks when they're afraid their territory is being invaded. Then there was Corrine's text, which made it seem as if she wasn't exactly fond of him. Not that Kyle was especially likable. Aloa went to her computer with a mug of coffee and soon found a 2006 story about Kyle Williams on the archive of a true-crime website.

Kyle had been twelve years old and living outside Hood River, Oregon, when his mother, a drunk, decided to run off with a truck driver she'd met at a local bar. According to the writer, she'd left the boy a pair of twenties and said she would be gone for the weekend, but ten days later, she was still MIA and Kyle had run out of money and food. A teacher had become concerned when Kyle stopped coming to school and went to his house, where she found dishes still on the table and a book open on his bed as if he had left midsentence. A neighbor said she'd seen the boy walking to the school bus stop three days earlier, but the driver didn't remember picking him up.

It was as if the boy had vanished.

Five years later, a hiker had stumbled upon a remote cabin in Oregon's coastal range and saw a stick-thin teenager in ragged clothes chopping wood while a bearded older man sat on a stump with a shotgun in his hands. The hiker said he thought he'd heard the man call the boy Kyle, or maybe it was Kevin, but the name sparked the memory of a story about a missing boy. He called the FBI, and Davenport and a partner had gone out to investigate.

Creeping through the woods, Davenport came upon the man beating the half-starved boy with his fists and had wrestled the suspect to the ground. It turned out the older man had kidnapped the boy from the bus stop, then chained, starved, and abused him for nearly half a decade.

It was as if the boy had been the prisoner in some horrific, secret war, Aloa thought.

There was a footnote to the article, which said Davenport had kept tabs on the boy, mentoring him and setting up a college fund, and that Kyle Williams was now working at an unnamed software company. Aloa guessed the wounded Kyle had latched on to Davenport as both savior and father figure. It would explain why he quit a good-paying job to take care of Davenport, and also why he seemed so protective. An experience like the one he'd been through would leave anyone with scars.

She added more questions to her research list—why did the list always get longer instead of shorter?—before dialing Quinn, the No. 2 chore. She asked if she could buy him a cup of coffee and he said he had questions for her too. They agreed to meet in one hour at a café near his office, and she found him just sitting down with a cup of black coffee when she walked in.

She appreciated people who were not only on time, but a little early. Years of newspaper deadlines did that to you.

"You first," she said after she'd settled across from him with a sixteen-ounce Americano. He wore slacks and a white dress shirt with a bomber jacket that should have been thrown away sometime around 1995. *Who was dressing him these days?*

"Tell me about Pablo Ruiz." He looked at her over the rim of his coffee cup.

"You know about him?"

"I may be a cop, but I know how to do a Google search."

"Sorry," Aloa said.

"You said you were at the Jungle looking for a drug dealer Corrine Davenport put away, then you asked me about William Lisowski, the guy in the duffel bag. I figured you'd made some connection."

"I may have," Aloa said. "From what I heard, Ruiz was a bad dude. Crazy-violent is basically what people described. One of the guys I met said people in the Jungle have been disappearing. It was around the time Ruiz arrived." She let him reach his own conclusion.

Quinn rubbed a hand over his chin. "We found another one this morning. Duffel bag, bolt gun, throat slit, barbed wire. One of the cops thinks he lived in the Jungle."

Aloa set down her coffee. "He?"

Quinn pulled a notepad from his jacket pocket. "Elvis Nash. Fifty-six years old. Arrests for public intoxication, disturbing the peace, drunken driving, possession of drugs, possession of drugs for sale, among other things. Lived in Charlotte, North Carolina, then drifted around before he landed here."

Sorrow lapped at Aloa's heart. Elvis had been no match for the pain that had followed him—and his death was even worse.

"He worked at the post office," Aloa murmured. "A hundred and thirty-four houses on his route."

"What?" Quinn asked.

"Elvis used to work at the post office. I met him when I went to the Jungle. He lived in a lean-to next to Ruiz. He said it was OK to look in Ruiz's tent."

"Christ, Aloa," Quinn swore.

"Relax. Ruiz wasn't around," she told him. "But I did find this." Aloa pulled out her phone and showed Quinn the images of the box with Ruiz's court papers and the photo with Corrine Davenport's face circled in red. "Elvis moved into Ruiz's place."

"He jacked Ruiz's tent?"

"Elvis said there are rules in the Jungle. If someone is gone for a week, then their stuff is fair game for everybody else. Ruiz had been gone for six days, according to him."

Quinn met Aloa's eyes.

"You think Ruiz came back, found Elvis in his tent, and killed him? Like he killed the others?"

"It's possible," Aloa said.

"And that he stabbed Corrine Davenport too?"

"Maybe he found a taste for killing after he murdered her."

They were both silent as they considered the possibility of a serial killer on the loose.

"Any ideas where Ruiz might be now?" Quinn asked.

Aloa thought of the hooded worshippers and of the reputation she'd once had as a reporter who didn't cut corners. She only had one source linking Ruiz to the church, and if Quinn raided the service and it turned out Ruiz was nowhere around, there could be all kinds of First Amendment blowback. Cops storming a group that could claim it was simply exercising its right to religious freedom would ignite the internet and Quinn would forever blame her for it. She decided she would tell Quinn only after she checked it out more fully.

"I'm still looking," she said.

Thirty minutes later, she stood on the street corner and rechecked her notebook. The address Quinn had given her for the spot where Elvis's body had been found was just to her left.

Why bring his body here? What was she missing?

She turned in a slow circle.

Once home to factories filled with sweat-stained laborers, the area was now populated by artisanal businesses and well-heeled office workers. She walked over to the stairwell where Elvis's body had been dumped and examined a small pile of trash that had been blown into the corner of the damp landing and a coffee can that saw double duty as an ashtray. Above her was a windowed office building, across was an interior design shop and a coffee importer. Nothing seemed to connect the location of the dead bodies to the weird church or to Ruiz. *Poor Elvis,* she thought. He didn't deserve to die the way he had.

Her stomach grumbled and she realized she'd missed lunch. With a frustrated exhale, she pulled out her phone and snapped photos of the area before climbing onto her bike and heading for home.

People whose only sin was addiction and poverty were dying, and if it was Ruiz who was killing them, he needed to be stopped.

Aloa waited until she'd seen twenty dark shadows slip into the abandoned factory before she stood up from the concrete barrier where she'd hidden herself.

She'd gone to a secondhand store that afternoon and bought a red flannel shirt and a pair of men's jeans. With only three women among the worshippers, she'd decided it was better to try to pass as a man and thanked her DNA for her height and, maybe for the first time, for her small breasts.

Her plan was to wait each evening to see if there would be a ceremony, sneak as close as she could, and watch the comings and goings to see if she could spot Ruiz. Her own hood and outfit would not only make her seem like one of the worshippers if she were spotted, but also permit her to trail anybody who fit Ruiz's height and weight in hopes they would pull off their own hood and reveal themselves. It wasn't a great plan, but it was the best she could come up with.

At home, she had removed her eye makeup and nail polish, put on the secondhand clothes, and the hood Erik had made. Her heart had given a nervous thump when she saw herself in the mirror, but now that she was here, she felt calm. That was the thing about being a journalist. Stuff you'd never do in regular life became OK when it was the only way to find the truth. It was why war correspondents put themselves in harm's way again and again, why journalists kept going to dangerous places.

She grabbed the tall walking stick she'd bought at a fancy hiking store and stripped of its colorful strings and charms and slipped on the hood. Ducking quickly through the hole in the fence, she strode toward the building through the hazy illumination cast by the lone spotlight and stepped inside.

Following the path through the junk-filled space, she could see a column of light from the half-open door where she'd witnessed the ceremony before. She made her footsteps quiet and, thinking she would creep closer when the ceremony actually started, she stepped off to the side by the hallway opening to wait.

"Ceremony's about to start," said a male voice so close it made Aloa jump.

She whirled to see a squat man in a hood, hoisting the zipper on a pair of camouflage pants as he came from behind a tumble of metal drums. "You're too late for a piss."

Aloa thought quickly. Even if she pretended she needed to pee, the guy might get suspicious if she didn't show up inside and come looking for her—or worse, he might wait for her to empty her bladder, which would put her female anatomy to a test it couldn't pass.

Aloa cleared her throat. "Oh yeah, sure," she mumbled in her huskiest voice and followed the man inside, praying there would be no head count or roll call.

The room was lit with candles as before, the inverted cross in its place in the center of the space. A few congregants gathered in clumps, but most stood off by themselves. One guy in particular drew Aloa's attention and she drifted toward him.

The description Steve Porter had emailed listed Ruiz as five foot eight and 175 pounds, and while this guy was closer to 164—one of an anorexic's talents was gauging weight to within a few ounces—Aloa supposed time on the street could account for the lost pounds.

The robed and hooded priest raised his staff and banged it twice on the floor.

"We gather in justice," he called. "We gather in the Lamb's name."

Quickly, the congregants arranged themselves in a circle and Aloa maneuvered herself so she stood next to the hooded worshipper she thought might be Ruiz.

"We gather to celebrate another victory," the priest said.

"In the Lamb's name," the worshippers said and thumped their staffs.

"We gather to rid the world of sin."

"In the Lamb's name," the worshippers recited and banged their sticks again.

Aloa had just spotted a crude tattoo on the back of her neighbor's hand—a melting clock that, in prison, signified the passage of time—and so nearly missed the last stick thump.

Could she have found Ruiz this easily?

Keeping an eye on the suspicious worshipper, she followed along with the ritual as best she could, giving thanks for the hood, which obscured the fact she was a woman and also her ignorance of the words being chanted. When the violinist began a slightly off-key tune, the priest took his place next to the cross, preaching about how drugs ruined the bodies gifted to mankind by the Creator and how those who peddled these temptations were animals who deserved to be killed and burned in the fires of hell. He spoke of a world where addicts were locked up until hard labor cleansed them of their sins. He spoke of self-punishment and purity, of handing out justice when it was needed, of pain and death for dealers who peddled temptation to others.

Excitement rippled through the crowd and Aloa stifled the urge to flee.

"Is there one among you who will show their readiness and their piety?" the priest called, lifting a length of chain wrapped in barbed wire from the foot of the cross.

"I will," cried a hooded man in neatly pressed denims who stripped off his shirt and took the chain. "I will be pure. I will serve the Lamb," he said and slapped the chain across his bare back, drawing blood.

"Again," cried the crowd.

Aloa swallowed the bile that rose in her throat as the man struck himself over and over.

"He is pure and ready for his task," the priest said when the man finally collapsed, exhausted and dripping blood, only to be carried off by two congregants who dumped him unceremoniously on the long table on one side of the room. But as the pair returned to the circle, Aloa's heart gave a thud of recognition. One of the hooded men wore a pair of run-down cowboy boots engraved with a coiled snake. Just like the hollow-cheeked man outside Elvis's tent.

Aloa forced herself to concentrate even though her mind was racing. She watched as the priest came around the circle with a chalice, announcing it was the Lamb's blood and asking for an oath of cleanliness and purity before each person took a sip. Aloa avoided his eyes when it was her turn. "I give my oath to you," she recited in a low voice and took a small taste of what seemed to be cranberry-grape juice. Behind the priest came the man in the cowboy boots, holding the metal symbol he'd unhooked from the inverted cross.

"I am your servant," each person said and kissed the edge of the emblem.

"I am your servant," Aloa dutifully proclaimed when it was her turn, but after she'd kissed the symbol, a tingle of foreboding ran through her.

She didn't know if it was her imagination or if the guy in the cowboy boots had hesitated before he moved on. Did he sense she wasn't a man, or worse, somehow recognize her from the tent city? Her civilian mind told her to leave, but her journalist's brain told her if she didn't confirm Ruiz's identity now, she might never get the chance again.

The violin sounded. The circle began to move.

"We follow your word," the congregants sang. "We die so that we may live."

Aloa recognized this part of the ceremony and moved along with the group. When they came to the end of the song, Aloa banged her stick along with the others. "Justice for all," she called out, her voice joining those of the other worshippers. She could hear the tattooed man next to her breathing hard.

"Remember those who have died for your justice," the priest said. "Those we have cleansed with your holy sword."

He lifted a tablet and voices mumbled the names on the list.

"Lester Holman. Billy Lisowski. Pablo Ruiz. Star Felice. Elvis Nash."

The dead.

Aloa felt herself pale. It wouldn't do any good to look for Ruiz. It was time to get the hell out of there.

Aloa slipped from the room the minute the ceremony ended and strode down the hallway into the factory space, resisting the urge to hurry or to look over her shoulder. No need to arouse suspicions if she didn't have to.

The outdoor spotlight shined through the building's highest windows, turning the abandoned factory into a world of hulking shadows and whispered pasts. Her Timberlands crunched glass and dirt as she followed the pathway through the machinery and metal that had once turned out handsome and sturdy ships.

A hundred yards to the door.

"Hey!" A voice pierced the semidarkness.

Aloa stiffened but didn't turn or change pace.

"Come back here. Show yourself," the voice commanded.

Aloa glanced over her shoulder to see a shape coming down the hallway toward her. Was it the snake-booted man?

"Identify yourself," the voice ordered.

Aloa knew she had exactly two choices at that point—to bluff or to run.

It took only a nanosecond to choose.

She dropped her stick and ran.

Behind her came a shout and the slap of boots. She strained her eyes in the semidarkness and yanked off the hood, which was blocking her view. Thanking her father for his lessons on focus and memory during their bird-watching excursions, she turned right and vaulted over a long workbench before ducking under a length of metal roofing, which leaned against a pile of lumber.

She grabbed the corrugated roofing sheet, causing the edge to slice into the soft part of her palm. Ignoring the pain, she shoved the roofing toward her pursuer.

She heard him grunt an oath as the metal crashed into bone and flesh with a sound like thunder. She turned and ran again, veering around some kind of giant cogwheel and finding another path through the detritus.

Fifty feet to the door.

"I see you," her hunter called. He was coming after her, leaping over a three-foot-high pile of pipes she'd been forced to swerve around and thus lose ground.

Windmilling her arms, she plunged right again and jumped over a low metal rod she hoped he might not notice. Another thump came and a shouted oath. She ducked low and threaded her way through the junk, praying he wouldn't see her. The old pickup truck blocked her way and she scrambled through the rusted-out cab. But instead of sprinting out the door as her pursuer would expect—and where open ground would allow him to catch her—she stopped and slid underneath the gutted vehicle. She hoped the darkness would hide her.

The truck shook as her hunter climbed through the cab and continued on. She calmed her breath, pulling her phone from her pocket, thumbing it to life and holding it against her chest. The darkness had given her an idea. *Plan B,* she thought.

The factory door slapped open. Another string of curses.

Footsteps came back in her direction and the truck shook again.

Aloa willed her fluttering heart to calm.

"I'll find you," the man who hunted her called out. Then, "Hey, you," he shouted to someone nearby, "come and help me. We've got an intruder."

Suddenly, a pair of cowboy boots appeared inches from her face, followed by a bent knee.

Shit.

The shadowed face of the snake-booted man appeared in her vision.

"Gotcha," he said, reaching to grab her.

"Maybe not," Aloa said and thrust her phone at her pursuer's face. The flashlight on her phone was small but powerful and the man roared, reaching blindly for her. But Aloa was already sliding out from under the truck and running.

Aloa knew she had only a few seconds before the snake-booted man regained his vision, so she turned right at the door instead of left toward the hole in the fence. She thanked the weather gods for a fog that seemed thicker and even more impenetrable than when she'd arrived. She sprinted across the empty lot that spread out from the warehouse, then slowed to quiet her footfalls. At the far corner, she listened, heard only silence, and scrambled over the chain-link fence. She dropped to the ground and jogged through an alley she thought led toward the waterfront and her trusty CB-350.

Back home, Aloa threw off the secondhand clothes, took a hot shower, and tended to the wound on her hand. If the worshippers' mumbled list was what she thought it was, then Pablo wasn't hiding. He was dead.

She debated calling Quinn, but it was late and she knew the congregation, along with all the accoutrements of the vigilante church, were already long gone. She poured herself a glass of wine and paced the length of the house. Streetlights shined gauzily through the fog and squares of light glowed from the apartment building across the way.

Calmer now, she went to her desk, opened her notebook, and began making a list of what she knew. Putting pen to paper always organized her thoughts. Partway through, she paused, set down the wine, and reached for her phone.

Her finger swiped through the photographs of the street where Elvis's body had been found: the office building, a parking structure, a row of converted live/work spaces. She stopped and swiped back one shot.

PETERSON AND SONS PACKING CO. read the faded sign painted high on the exterior of a restored brick building.

Aloa skimmed again through her list, felt a stir of excitement, and turned to her laptop. If she was right, she knew where Pablo might be found.

DAY 9

Rick Quinn ducked under the yellow crime-scene tape and headed toward the sidewalk where Aloa waited. His face was grim.

"All right," he said, stopping in front of her, "time to tell me how you found him."

"Is it Ruiz?" Aloa asked. She'd arrived early at the industrial area to avoid the questioning eyes of workers coming in for their shifts. She'd parked her bike and begun to stalk the neighborhood, checking dumpsters and peering into the branches of the few trees that were there. She'd walked the entire perimeter of a long concrete building and ducked down to look under what appeared to be an abandoned tractor-trailer rig. She finally found what she was looking for in a thick clump of berry vines behind a vacant factory building at the far end of the street: a green duffel bag leaking the sickly sweet scent of decay.

"We're pretty sure it's Ruiz," Quinn said gruffly. "Now talk. And don't play Ms. I-Can't-Reveal-My-Sources with me."

"I'm not sure I like your tone," Aloa said.

"I'm not sure I like you going around the city finding dead bodies."

"Just one dead body," she corrected.

"Don't make me arrest you for interfering with an investigation."

For a moment they glared at each other.

Aloa knew Quinn could, and would, make good on his threat if she forced him into a corner. "All right. You win," she said finally and pulled out her phone, showing him a photo of the spot where Elvis's body had been found. "See that faded old sign on that building? The one that says Peterson and Sons Packing Co.?"

Quinn nodded.

"I was thinking about how each of the vics died—shot with a bolt gun before their throats were slit—and it hit me: that's how pigs and cattle are slaughtered."

"So?" Quinn asked.

"So that old sign on the building meant there used to be a meat-packing plant where Elvis's body was found. I did a search for slaughterhouses in the city and came up with an 1860s map. Sure enough, the bodies of Billy, Elvis, and the woman named Star were each found where a slaughterhouse or meat-packing plant used to be." She swung her finger in an arc. "And this was Butchertown. There were five or six slaughterhouses here."

She'd read reports about San Francisco's rapid rise in population from 1860 to 1870 and how residents began to complain about the noise and smell of the slaughterhouses in their midst. The area around Mission Creek, called Old Butchertown, was especially bad. The slaughterhouses there would dump their waste into the slow-moving waterway, which required two or three tides to eventually wash the offal into the bay. The stench of rotting flesh and curdling blood was horrific. Public health officials, believing noxious odors could affect a person's health, cracked down.

Eventually, the city forced slaughterhouses farther south. There, the abattoirs were built on stilts over the bay waters. The spot where Aloa and Quinn stood was at the heart of the city's second Butchertown.

"I guess I was right," Aloa said.

Behind Quinn, a swarm of technicians and police officers scoured the crime scene, gathering evidence and taking photos.

"How long do you think Ruiz was there?" Aloa asked, remembering the bag's smell.

"A couple of weeks, at least," Quinn said.

"Before Corrine Davenport was killed," Aloa said.

"Yup."

There went her Some-Other-Dude-Did-It theory.

"I don't suppose you also have an idea who's killing these folks?" Quinn folded his arms across his chest.

Aloa squinted into the gloom, the image of the strange ritual with its inverted cross and weird symbol rising in her head.

"I might," she said. "You saw the circle-with-a-triangle spray-painted on the duffel bag?"

Quinn nodded. "It was on the other duffels too. We were keeping that quiet, though."

Aloa knew police often held back certain details, but if she'd known about the symbol, she would have alerted Quinn to the church—and Elvis might still be alive. She gave a silent curse.

"So I need to tell you that there's this church, actually more of a cult, called the Church of the Sacrificial Lamb and they have these weird ceremonies," Aloa said.

For the next twenty-five minutes, Aloa laid out what she knew and had witnessed, describing the symbol she saw and sketching a map of the abandoned factory and its makeshift church. She told Quinn she'd witnessed two of the ceremonies and that they'd happened right after the killings of Star and Elvis.

"Are you dumb or do you just have a death wish?" Quinn had exploded when she'd finished telling him about the snake-booted man and how she'd escaped him at the abandoned factory.

Aloa lifted her chin. "I was trying to confirm what I'd heard. Or would it have been better if I let you storm into a church service and be wrong?"

Quinn looked skyward and blew out a long breath.

"Be at the station at two. We'll need a formal statement and also to see if we can get a sketch of the guy in the cowboy boots."

"Fine," she said.

"Good," Quinn said.

He turned and ducked back under the crime-scene tape. "And don't be late," he warned.

Aloa undressed on the laundry porch, shoved her clothes into the washer, and went to take another shower. The smell of dead body was still in her nostrils and in her mouth, and she scrubbed herself under the stream of hot water before slathering her body with lavender-scented lotion. It was an old cop trick, trading one strong scent for another, but it was only partly successful, and she knew lunch, and possibly dinner, were out.

She made a pot of coffee and threw herself into the chair at her desk. If Ruiz wasn't the killer and it wasn't Burns Hamlin either, then who was it? Could it be somebody from Christian Davenport's past?

She called the regional office of the FBI, where an officious-sounding agent told her the agency wasn't investigating the case and even if they were, they wouldn't say anything about it to a reporter.

"Have a nice day," the agent said and hung up before Aloa could get in another word.

"Well, you've just made that impossible," Aloa muttered.

She sat back in her chair and tapped the end of her pen against her teeth.

There were always ways around an obstacle.

She flipped through her notebook, spotted the name of Davenport's superior officer while he was at the detention center in Afghanistan, and smiled. It took her an hour of research plus another call to Steve Porter before she found the number for Retired Army Lt. Tim Everson.

"I don't talk to reporters," Everson said after Aloa identified herself and told him the reason for her call.

"Mr. Davenport was the one who told me about you. We've been talking."

"How do I know you're not lying?"

Aloa kept her patience. "He told me that he asked you to help him kill himself but that you wouldn't do it. You told him a real warrior stayed alive to fight."

Long seconds of silence followed. "OK, ask your questions. But just so you know, I might not answer."

"Fair enough."

According to Everson, Davenport had never mentioned any threats against him as a result of the cases he'd worked, and while there were a lot of people in the Middle East who probably hated Davenport, they were either in prison, dead, or scratching out a living in a village somewhere and couldn't afford to fly halfway around the world to kill Davenport or his wife. "He was a hero. He didn't deserve what happened," Everson finished.

"Tell me more about him," Aloa said.

"Chris was good at what he did. He was smart, driven," Everson said. "He could find the needle in the haystack, then figure out what thread it was connected to. He could match wits with the best of them, stay in the booth for as long as it took. Real interrogation isn't like in the movies, Ms. Snow. Real interrogation is about patience and intelligence and paying attention. It's about being willing to live every day in a pit of deceit and hate and stink. Try spending hours listening to some guy talk about how infidels deserve to be killed and their women raped and not reacting while you pick up the bits and pieces he drops and figure out he was a weapons smuggler or a bomb maker for the bad guys. Chris could monster better than anybody I knew."

"Monster?"

"Stay in the booth with them. Ten, twelve hours of questions. It's not torture if you're doing it, too, right?"

Unless the interrogator had had a good night's sleep and wasn't afraid for his life, Aloa thought.

"Chris helped cut off a Taliban supply line that way, and he was a ballsack hair away from getting us to Osama bin Laden's video guy, but then the CIA sends in some girl who tells the guy he's going to rot in prison unless he talks. Two weeks of work down the drain in less than ten minutes."

"I'll bet Christian wasn't happy."

"I told the gal she'd better keep on the other side of the base for a while. Some people thought Chris was arrogant, that he played fast and loose with the rules. But he got the job done."

"How did he play with the rules?"

"You know, he pushed things. He liked to start work at two a.m. He'd figure out what the guy was afraid of and dig into that. Like if he sensed the guy had a thing about dogs, he'd have an MP bring one to bark outside the door. Or maybe he'd tell the guy he didn't hurt people but that there were other people who did and give him a blow-by-blow of how it might feel to be stuffed in a four-by-four wood box and left for a day or two. He had one guy curled up in a ball under the table, blubbering the name of his recruiter and his training camp after only four hours."

"Was there a prisoner there he couldn't break, one who willed himself to die?" Aloa asked, remembering her conversation with Davenport.

Everson gave a low snort. "If you call stabbing yourself in the throat with a pencil willing yourself to die, then yeah. The brass was all over us for that one."

"Did that kind of thing happen often?"

"Nope. That was the only time Chris's name came up in an investigation."

Aloa sat up straighter. Davenport had been investigated for a prisoner's death?

"What happened with the investigation?"

"Nothing, which is exactly what should have happened."

"No evidence he had anything to do with the guy's death?"

"I don't like what you're saying."

"I understand there were problems with prisoner interrogations in Afghanistan, that's all. A couple of people died, right?" She'd read reports in the *New York Times* about the cruelties: inmates left naked in freezing cells, waterboarding, detainees who'd died under suspicious circumstances.

"Is that a question?" Everson said. "Because it sounds more like you're one of those bleeding-heart liberals who don't know a thing about war or care about our freedom. Chris did a great service. He saved the lives of American soldiers, of fathers and sons and brothers. He should be considered a hero, not a scapegoat."

"He left after one tour. Was he forced out after the prisoner died or did he leave on his own?" Aloa asked.

"I'm done talking to you," Everson said.

The line went dead.

Aloa slowly set down the phone.

Aloa's phone rang twice in quick succession after the call with Everson. The first call was from Rick Quinn, who said he and a tech had gone to the old factory and found evidence of bloodstains in the room she'd described, and that an undercover cop also had heard something on the street about vigilantes going after drug dealers—which was as close to an apology as she was going to get for his anger and for his accusation that she'd stepped on his case.

"How about lunch?" he said. "I can take your statement there instead of you having to come to the office at two."

"I'm busy." She wasn't about to admit the lingering smell of dead body made eating impossible.

"How about a beer, then? I get off at four. You could give me your statement then." He named a spot where cops and reporters mingled after hours. A working place, not a date place. Good.

"Sure," she said.

"And a cigar works best," he said.

"What?"

"To get the dead-body smell out so you can eat again. I'll bring you a couple of Gran Habanos."

She could hear the smile in his voice.

The second call came as she finished reading an investigative piece on death, torture, and the CIA during the Iraq War.

"Hey, Doc," she said, tucking the phone between her shoulder and ear.

"I can't talk long," he said. "We're on the move. Me, Tick, P-Mac, and the kid."

Aloa stopped working. "By 'kid,' I hope you don't mean Burns Hamlin."

"We couldn't wait. Tick said the pigs were closing in," Doc said.

"Where are you?" she demanded.

Doc ignored her. "If something comes up, you call this number. Let it ring twice, hang up, then call back. One of us will answer."

"Running is the worst thing you can do," Aloa said.

"Two rings, hang up, then call back," Doc said.

"This is such a bad idea, Doc," Aloa said, but she was already talking to empty air.

Aloa stared at the phone and cursed. Tick had called as she was about to get into the shower and she'd told him Ruiz was dead, but that it didn't mean there weren't other possibilities. Why hadn't she kept her mouth shut until she could explain more to him?

She slammed into her bedroom, changed into her running clothes, added the pink beanie, and let herself out the front door. She needed to think, to get the dead bodies out of her mind—and her nostrils.

Her feet took her down to Fisherman's Wharf. She ran hard, pumping her arms and skirting the few hardy tourists who'd ventured into the fog. Seagulls hunkered on railings, resigned to a day without overflowing trash cans to loot. According to the news, the city was struggling under the weight of what had turned into a slow-speed disaster. School had been canceled. Businesses closed. Hospital beds were full. Hotel beds were empty.

Aloa ran the path around Aquatic Park, the protected lagoon now empty of the hardy swimmers that usually plied its calm waters. Breath filled her ears, salt and sea replaced the scent of death. She lengthened her stride. Two miles in, an idea sparked. By mile three, it had caught and spread. She turned and headed for home.

Aloa knew the best sources weren't always at the top of the food chain. Sometimes it was the clerks and the janitors, the housekeepers and hairdressers—the invisible people who saw things, who heard conversations, and who had a better sense of right and wrong than the people they worked for—who could lead you to the truth.

Aloa hoped this would be the case as she parked her bike in front of San Francisco's Hall of Justice, a concrete block that looked like it belonged in some outpost in Siberia. She found her way to the district attorney's office, where two women sat behind a small reception counter—one young and one older. The younger woman was on the phone. The older one, gray-haired with skin like a cracked and drying creek bed, looked up.

"Can I help you?" the woman asked. Her hair was cut short and close to her head. Her lipstick was pink.

"I hope so," Aloa said. "My name is Aloa Snow, and I'm a reporter working for Novo, a news website, and I was hoping to talk to you about Corrine Davenport."

"You mean you want to talk to her old supervisor," the woman said.

"No, I'd rather talk with you, if that's all right." Aloa smiled. "I'm guessing you know more about what goes on than anybody else here. And that includes the big boss."

"I've been here thirty-eight years," the woman said.

"So you remember Corrine Davenport?"

"Poor thing. Life just didn't treat her right."

"It must have been tough," Aloa agreed. "Did you ever see her after she left here?"

"I liked her. We stayed in touch." Intelligence shined from the woman's pale-blue eyes.

"Did she ever talk to you about anybody who gave her trouble?"

"Besides Kyle and that husband of hers?"

Aloa glanced at the nameplate in front of the woman. "Could I buy you a cup of coffee or lunch, Ms. Pianelli? It would be really helpful to hear more."

"It's Wendy, and I was going to take a smoke break in ten minutes. Meet me around the corner, where we have to huddle like lepers so we don't destroy the lungs of innocent bystanders." She winked at Aloa.

"I'll see you there," Aloa said.

Wendy, dressed in a purple down coat, appeared eight minutes later and, lighting up within seconds of her arrival, blew a stream of smoke into the icy air. "I'm going to die of pneumonia before these cigarettes get me," she said.

"It's freezing," Aloa agreed. She'd crammed the pink beanie on her head and wrapped her neck in Erik's yellow scarf. Between her and Wendy's purple jacket, they looked like a gathering of Skittles in the fog.

"Tell me about Kyle," Aloa said, pulling her Moleskine out of her pack. It was always better to start out with an open-ended question and see where it might lead.

"He's a piece of work, I'll tell you. Corrine said it was like living with a mean little lap dog. One that bit." Wendy took a long drag on her cigarette. "If you ask me, she should have gotten out of there. But she was loyal and felt guilty for what she'd done. It was a bad combination." She flicked the ash from her smoke into a small tin she carried.

"If that's true, why'd she keep Kyle around?"

"Because she was exhausted, because she wanted a life. She'd wanted to hire a day nurse early on, but that husband of hers wouldn't hear of it. He said he didn't want a stranger in the house, so she quit to take care of him. It was Kyle or nothing."

Not the same story Davenport had told.

"Those first years were rough," Wendy said and blew a funnel of smoke from the corner of her mouth. "It was like she couldn't do anything right. I understand you'd be angry if one second you were healthy and the next second you couldn't even scratch your nose, but he was a first-class jerk. He'd complain his tea wasn't hot enough, that she'd used the wrong detergent for his clothes, or the temperature in the room was all wrong. She got up in the middle of the night to turn him so he didn't get pressure sores. She wiped his behind and gave him baths and kept the house spotless because he was such a neat freak. She told me that, once, she mentioned how tired she was to one of Christian's doctors, and that he was livid when they got home. He accused her of disloyalty and weakness."

Wendy took a long pull on her cigarette and held the smoke for a moment before releasing it into the air. "That's when he made her get that weird tattoo."

"Wait," Aloa said. "Christian told me the tattoo was her idea and that he tried to talk her out of getting it."

"Oh, god no. She hated that thing, but that husband of hers insisted. Something about proving she loved him, which, strangely, she still did. Maybe it was like those hostages who supposedly fall in love with their captors. I don't know. Then he hires Kyle as his assistant. To help her, he says, and, for a while, it works. But then it was like two people humiliating and mistreating her instead of just one."

Aloa frowned. "How did Kyle mistreat her?"

"Not exactly mistreat, I guess." Wendy pinched a fleck of tobacco from her tongue. "He came in and rearranged all their furniture and ordered new clothes for Christian, saying it would make Christian feel like less of a patient. He nudged Corrine out of the way when it was time for Christian's bath, criticized her for the way she did his physical therapy, and insisted she was hurting her husband's health by not buying organic food."

Wendy leaned in. "Once, Kyle gave her a schedule for spin classes at a nearby gym. 'Christian thinks you've gained a few pounds,' he said."

"No wonder she fell for her poetry teacher," Aloa said.

"I think Kyle would have been happy if she were out of the picture."

"You mean like get rid of her."

Wendy shook her head and took another drag from her cigarette. "That was the first thing I thought when I heard she'd been murdered, but I guess I was wrong. From what I hear, everything points to that professor of hers." Her blue eyes sparked. "But I do know that Corrine had a big life insurance policy, her husband was a jerk, and that Kyle was a little punk who enjoyed humiliating her. It wouldn't surprise me if Kyle . . ." She paused and stubbed out her cigarette in the little tin. "No. I shouldn't say that. It's just that . . ." She stopped.

"Go on," Aloa said.

"Oh, what the heck. Don't say I told you, but you should look up this guy named Aat Bon Tae." She spelled the name for Aloa. "He lives in Dogpatch. You'll see what I mean."

She snapped the lid on the tin with the cigarette leavings and tucked it into her jacket pocket. "I have to go. I want to grab a Diet Coke before my break is over. Call me if you find something."

Aloa promised she would.

Aat Bon Tae was a slender man with long dark hair and bright eyes framed by a pair of black-rimmed glasses. As soon as he heard Aloa was a reporter who wanted to talk about Kyle Williams, he invited her in.

"That dude is trouble, man," he said.

He poured Aloa a mug of coffee and they sat in the living room of the cottage, which, he explained, had been built in the late 1800s to house immigrant workers and now was priced somewhere in the million-dollar range.

"Crazy, huh?" he said.

"That's one word for it," Aloa agreed.

The room held a low-slung couch, a desk, and a basket full of Legos that told of the presence of at least one child. Beyond it was a modern kitchen with a gleaming stainless-steel refrigerator, granite counters, and a table with metal loft-style chairs.

According to Bon Tae, he and Kyle had met when they worked for a big tech company and had come up with an idea for an app that would connect aging homeowners with young people who needed a place to live. Called SharePair, the app was designed to provide affordable housing for a young person or couple in exchange for helping the elderly with shopping and light housekeeping. The arrangement provided the homeowner with an antidote to loneliness and the young person with stable, cheap housing. At one point, they were working so many hours Kyle moved into the apartment where Bon Tae had lived with his wife and their sixteen-month-old son. Sometimes Kyle would watch the baby if Bon Tae had to travel and his wife was at work.

"We trusted him," Bon Tae said.

"Did you know about his background?" Aloa asked.

"Not until later. If we would have known, I don't think we would have left Sam with him."

By year two, the company had raised $2 million in funding and connected its first hosts and renters. A newspaper story about a young teacher who brought his ninety-two-year-old landlord, a WWII vet, to his high school history class to talk about the liberation of Buchenwald concentration camp, put the app in the public eye. Six months later, a national magazine recounted how one renter had so fallen in love with her aged housemate, she'd nursed the woman through stage-four ovarian cancer. The result was another round of funding and a prediction that SharePair would revolutionize the way Americans lived. Everything looked good.

"We had enough funding to hire a few employees and to buy this house," Bon Tae said. "When we moved, Kyle came too. We had so much stuff going on, it was better to have both of us around at the same time. Our boy, Sam, loved him."

Bon Tae's hands curled around his coffee mug.

"Then everything hit the fan," he said. "We got named in this lawsuit. Supposedly, one of our clients had persuaded her elderly roommate to put her in his will. Four months later, some eighty-year-old dude tried to rape the twenty-two-year-old housemate we'd matched him with." Bon Tae's eyes narrowed. "Kyle said it was my fault for making him rush the app, but it was his incompetence that left a hole in the background checks. We got in a big fight, and Kyle lost it. He threw my computer out the window."

"Wow," Aloa said.

"Yeah. My wife was hysterical. I told Kyle to pack his bags and get out. An hour later our kid, who was four, had a seizure." Bon Tae set down his cup and ran a hand through his hair. "The docs found THC in his system. My wife used edibles, weed-laced cookies, to sleep. But I swear they were always in a jar on top of the refrigerator. We told the docs that, but Child Protective Services came anyway and took Sam, and we didn't get him back for two months. We had to do counseling and drug testing and these ridiculous supervised visits."

Bon Tae's gaze met hers.

"We could never prove it, but I know it was Kyle who gave the cookie to Sam. He was a vindictive little prick. He knew where to hurt me the most."

"Did you file a police report?" Aloa asked.

"We told Child Protective Services, but they said it didn't matter who did it. It was our fault for keeping the edibles in a place that wasn't safe."

"How's your son now?" Aloa asked.

"We think he's fine, but we won't know for sure for a few more years." Bon Tae set his coffee mug on the small table. "Until then, I wake up every day thinking about how to make Kyle's life as miserable as I can."

Aloa waited. Silence was often the best way to draw out confidences.

"I lost track of him for a while," Bon Tae said finally. "I heard he went to Seattle to work. Then, one day, I saw him at the CalTrain station and followed him to this house. I talked to an old friend of his, heard he was caretaking this handicapped dude, and went up and told the dude's wife what Kyle had done to my boy."

He smiled. "She told me she was going to fire his ass."

"When was that?" Aloa asked.

"I'd say it was three weeks ago, give or take a few days."

A week before Corrine's murder.

When Aloa told him the "dude's wife" was now dead, Bon Tae got serious. "I wouldn't put it past him," he said of his old partner.

Aloa knew that while Bon Tae's hatred of Kyle Williams could have tainted his story, the fact that Corrine Davenport may have been planning to fire the assistant opened up another possible motive for her murder.

Just how solid was Kyle's alibi?

She left the house, threw her leg over her motorcycle, and pulled into the street.

The fog was like a malevolent tide. It rose and fell, giving hope for sun, then taking it away. By the time she was halfway to the downtown bar where she was to meet Quinn, the fog had descended again. It turned the city vaporous and sinister, sending frigid air slicing through her jeans. She tried to concentrate on the road, but her mind kept returning to the story of Kyle and the little boy.

She remembered how Kyle never met her eyes when she visited, his almost ferocious protectiveness of Christian Davenport. An image came of Kyle making tea and a mental light bulb clicked on. The cranky witness across the street had told Aloa she'd seen the late-night caller lift a hand to knock on the Davenports' door and knew he was up to no good. "He was a lefty," she'd sniffed.

At the time, the comment hadn't registered amid the litany of the woman's complaints about the deterioration of the neighborhood, but now it did. Kyle had prepared the tea and handed it to her with his left hand. He was a "lefty."

Burns Hamlin was not.

"Omigod," Aloa thought, just as a barefoot man in a ragged coat stumbled from the curb into the path of her bike.

Aloa sucked in her breath and squeezed the brakes hard. The bike's back tire broke loose on the damp pavement and she put her foot down to steady the machine. It came to a halt inches from the man, who lurched backward onto the sidewalk.

"Watch it," she started to yell, but before she could finish there was a squeal of brakes and suddenly she was flying.

She saw gray sky, blue metal, and a pair of panicked eyes behind windshield glass. Her body crashed into hard asphalt, sending a bone-rattling vibration through her. She heard a scream, an engine roar, and, before she could figure out what was happening, something smacked against her shoulder. An arrow of pain pierced her forearm and she was dragged a few feet along the pavement. Another scream sounded and her head thudded against the pavement. Blackness descended.

She came to with her helmet gone and a pair of hands holding her shoulders against the pavement. "Lie still, miss," said a voice that seemed to belong to the hands. Or maybe not. "The paramedics should be here any minute," the voice said. "You're going to be all right."

Her ears rang and her limbs seemed to be separate from her, as if they had decided to take a long rest instead of doing their job and getting her to her feet. She groaned.

From the distance came the sound of sirens and, later, other sets of hands.

A man's face appeared in her vision. He had kind brown eyes and a calm voice. "Hi, my name is Bryce and I'm a paramedic. Can you tell me your name and where you live?" he asked.

"Aloa Snow," she said and gave her address. Her vision swam and she closed her eyes. The world took a slow spin around her.

"And how many quarters in a dollar, Aloa?" the paramedic asked.

She let the dizziness pass and opened her eyes.

Why was he asking about money?

"How many quarters?" he repeated.

"Four," she said. "Where's my bike?"

"Don't worry about your bike. Can you wiggle your fingers and toes for me, Aloa?"

She did what he requested as the ringing in her ears cleared and the world grew more solid.

"Somebody hit me," she said.

"That's right. It was a truck, a small pickup," said the paramedic. "The guy left but the cops will find him. Don't worry."

He pressed his hands on her abdomen, her sides, her legs.

Aloa lifted her arm and sighed. Her leather jacket looked as if a herd of cats had decided to sharpen their claws on the sleeve.

"Everything looks good, Aloa," the paramedic said, "but we need to get you to a hospital to make sure."

"No hospital." Aloa groaned. Her mom's weeklong stay in the hospital before she died, with its smells and hurried doctors and beeping machines, had made Aloa want to never set foot in one again.

"You may have a TBI, a traumatic brain injury. Those can be serious," said the paramedic. "Your helmet was cracked. That means you took a pretty good hit."

Aloa tried to push herself into a sitting position but the paramedic held her down. "I don't care. I'm not going to the hospital," she said.

"The ambulance is almost here," said the paramedic.

"I can't afford an ambulance." Aloa's voice rose and an unexplained panic surged through her. "I know my rights. You can't make me go to the hospital."

"You really need to see a doctor," said the paramedic in the same calm voice.

"I'll go to a clinic," Aloa insisted. "You said yourself everything looks good."

The paramedic sighed and sat back on his heels. "Do you have someone who can drive you?"

"I'll call an Uber."

"That's not what an Uber is for," the paramedic began.

"I'll take her," said a voice.

Aloa looked up the dark pair of slacks to a white shirt and a face she knew.

"Quinn?" she said.

Three hours later, Aloa was perched on an exam table with Quinn leaning against the wall in one corner of the room and a bespectacled doctor explaining that besides a couple of nasty bruises and a cut on her arm, she'd also suffered a concussion.

"You're one lucky girl," he said when he'd finished.

"In case you didn't notice, I'm a full-grown woman," Aloa snapped. A strange and powerful anger had risen inside her. Like PMS times three.

Quinn grinned from the corner. He'd heard the hit-and-run call on the radio, thought the description of the victim and her motorcycle sounded a lot like Aloa and her bike, and decided to check it out on his way to the bar. He'd helped her into his car and taken her to the clinic where she now sat.

The doctor looked at Quinn and crossed his arms. "She doesn't realize how close she came to a drawer in the morgue instead of an exam table in the clinic."

"Hey, I can hear you," Aloa said.

"What I was saying, Miss Snow, is that you could have easily been killed. Motorcycles are dangerous. Thousands of people die every year on them. You came very close."

"Yeah, and people die of bee stings and spider bites. Should I stay away from insects too?" Aloa said.

The doctor ignored her, addressing Quinn. "While her concussion isn't severe, it's still serious. She needs to rest and stay hydrated, and someone should monitor her for symptoms like vomiting, confusion, and slurred speech for the next twenty-four hours. You may also see emotional changes: anger, hostility."

"In other words, she'll be herself," Quinn said. His eyes sparkled with humor.

"Not funny," Aloa muttered.

"She also may experience periods of forgetfulness, and lethargy over the next few days," the physician continued. "She definitely shouldn't drive or make important decisions, and I'd cut back on computer and TV time. And I'd also recommend giving up that motorcycle of hers."

Not a chance, Aloa thought, even though she'd seen the tow truck haul off her crumpled bike and wasn't sure it was even fixable.

Quinn grinned and shoved himself away from the wall. "Come on, Evel Knievel," he said, "let's get you home."

Quinn somehow managed a miracle and found a parking spot a few yards from Aloa's house. He followed her through the front door and into the living room.

"Did you forget to pay your electric bill or something?" he said as he set her daypack on her desk. "It's like a refrigerator in here."

"Cold house, warm heart," Aloa said and sank onto her couch.

Quinn smiled. "How about I make you something to eat?"

Either the concussion or the run had wiped out the dead-body smell and Aloa realized she was hungry. "Sounds good. Thanks," she said and settled back on the couch, propping up her head with a pillow and tugging a throw over herself.

Her hip ached, her arm stung, and her head pounded dully as she lay there, listening to the hiss of flame, the clank of pans as Quinn worked in the kitchen. Part of her suddenly longed for him, for someone, to always be there to take care of her.

She told herself it was the concussion talking and shoved the thought into her mental spam folder where it belonged.

She heard Quinn take a phone call about the Sacrificial Lamb murders. A short time later, he came into the living room.

"Omelet with prosciutto and spinach," he said. "There wasn't a lot to work with."

"I didn't know you could cook," she said, sitting up.

Quinn handed her a fork and the plate.

"There's a lot you don't know about me," he said.

"So tell me," Aloa said and took a bite of the omelet. It was good.

146

Quinn shook his head and dropped into her grandmother's rosé chair.

"The doc said I shouldn't watch TV or get on the computer. How am I supposed to entertain myself?" she said.

He sighed. "OK. What do you want to know?"

"Where you grew up. How you became a cop. Start there," she said.

Quinn stretched his legs, crossing them at his ankles. "All right. Let's see. I didn't grow up anywhere, really. My dad was a guitarist; played in a bunch of second-tier rock bands. We had this Ford van we lived in, pretty much going from gig to gig. The only time we stayed put was when the van broke down, in which case we'd hang out until we saved enough money to fix it. My mom called herself an artist, but she spent most of her life so stoned, she really didn't function."

"I'm sorry."

"No need. My dad, Craig, was pretty solid. He made up for her being MIA most of the time."

"School?" she asked.

"Craig taught me to read," Quinn said. "After that, I was pretty much on my own. I left them when I was fourteen. We were outside San Diego when the transmission blew. When it was fixed, they left and I didn't. I was tired of moving around. I forged my dad's signature and enrolled in high school. I lived on the beach and stole food from the cafeteria. I showered at the gym. A cop named Winston Graham found me camped out and took me home instead of hauling me to juvie. I lived with him and his wife and two kids through junior college. He was a good man. He helped people. I guess that's why I became a cop. What about you? What's your story?"

Aloa thought about the many ways parents could fail their children—from neglect to violence to selfishness—and set her plate aside. She told him about her own father and how he died on a run through the woods, and about her grandmother Maja, who lost her husband when she was forty and spent her days doing hair and makeup for the dead, a clientele that never tipped, but also never complained.

"She saved her pennies and built this house," Aloa said. "She was so proud of it. On Saturdays, she'd tie up her hair, get on her knees, and wax every inch of the floor. She always said that you needed a clean house and a clean conscience, in that order."

"I'm not so good in either department," Quinn said.

"I've got a few dusty corners myself," Aloa said.

She told him about her scholarship to UC Berkeley, about her mother's death, and about losing a job she loved. She didn't mention her eating disorder, her stay in the psych ward, or Michael.

Her conscience-scrubbing could come later.

Afterward, Quinn made them cups of tea. Darkness pressed against the front window.

"Don't you have to get home?" Aloa asked.

"I wouldn't call a couch in my cousin's house a home," he said.

"What about . . . ?" Aloa began.

"My wife?" He twisted the platinum band on his finger. "We're not exactly together at the moment."

The tick of her grandmother's clock suddenly felt too loud in her ears.

"I'm feeling a little, I don't know, claustrophobic," Aloa said. "Do you mind if we go outside?"

The concussion seemed to be playing with her emotions, making them appear and disappear with only the slightest nudge.

Quinn shrugged into his jacket. Aloa wrapped herself in the throw and they went out to sit on the Vallejo Street steps. The fog had lifted so it was now a high cloud. She could see the glow of lights below.

"Nice," Quinn said of the view.

Aloa's head gave a slow spin and she closed her eyes until it stopped. Then: "I guess marriage is harder than it looks," she said. She wasn't sure if it was an apology for asking too personal a question or something she actually believed.

Quinn stretched his arms so his hands hung over his knees. "Yeah, especially if you find out you owe about sixty thousand dollars on two credit cards you never knew about and that your wife and an old boyfriend have been texting back and forth for the past eight months." He stared into the night. "It's kind of hard to trust anything she says right now."

"Ouch, that's rough."

"We went to counseling." He shrugged. "She says it was my fault for not being home enough."

"We probably should talk about something else, huh?"

"Good idea." A truck rumbled past on the street below.

"How come you didn't consider Kyle, the assistant, as a suspect?" she asked.

"We did. His roommate said he was home during the time Corrine was killed. The girl had no reason to lie for Williams as far as we could tell."

"I don't think he liked Corrine. He was a real jerk to her, from what I've heard."

"You can't arrest people for being jerks. Otherwise, all the jails would be full."

"You know, the professor has an alibi too."

He looked sideways at her. "What do you know?"

She thought about her promise to Hamlin. "I can't tell you at the moment."

"Not that again," Quinn said.

"But I will the moment I figure out a few things," she added quickly. She touched her fingertips to her forehead.

Was it the concussion that made her feel so fragile, so combustible?

"And when will you be figuring those things out?" Quinn asked.

"Soon, I hope."

"Well, while you're at it, why don't you ask Hamlin why he bought a boning knife on Amazon right before Corrine Davenport was killed?"

Aloa pushed down a flash of surprise. "But unless you find the knife with her DNA on it, it doesn't prove anything, right?"

"We're serving a search warrant as we speak." Quinn's phone rang and he fished it out of his pocket. He looked at the caller ID. "Speak of the devil."

He answered.

"Are you kidding me?" he said after a few moments of listening. "When? Did anybody get a plate number?" He waited. "Well, find the hell out."

He swore, disconnected the call, and stood.

"Looks like Hamlin skipped," he said.

What have you done, Tick?

"A neighbor saw him leave with a suitcase this afternoon. He came out with an old guy in a porkpie hat and they got into a VW van." He turned to her. "You wouldn't happen to know anything about that, would you?"

She massaged her temples. "Not really," she said.

"I'm not stupid, Aloa. I know what kind of car your gray-hairs drive. What did you do?"

"Nothing. Well, maybe something." Aloa looked up. "Tick called."

Quinn waited.

"He's Burns Hamlin's dad."

"Mother of God," Quinn exploded.

"I just told him my best suspect was dead; that he couldn't have killed Corrine. I was going to explain more later but he must have panicked."

"So basically, you told Tick we were coming for his son," Quinn said.

"He promised he wouldn't run."

"Well, you can see how well that worked out." Quinn folded his arms across his chest. "What else did you blab about? Did you tell him we had his cell phone records?"

Aloa felt anger spark. Part of it was aimed at Quinn's tone, the rest at herself for not stopping Tick. "Anybody who watches TV knows the cops look at your cell phone locations."

"Christ," Quinn said. "I can't believe this."

He paced down two steps before coming back in front of her. "Why did I ever think I could trust a reporter? I should have known better."

Aloa got to her feet. "Listen, Quinn—"

"No." He held up a hand to her face. "I thought you were different. I thought you were one of those who wanted the truth more than big headlines. You're no better than the rest of them."

Aloa had spent years fighting to have her voice heard in a testosterone-soaked profession and she wasn't about to be shushed now. Not by Quinn. Not by any man.

"Put that hand down before I do something you and I will both regret," she said.

Slowly, Quinn lowered his palm.

Aloa leaned toward him, her voice rising. "I'm not a headline hunter, Quinn. The only thing I want is to make sure the bad guys get what they deserve and the innocent aren't railroaded."

"It isn't being railroaded when all the evidence points in one direction," Quinn said.

"It is if you forget the track runs both ways."

"Hamlin is guilty and you know it. What about the texts, the cell phone, the voice the husband heard?"

"I think he's innocent," Aloa said. "You just need to look a little harder."

They were shouting now.

"And how can I look when you run around mouthing off to my suspect about important evidence, when you screw up my case?"

"A case against the wrong man," Aloa said. "And don't yell at me."

"It's the only way I can get past that giant ego of yours," Quinn said.

Her anger seemed to take on a life of its own. It was volcanic, unstoppable.

She tossed the throw from her shoulders. "Don't talk to me about ego, Mr. Blowhard. Yours is so big you can't see around it to the fact you're about to make a huge mistake."

"My only mistake was trusting you," Quinn shouted. "Now, I've got to go clean up the mess you made."

"Good. Go," she yelled, "and take your big head with you."

"I'm taking you to the station. The doc said you shouldn't be alone."

"The only way I'll go to the station is if you arrest me."

"Don't think I wouldn't like that."

Aloa snatched the throw from the ground. "I'm going back to the house. Alone," she added.

"So I can find you dead tomorrow? Hell no," Quinn said.

He reached for her arm and she shrugged him off.

"Leave me alone."

"I will not," Quinn said.

In the end, Aloa agreed to let Quinn escort her to Justus, where Erik and Guillermo fussed over her and put her to bed in their guest room, bringing her a tall glass of ice water and two Tylenol and promising to check on her every hour.

"Sleep tight, but not too tight, sweetie," Erik said as he closed the door gently behind him.

Aloa fell into a restless sleep, awakening once to find Baxter the cat curled up against her ribs and another time to feel Erik gently tugging the covers up over her shoulders.

"I'm fine," she whispered when he came in a little before 5:00 a.m. to check on her again. "You don't need to keep watching me."

"You scared us, honey," Erik said. He perched on the edge of the bed. "You could have been killed."

"But I wasn't." She took his hand. "Thanks for taking care of me."

"That's what big old queens are for." He smiled. "You're family, honey. Don't forget that."

A lump grew in her throat and she swallowed it away. Damned concussion. "I won't," she said. "Now, you should get some sleep. You have to work today."

"You promise you're fine?"

"I am."

"And you'll do what the doc said and stay here and rest?"

"Scout's honor," she said.

But at 7:30 a.m. she awoke with an idea so strong her brain seemed to crackle like lightning with it. She lay still for a moment before climbing out of bed. She slipped into her clothes—jeans and a college-era denim jacket she'd found in her closet—left a note for Erik and Gully saying she'd gone back home, and tiptoed down the stairs carrying her Timberlands in her hand.

She walked a few doors down the street, pulled out her phone, and summoned an Uber.

DAY 10

The Davenports' neighborhood was just waking up as Aloa's driver crested the hill and asked if she wanted to drive around the block one more time or if there was another place she wanted to go.

Aloa studied the steep street. She watched a man in a plaid robe walk a nervous Chihuahua, and a woman in a suit and high heels get behind the wheel of a Mercedes and pull away. But there was no sign of a small blue pickup like the one that had hit her.

"Just let me out," she told the driver.

She'd awakened that morning with the sudden realization of where else she may have seen the panicked eyes that belonged to the hit-and-run driver. It was at the Davenports' house when Kyle Williams had opened the door that first time. The memory had made her sit up and let the thoughts flow: Kyle's overprotectiveness of Davenport, the left-handed man at the Davenports' door, his mistreatment of Corrine Davenport, his years at the hands of a psychopath, and Bon Tae's tale of a nature so vengeful he would hurt a child.

If it was Kyle who tried to kill her with his truck—and that was still an "if" until she could confirm the blue truck belonged to him and examine it for damage or blood—there could be only one reason for the assault: he was Corrine's killer and he was afraid Aloa was getting too close.

She'd gathered up her clothes, remembering Kyle had an alibi, but also knowing there were ways to manipulate witnesses, and dressed quietly. She'd debated calling Quinn, but realized the Brain Farm had made that impossible by absconding with Hamlin. Not only did Quinn blame her for what happened, but he was so angry he wouldn't believe any theory she came up with at the moment.

That left her with only two options: She could break her promise and reveal Hamlin's alibi, something that would violate the moral code she'd adopted of trustworthiness in all things. Or she could prove Kyle was the killer.

She looked down the street at the Davenports' house and got out of the car. There might be a way. But it would be tricky.

She watched the Uber pull away and took a few steps, but a sudden wave of vertigo washed over her and she had to put her hand on the hood of a parked Volvo, waiting for the dizziness to pass. Her head had stopped pounding, but her brain was behaving like a cell phone with bad service. Stretches of clarity would be interrupted by a moment of buzzing blankness. She closed her eyes and waited for the spinning sensation to end before continuing. She hoped it was intuition and not the concussion that had led her here.

She knocked on the Davenports' door, heard footsteps, and saw Kyle blanch when he opened the door to find her standing on the porch.

"Oh," he stammered, "it's you."

"I'll bet you're surprised to see me," Aloa said.

His Adam's apple took a deep bob. "Well, it's barely eight o'clock."

"That's not what I meant," she answered.

He cleared his throat and straightened his shoulders. "Yes, well," he said. "Whatever you meant, you can't come in. Christian isn't ready for visitors." He started to close the door.

Aloa put up a hand and stopped the door's swing. "You can't run forever, you know," she said.

An intercom crackled. "Who's there, Kyle?"

"Nobody," Kyle said. "Go away," he hissed at Aloa.

Instead, Aloa called out. "It's Aloa Snow. I'd like to talk to you, Mr. Davenport." She raised an eyebrow at Kyle.

"You can't do this," Kyle said under his breath.

"Watch me," said Aloa as Davenport's voice came back over the intercom.

"Well, if you don't mind a little quadriplegic skin show, come on back," he said.

Aloa smiled, pushed her way past Kyle, and went into the bedroom where she guessed Davenport would be. He was lying in his hospital bed, his hair damp and tangled, a sheet lowered to below his navel, revealing prominent ribs and hip bones that stood up like cupped gravestones—an image of wasting she recognized too well. She looked away.

Kyle shoved past Aloa to draw the sheet over Davenport's chest. "You need your bath and your breakfast," he said.

"It's fine, Kyle," said Davenport. He smiled at Aloa. "I have trouble regulating my temperature. Sometimes I'm too cold and sometimes I feel like I'm in the tropics. Right now, it's the tropics." He lifted his chin toward a straight-backed chair in a corner of the room next to a clutter of medical equipment. "Have a seat, Ms. Snow."

"Christian, you know what happens when your schedule gets thrown off," Kyle objected, smoothing Davenport's hair off his face and drawing it into a topknot he secured with a small elastic band.

"I'm sick of schedules. Let's live a little, huh?" Davenport smiled at Aloa but the grin faded to a frown. "You found out something. Something I won't like," he said.

Davenport's perception was spooky-good.

"I have a few questions," she answered. "I guess whether you like them is up to you."

She waited while his eyes searched her face.

"OK," he said slowly. "Ask your questions and I'll see whether or not they make me happy."

Aloa inhaled. "So tell me about your marriage. Were you and Corrine happy?"

"This is ridiculous," Kyle interrupted, smoothing Davenport's sheets and adjusting his pillow.

"It's all right, Kyle. Apparently, Aloa thinks I'm either faking this useless body of mine or I somehow rose up and ninja-killed my wife. And would you stop fussing over me, please."

Kyle lifted his hands and stepped away.

"I just want to get a better feel for your wife's state of mind," Aloa said.

"Sure. Lay a foundation, right?" Davenport said. "So do you remember me talking about *gaman*? The Japanese virtue of endurance and self-denial?"

Aloa nodded.

"While it sounds like some really noble thing, it's also a recipe for darkness. Imagine being expected to endure suffering no matter what it did to you inside. Imagine not speaking up or asking for help or thinking you deserve better. Then, imagine being married to someone like that, someone who bottles up her emotions so you don't know if she's happy or sad or hates your guts. I could do something like forget Corrine had made a special dinner and stay late at work, or jump on a plane without telling her, and she wouldn't say a word. She'd just look at me and go unpack my suitcase or make another dinner. It made me feel like a jerk. We worked on it, though. She went to counseling and got the job with the DA's office. She was getting better. Then the accident happened and we were back to the same old thing."

"So if you told her to get a tattoo to prove her love, she'd do it?"

"I told you that was her choice."

158

Who was lying? This man in front of her or Corrine, who'd told Wendy her husband had forced the symbol on her?

"How about right before she died. Was she depressed? Worried?" Aloa glanced at Kyle. "Wanting to make changes?"

"Having to tell your husband you cheated on him isn't exactly a recipe for happiness. She was ashamed, sad. She said she had a lot on her mind and was having trouble sleeping, but she and I were good. She was determined to fix her mistake."

"You said before that it wasn't a mistake."

"That was her word, not mine."

"Maybe she thought it was a mistake because it was she who fell in love."

"She wasn't in love with Hamlin," Davenport said. "What are you getting at?"

Aloa weighed her options. "I think everybody is wrong. I'm pretty sure it wasn't Hamlin who killed your wife."

Davenport arched an eyebrow.

"Hamlin was somewhere else when Corrine died," she said.

"But I heard his voice," Davenport said.

"You said yourself you were angry with Hamlin and that you wanted to punish him. You had a lot of time to lie there and think about it that night. Maybe you heard what you wanted to hear."

For a moment, the only sound in the room was the quiet hum of an air purifier.

"So Hamlin didn't kill her?" Davenport asked.

"That's right," Aloa said.

"Do you know who did?"

Aloa paused. "I think I do."

"OK. Well then." Davenport frowned. "Kyle, why don't you bring us some tea? I think I need a little fortification and Ms. Snow looks a bit pale. Let's try some of that special Yan Wang tea. I think it's exactly what we need on a day like today." Davenport turned to Aloa. "It's very rare. I have to order it through this dealer in New York."

Kyle didn't move.

"Go," Davenport ordered.

"So, Ms. Snow," said Davenport after Kyle had left, "are you saying I've accused an innocent man?"

"I'm saying things aren't always the way they seem at first," Aloa said.

"And you're sure about this other person? The real killer?" he asked.

"I'd like to ask a few more questions before I answer," Aloa said.

Davenport's lips twitched into a smile. "The eighth rule of interrogation: the 'we know everything' gambit. Hanns Scharff pretty much rocked that method in World War II: let the subject believe you already know everything and hope they'll slip and fill in the blanks for you. For me, it really only worked if the subject wasn't all that bright. But go ahead. Give it a try."

Aloa ignored the dig. "So it was only you and Corrine here on the night she died?"

"Would you mind raising my head? My neck muscles can't take this angle for too long," Davenport said.

Aloa found the right button on the hospital bed and did what she was asked, glancing at Davenport's soft, unmoving hands. *What would it be like to be so helpless?*

"Thanks," Davenport said. Then: "That's right. Kyle had gone home. We had dinner and watched a movie."

"He didn't come back?"

"If you saw the police report, you know his roommate alibied him. He was at home."

"Then who was the left-handed man your neighbor saw knock on your door?"

"It was Hamlin."

"Hamlin is right-handed," Aloa said.

"The old lady could be wrong."

"Maybe, but it seems strange there was no DNA evidence putting Hamlin inside your house."

"The detective said the murder happened fast."

"How does your intercom system work?"

"Voice-activated. Kyle set it up."

"Interesting," Aloa said. "Then why didn't you activate the intercom when you heard Corrine and a man talking? You said you couldn't hear, but you could have listened in."

"Like I said, it happened fast. I guess I didn't think."

Aloa changed tacks. "What kind of vehicle does Kyle drive?"

Davenport frowned. "What does it matter?"

"Here we are," Kyle interrupted, coming into the room with a black lacquer tray that held two cups of tea. He pulled over a small table and set Aloa's tea on the shiny surface, then busied himself arranging Davenport's beverage, blocking Aloa's view of his boss.

"Try your tea," Davenport said when Kyle finished. "Tell me what you think."

Aloa took a tentative sip of the dark-gold brew. It had an unusual but appealing taste. A combination of mushroom and earth and something brothy. Warmth filled her.

"It's good," she said.

"Expensive as hell," he said. "Can you taste the minerals? Imagine a sidewalk after a summer rain."

"Sorry. No."

"Try again."

She took a small sip. "Maybe."

"That's all right," Davenport said. "Not everyone has that kind of palate. I doubt you'll have another opportunity to try it, anyway. It's so rare customers can only order two ounces at a time, and then only once every two months."

Rare or not, Aloa set aside her cup.

"So you want to get down to business, do you?" Davenport asked.

"Please."

"Kyle, why don't you leave us alone for a few minutes?" Davenport said.

"I don't—" Kyle began.

"That wasn't a request, Kyle," Davenport said more forcefully. "Go on. Maybe start packing up Corrine's things like I asked you to. And make sure you close the door behind you."

"All right," Kyle said, throwing a glance over his shoulder at Aloa as he left.

"Now," said Davenport when Kyle was gone, "why are you asking about Kyle's truck?"

"Details. You said it yourself. That's how you found the little girl's kidnapper, how you almost nailed Bin Laden's videographer."

Davenport's eyes narrowed. "Wait. How did you know about Bin Laden's videographer?"

"I talked to your lieutenant, Tim Everson."

"And why would you do that?" Davenport's voice hardened.

"Background. Sometimes you find out things you didn't expect."

"Like what?"

Aloa considered her answer. "Like an army investigation."

Outside, wind rustled the ferns and grasses. Maybe the fog would finally clear.

"And you have no secrets, Aloa?" he asked.

"I try to be open about them."

"Like your time in the psych ward? Did you think there weren't records?"

Aloa's head gave a thud and she reached for her teacup. She could count on one hand the number of people who knew about that part of her past. She took a long pull of the tea. She needed a moment to process.

"How did you get them?" she asked finally. "Medical records are private."

"Friends in the bureau. Not everybody likes journalists."

"That time has nothing to do with this case."

"It does if you're damaged; if, say, you've got mental health issues that screw around with your idea of what's true and what isn't, that lets you make up things like news sources."

Don't fall for his diversion.

"We're all damaged in some way. You, me, Kyle. Especially him." A ripple of vertigo ran through her, then passed.

"Kyle's doing remarkably well for what he went through," Davenport said.

Aloa opened her mouth, but her next question seemed to have scurried to some dark corner of her mind.

The concussion at work?

"Tell me about him." It was an old reporter's trick: ask a generic question while you gathered your thoughts.

"If that's the way you want to go," Davenport said. "He was a good kid, but pretty naive. His kidnapper saw him at the bus stop, offered to buy him a donut and drive him to school. He trusted the guy, just like he'd trusted his mother to come back, and ended up chained like a dog for the first year, abused, tortured—it was the worst I've ever seen, which is why I helped him. He needed to have a connection with someone he could rely on, someone who wouldn't hurt him. I got him a shrink and they worked on a lot of stuff, including his shame at not escaping, even when his abuser took him to town. That was the hard part for him, the part nobody understood. But I did. I read him. I know why he stayed. He had nowhere else to go."

The room suddenly pulsed in and out and Aloa grabbed the chair to steady herself.

"Are you all right?" Davenport asked.

"I had a little accident yesterday," she said.

Was it yesterday? What day was it?

"Sorry to hear that." Davenport stared at her for a few silent moments. "Did you ever wonder why life is so full of suffering, Aloa?"

She frowned.

"Ever since I found Kyle at that cabin, I've asked myself that question, but it's only now that I'm beginning to figure it out."

His words seemed to echo in her head.

"It's because we need suffering to bring insight and we need insight to bring transformation. Otherwise, we just go on with our soulless little lives: going to work, eating dinner in front of the TV, buying crap we don't need in order to make ourselves feel better. But we never do feel better, do we? That's because by trying to avoid suffering, we miss finding our true selves. I've suffered and so have you, Aloa. You worked hard. You denied yourself pleasure. But you pulled back before you reached transformation." He *tsked* in disapproval. "Why, Aloa?"

Outside, the wind wrinkled the water in the swimming pool. Aloa watched the ripples. They seemed to shimmer and curl like snakes.

"We found your college records too. Eighty-nine pounds. Light as a feather, weren't you?" Davenport's voice was low. "A little bird who tried to fly."

Fly. Fly. The word echoed in her head.

"But you didn't fly, did you? You reached for the sky, but you let the earth pull you back. Fame, money, power. That's what you craved and it made you mediocre. Just like the rest of the mindless people in this country. You screwed up. You made a mistake." His gaze flickered over her. "Are you sure you're not making a mistake now?"

Aloa closed her eyes. Images flashed behind her lids: a dark crow, her father's body in the forest.

What was happening?

"I wanted to trust you, Aloa," Davenport said, "but these half-baked accusations you're making? They tell me you're still so desperate to make a name for yourself that you're ready to hurt innocent people. Shame on you."

Shame. Shame.

The room pulsed in and out as if it were breathing.

"I see what you're trying to do. Don't kid yourself that anybody is going to let you back in the game, even if you think you're some kind of justice-seeking superhero. Nobody trusts you. Nobody respects you and now you're blowing it again with your so-called investigation. You'll be ruined again if you keep it up. Believe me, I know."

The room tilted and Aloa slid from the chair to the ground, grabbing at the floor to steady herself.

Davenport's words floated in. "Are you all right?"

She opened her mouth but no words came out.

"I'll get help" was the last thing she heard.

Hands touching her. A car door slamming. The world speeding past in a blur.

Shame Fame Fly Sky. The words were like a merry-go-round in her head.

She heard a muted roar and began to walk, the sound pulling her forward to the edge of a cliff. She was high above the sea.

She stared down into the churning blue-and-white water.

"Come," whispered a voice in her head.

Her body seemed loose and unconnected, as if she might float away.

She shrugged out of her denim jacket and pulled off her boots.

Light as a feather.

She reached into her pocket, felt the note tucked there, and slid it into her left boot so the breeze wouldn't take it.

She straightened and swayed slightly. The image of her father, long dead, floated into her memory.

Fly, the voice said.

She walked a few steps to the cliff's edge.

She felt the tug of gravity; the waves beckoning her to come.

She inhaled a long breath, spread her arms wide, and leaned.

The gust of wind slammed hard into the land, pushing upward along the dirt and rock, throwing a lone seagull into the air. The gull struggled, flapping its wings, but it was no match for the strong current of air and Aloa felt one of its webbed feet suddenly slash against her cheek. She threw up her arms to shield herself and stumbled backward from the cliff's edge, landing hard on her back. The gull cried and wheeled away. For a moment, she couldn't breathe.

The earth tilted and rolled. Aloa dug her fingers into the ground and closed her eyes. Her body was warm, then cold. Images scrolled through her mind like some crazy movie. Birds. Eyes. A bleached skull. She called out. Or maybe she didn't. After some time, the images died but her body still refused to move. A shaft of sunlight touched her, then disappeared. Children laughed. She pushed herself to her elbows and, finally, sat up.

The wind pushed against her and she shivered hard, almost to her bones. She pulled her knees to her forehead and wrapped her arms around herself. Her mouth was dry and her heart pounded. Her stomach roiled. She leaned over and vomited, then huddled into a ball again.

"Are you OK, miss?" someone said near her ear.

She lifted her head a few inches to see a round face, brown eyes, a light mustache over full lips. She couldn't find the words to answer his question.

"I was your driver," said the man. "I brought you here but you looked ill. I had another fare, but I became worried and so I came back."

She studied him. No memory came.

"Are you sick? Shall I take you to the hospital?"

She shook her head.

The man plucked her denim jacket from the ground nearby and wrapped it around her shoulders. "Perhaps you have friends. Someone to help. I cannot leave you here."

A thought formed through the murk. "Tick," she said.

The driver frowned. "You are wanting a clock?"

Aloa closed her eyes. Shook her head and laid her forehead back on her knees.

"If you give me a number I will call someone," the man said.

He waited.

"Please. A number," he said, "or I must summon the authorities."

Aloa mumbled the first phone number that came into her head, wondering who it belonged to even as she recited it.

The man pulled out his phone. "Ah yes," he said after a few moments. "My name is Arjun and I have a woman here who is very much in need of assistance."

Aloa came awake on a purple velvet couch with the Brain Farm bending over her and what felt like a team of miniature workmen jackhammering inside her skull. The room where she lay was painted a hideous shade of lavender with prayer flags and Indian tapestries on the wall. She closed her eyes.

"Where am I?" she asked.

"In an apartment in the Castro," Doc said. "I got a call from your buddy, Michael, saying you needed help. He was in Hong Kong so we hauled ass and picked you up."

She groaned.

"What the hell were you doing, Ink?" Tick said. "You were higher than a kite."

The jackhammers pounded. A hazy memory formed. "I went to find the eyes," she said.

The men shared a glance.

"Still high," P-Mac said.

"Coffee," said Tick, straightening.

"B12," said Doc.

"I'll get her boots," P-Mac said.

An hour later, Aloa had downed three cups of coffee, swallowed two B12s, and was now marching laps in the alley behind the house with Doc holding her arm.

"Seventy-six," Tick called from his perch on the back porch as Aloa passed.

"Can I stop now?" she asked.

"You gotta do eighty," said P-Mac, who'd escorted her outside and was now leaning against the wall, smoking a fat joint he'd rolled.

"Why eighty?" Aloa asked.

"Do not question the master, grasshopper," P-Mac said, holding the smoke inside his lungs so his voice came out tight and low.

"I'm fine," she said.

"Seventy-seven," Tick called out.

"How are you feeling?" Doc asked.

"Better."

More marching.

"That's eighty. Get her in the apartment," Tick said.

Inside, Doc scrambled her some eggs and made her swallow a couple of ibuprofen along with a tall glass of water. Her arms and legs ached dully. The men crowded around the small wooden table watching her eat. When she was finished, Tick leaned forward. "You gotta be careful with what you buy on the street, Ink. You could have killed yourself."

"Yeah, you were tripping like Tim Leary when we got to you," P-Mac said. "What was it? Acid? Molly? Shrooms?"

Aloa searched her brain. "I don't think I took anything."

"More coffee," Doc said, getting up and pouring her a mug of something that resembled coffee but tasted more like battery acid. "Drink," he commanded.

Tick leaned in, folding his elbows on the table. "Tell us everything that happened after I called and you told me you hit a dead end with that drug guy. And before you ask, my kid isn't here. We've got him stashed."

Aloa rubbed her temples, letting the memories form and details emerge from the muck in her brain. She told the Brain Farm about Wendy Pianelli's story of the dysfunctional Davenport household and Aat Bon Tae's tale of revenge. She described the drunk stumbling into the street, the truck hitting her, and the gray eyes she thought belonged to Kyle. She told them about going to the house and meeting with Davenport.

Suddenly, she sat up straighter. "Holy hell," she said. "That little bastard drugged me."

The men stared at her.

"Kyle Williams. Davenport's assistant." Her voice rose. "Davenport told him to bring us tea. After I drank it, the room started going in and out. Like it was breathing."

"Color. Taste. Smell. Tell me everything," P-Mac ordered.

"Tiger's-mouth root," P-Mac pronounced after she'd described the brew's taste, the snakelike images in the pool, her father's voice, and the strange vertigo. "Crazy-ass stuff. Comes from this plant in northeast China. The ancients believed it allowed you to talk to spirits. It's a helluva trip, apparently. I saw a guy on that stuff in Nam. He thought his dead lieutenant came back and told him to swim to Cambodia. They pulled him out a mile downriver, naked, half dead, and covered in leeches."

Tick made a *tsking* sound. "That's not how I would have done it."

"Oh?" said P-Mac. "And how would you have killed her, Mr. Master Assassin?"

"I would have poisoned her," Tick said. "It's a lot more reliable than drugging somebody and hoping they fall off a cliff. A little polonium-210, maybe some ricin on the end of an umbrella."

"Wait, that's it." Aloa leaned forward, her elbows on the table.

"There was an umbrella?" P-Mac frowned.

"No. The jerk wanted to make it look like suicide," Aloa said. "Davenport had gotten my medical records and knew I'd spent time in the psych ward. I'm sure Kyle read them and figured he could slip that stuff in my tea and send me off to the cliffs knowing how disoriented I'd be. The place where I got dropped off isn't that far from the edge. I'll bet he followed me, and if I didn't jump or fall, he'd have figured out a way to give me a shove."

Nausea tickled her throat at the thought of how close she'd come to jumping.

"And a tox screen would just make it look like you'd gotten high before you took the big plunge," P-Mac said. "Boom, investigation over."

Doc looked stricken. "So that's what this was," he said and pulled a crumpled piece of paper from his pocket. "I found it in your boot."

"What's it say?" Tick leaned in.

Doc read the note. "This is the most honest thing I'll do."

Nausea pricked again.

"That asshat. He even wrote a suicide note," said Tick and banged a fist on the table. "I say we give him a taste of his own medicine."

"No," Aloa said.

"Why not?" P-Mac said.

"Because first we're going to prove he's the one who killed Corrine Davenport."

Aloa stripped off her clothes and climbed into the shower, washing the dirt and the feel of violation from her hair and skin. The bastard had slipped her a drug that stole her will and left her as vulnerable as a newborn.

Is that how he had felt, chained in that cabin with his abuser?

She scrubbed herself with a washcloth until her skin was pink. She stepped out of the shower and looked in the dingy mirror over the sink. She touched the red stripe on her cheek where one of the gull's webbed feet had scratched her. What if the ancients were right? What if it *was* her father's spirit she'd communicated with out on that cliff? The skin on her forearms prickled. Had her father, the bird-watcher, sent the gull to save her?

She dressed quickly, pulling on a T-shirt and a pair of jeans she borrowed from the apartment owner. She squeezed some toothpaste onto her index finger and scrubbed at her teeth, tugging her mind away from the sadness that came at the memory of the way her father had died: alone in the woods, his heart stopped like an old clock. She should have been there.

She towel-dried her hair and went into the purple living room where the Brain Farm waited.

"What's next, boss?" Tick asked.

Doc piloted the old VW van to a forest of newer condos and apartment buildings in the Bayview-Hunters Point neighborhood where, according to Tick's research, Kyle's ex-roommate lived.

Above the van, a wind was blowing and the sky was clearing. Doc said he'd heard on the news that the wind had come from the north, driving fifteen-foot swells that had nearly capsized a sightseeing boat off Vancouver Island and swept over Washington and Oregon. Now it was scattering the fog and drying the ground. Meteorologists were predicting the fog would be completely gone by night.

Aloa thought of how the wind had shoved at her on the cliff and the gull had flown upward. She touched the small scrape on her cheek.

"It's that way," Tick said from the back seat of the van, pointing upward toward a cluster of modern-looking buildings painted in shades of rust and cream. The condos and apartments looked over the bay and an abandoned WWII navy shipyard that was also once the site for the testing and decontamination of target ships used in the nuclear tests at Bikini Atoll in 1946.

Such a beautiful spot to put a place meant for war, Aloa thought as Doc pulled the van up in front of the ex-roommate's address.

Aloa climbed from the van and went up the short walkway. A potted palm sat on the small porch. She knocked on the door and waited.

Anna Kim was a small woman with chin-length black hair. She wore leggings, an oversize flannel shirt, and had so many piercings in her ears and nose Aloa thought she would probably set off airport alarms as soon as she walked in the door. When Aloa said she was a journalist doing a story on the murder of Corrine Davenport for Novo, Kim let her in.

"I've only got ten minutes," she said, "then I have a conference call."

Kim was a freelance graphic designer who said Kyle had been the perfect roommate. She gestured toward the small bedroom off the living room where Kyle had presumably slept. "Gone all day. Slept all night. Paid his rent on time. I was bummed when he moved out. His schedule changed and he had to take care of the dude he was watching full time. He decided to live in his house instead of mine."

"Were you friends?" Aloa asked.

"We got along."

"You remember the night Corrine Davenport died?" Aloa asked.

"I do. Kyle was here."

"How can you be so sure?" Aloa asked.

"After it happened, I remembered this," said Kim. She walked over to a neat worktable containing a keyboard, two computer screens, a potted fern, a French word-a-day calendar, and a coffee table book on the cafés of Paris. The workstation was shoved against a picture window and abutted a green couch set behind a low coffee table. Kim tapped the keyboard and a selfie of her and Kyle in their pajamas appeared. The two of them were sitting on the couch saluting the camera with two glasses of red wine and a bowl of popcorn.

"We were watching reruns of *Wild Travels*," Kim said. "We both like that show. I posted it on Instagram."

She tapped a few more keys and Aloa leaned into the shot to read the caption Kim had posted. "Having a wild night," it said. "#pajama-gram #tristelundi #winetime."

"Did the cops ask for it?" Aloa asked.

"I showed it to them."

"What time was this taken?"

"I think it was ten forty-five. Maybe eleven."

About the same time Corrine was being murdered.

"Did you notice anything different about Kyle that night?"

The woman frowned. "What are you getting at?"

"Nothing. I'm just wondering if he seemed upset or nervous that night. Maybe he needed a glass of wine after a bad day or something."

The woman hesitated for a few seconds before answering. "No more than usual. There was always a lot of drama in that house."

"What kind of drama?"

Kim squinted at her. "What's this about again?"

Aloa knew she needed to tread carefully.

"I'm looking for details. You know, to fill in blanks in the story: what the family was like, their daily routines."

The answer seemed to satisfy Kim.

"From what Kyle said, the wife was supersensitive and the paralyzed guy was pretty demanding. He'd get angry and the wife would run around trying to make him happy, then I guess she had an affair or something. That's what Kyle told me, anyway. It was a pretty messed-up scene."

"Did Kyle ever say he was worried about getting fired?"

She considered the question. "I don't think so. Kyle was really good at all that caregiving stuff and was pretty attached to that paralyzed dude. He did everything for the guy."

"Have you seen Kyle since he moved out?"

"He came by once, to drop off some money he owed me." Her gaze went to the time at the top of the computer screen. "Sorry, but I've got to make my call."

Aloa climbed into the waiting van and slumped in the passenger seat.

"Well?" P-Mac asked as Doc fired up the van with a sound somewhere between a smoker's cough and a hog's squeal.

"The roommate insisted Kyle was home that night but, I don't know, something about it seemed off," Aloa said.

"How so?" Doc asked.

"That's the problem. I'm not sure." Aloa tugged at her bottom lip. "She did an Instagram post of her and Kyle at home that night. They were drinking wine and eating popcorn. She said they were watching *Wild Travels* reruns on TV."

"Pretty convenient," said Doc.

"Exactly," Aloa said. "It was almost like Kyle staged the photo and convinced her to post it. Like maybe he blackmailed her with something or paid her off. She's a freelancer. She probably needs the money. But how can I prove he did that?"

"How about we kidnap the little asswipe, slip him sodium thiopental, and see what he has to say?" P-Mac said from the back seat.

Doc grinned. "Hey, I know a guy who knows a guy who might be able to get us some of that stuff."

"We could say we have a delivery and grab him when he answers the door," P-Mac called out.

"How about a FedEx truck?" Tick said, leaning forward. "We follow a truck and when the driver gets out to deliver a package, we jump in. I hot-wire the engine. We're out of there in thirty seconds or less. We nab the jerk and boom."

"Just like Berkeley, 1969," P-Mac said.

"Christ," said Doc, "we said we were never going to talk about that."

P-Mac thumped the back of Doc's seat. "Good times, though, right?"

Tick laughed. "Do you think that capitalist pig ever figured out what happened?"

"Guys," Aloa interrupted, "I hate to bust up your kidnapping party, but we're not abducting Kyle."

"But—" Tick said.

Aloa turned. "No. We're going to go at this logically. We're going to think."

She swept her glance over the men. "And I don't want to know what happened in Berkeley in 1969, OK?"

Doc steered the van through the city toward the Castro, a circuitous route that took twice as long, but also avoided the very real possibility that the old van's gutless engine would wheeze to its death on one of San Francisco's famous hills.

The wind had pushed away the fog earlier than expected, bringing the city back to life. Delivery trucks honked, businesswomen strode along the sidewalk in high heels, the homeless huddled with their possessions on the sidewalk. Aloa thought of Elvis and of Keisha trying to raise her little girl under a freeway. It was a hard life and one with no easy options for escape, despite what some believed. She wondered if the Sacrificial Lamb deaths had hit the news yet. Tick, always suspicious about the government and police tracking citizens, had confiscated and shut down Aloa's phone when they rescued her from the headlands, which had turned her into a hermit on an island in the sea of technology.

An idea flickered, then disappeared. She willed it back, rewinding her thoughts.

"That's it," she said and slapped a hand on the dashboard of the van.

Doc startled.

"It was Monday, not Tuesday," she cried.

"Are you OK, Ink? You having a flashback or something?" P-Mac asked from the back seat.

She turned. "No. It was the hashtag on the Instagram. It said *tristelundi*."

"French for 'sad Monday,'" Doc translated.

"Exactly. There was a French word-a-day calendar on her desk. The Instagram shot of Kyle in his pajamas must have been taken on a Monday, not Tuesday when Corrine died. Either the roomie forgot she'd posted it the day after they'd watched the show or I was right and Kyle paid her to give him an alibi, but she screwed up."

"Release the hounds," Tick cried. "We've got him now."

P-Mac gave a loud bay from the back seat.

"Ah hell," Doc said.

"You don't like my hound-dog impersonation?" P-Mac asked.

"No, it's Tall Boy, and it looks like he's got some news," Doc said. He swerved the van toward the sidewalk where a young guy with corn-rows and baggy pants gave a quick chin lift to the vehicle.

"Uh-oh," Tick said.

The kid leaned in the window. "Narc in the park," he said, his gaze twitching up and down the street.

"What time?" Tick demanded.

"'Bout an hour ago. Unmarked. Across the street from where you're staying." Tall Boy looked at P-Mac. "You got what you promised?"

P-Mac rooted around in the cargo compartment of the van and reached past Doc out the window. "Here you go. Just like we said." He handed Tall Boy a thick paperback with a black cover. *The Pragmatic Programmer: From Journeyman to Master* read the title.

"Solid," said Tall Boy. He took the book and loped away.

"Who was that?" Aloa asked.

"Brilliant kid. We're trying to get him into Stanford," Doc said.

Tick took off his cap and slapped it against his thigh. "How in the hell did the cops find us?" he said.

"It doesn't matter," P-Mac said. "What matters is that we beat feet out of here." He tapped Doc on the shoulder. "Hit it," he said.

Doc stomped on the accelerator. The van jerked forward and died.

"Damn," Tick said. "Where'd you go? Miss Daisy's Driving School?"

"Shut up, old man. I got this," Doc said. He pumped the gas and turned the key. The engine coughed and died. Horns honked.

"Come on, baby," Doc urged the van.

"You're going to flood it," P-Mac called as the engine sputtered and died once more.

Doc shot him a look and tried another time: a cough, a wheeze, and, with an almost-human groan, the engine caught.

"Miss Daisy, huh?" Doc said and pulled away in a burst of speed, swerving the van around the next corner and racing down an alley so narrow it felt like they were being shot through a gun barrel. Aloa watched concrete walls flash by with what seemed like millimeters to spare.

"I told you not to take that call," Tick was shouting from the back seat.

"And leave our girl here twitching on a cliff? No sir," Doc said over the van's engine.

"He's right, Tick," P-Mac said. "We had to do it."

"Watch out," shouted P-Mac as a guy in sweatpants and a stained T-shirt started to step from a doorway into the alley.

Doc hit the horn and the man leaped backward.

Aloa saw his face as they passed the doorway. His eyes were wide and his mouth open in an *O*.

The van went about twenty more feet before it bounced onto a side street and Aloa heaved a sigh of relief that the van and everyone around it had survived intact.

"What now?" Doc asked.

"We get the kid and head for Mexico. Like we were going to do before," Tick said.

"Bad plan," Aloa said.

"Why?" Tick demanded.

"Because a) you'll never make it across the border and b) if they catch you, we'll all go to prison."

"When freedom is in jeopardy, prison is a palace," P-Mac said. "Mahatma Gandhi."

"Call it whatever you want, I still don't want to go there," Aloa said.

"We'll drop you off. We'll say we never saw you," Doc said.

"Too late," Aloa said. "I have an idea."

Doc piloted the van south of the city and stopped in front of a gray warehouse.

"This isn't a car rental place," Aloa protested.

"Better," Doc said. He eased himself from the van with a cracking of knee joints and approached a large metal rolling door. Aloa watched him push a button and talk into what looked like some kind of intercom, resulting in the door rolling upward. Doc hoisted himself back into the van and drove forward.

Inside the warehouse, a half dozen workmen in blue jumpsuits swarmed over an array of cars: a black Mercedes, some SUVs, a couple of Porsches, a green Prius.

What was a Prius doing here?

"Tell me this isn't a chop shop," Aloa said.

"All right," Doc said, "this isn't a chop shop."

He opened the door.

"Omigod," Aloa said and followed as the Brain Farm let themselves out of the van.

"Porky wants you guys to sit over there," said Doc, pointing to an old bench car seat set in a corner of the warehouse, before disappearing into the bowels of the shop.

Pneumatic drills burped, sanders hissed, tools clanged.

Aloa opened her mouth.

"Don't ask," Tick said.

A few minutes later, a shiny black Escalade rolled forward through the center of the warehouse with Doc at the wheel.

"Get in," he said.

Aloa opened the passenger door, her nostrils filling with the scent of leather and new car. "If this is stolen . . . ," she warned.

"What do you take me for, a rookie?" Doc said in a tone that let her know his feelings were hurt. "This is Porky's car. I helped his kid get into UC Berkeley. He's gonna give the van a new paint job, take out a few dents, and maybe get her a new license plate. We'll pick her up in a couple of days. Meanwhile, if there's a be-on-the-lookout for the van, we're safe."

"Sorry, Doc," Aloa said and meant it.

The door rolled open and they pulled away.

Hamlin looked terrible. His hair was wild and unwashed. His beard had gone past hip and moved into bum territory.

"What's she doing here?" he demanded when Aloa and the Brain Farm walked in the door of an elegant house in Pacific Heights, one of the richest neighborhoods in the city.

"Saving your butt," P-Mac said.

"Who lives here?" Aloa asked, surveying the two-story foyer and the curved staircase. To the right was an impressive library. To the left was a huge living room.

"An old girlfriend," Doc said. "Met her back in the day."

"Is she here?" Aloa asked.

"In Europe at the moment," Doc said.

Aloa was pretty sure that was a Jackson Pollock on the wall.

They went down a hallway into the kitchen, Hamlin eyeing her suspiciously. Doc rummaged around and came out with a bottle of red wine and five glasses.

"No thanks," Aloa said.

They sat down at a glass table in a gorgeous breakfast nook and Aloa went over the plan she'd devised.

Doc listened and then dialed.

"May I speak to Mr. Kyle Williams?" he said. "Yes, this is Detective, um, Jack Coltrane."

"Really?" Aloa mouthed.

Doc shrugged.

She hoped Kyle didn't know jazz.

"Yes," Doc said. "I'm with the Marin County Sheriff's Department and I'm afraid I may have some bad news." He paused. "It's regarding a woman. Her name was Aloa Snow." Doc gave Aloa's date of birth. "Do you know her?" He paused. "I'm sorry, but I'm afraid her body was found early this afternoon. Yes, um, it appears to be a suicide but we need to check all possibilities." He listened.

"What's he saying?" Tick whispered.

Doc held up a hand to quiet him. "Yes, it is upsetting, but if we can just have a few minutes of your time," Doc continued. He rustled an old *New York Times* that was on the table. "According to my notes here, Mr. Williams, a witness saw the victim leave an Uber vehicle before she jumped. We traced the fare to your account and the driver gave us the address for the pickup."

He raised an eyebrow at Aloa and she gave him the OK signal. Arjun, the Uber driver, had told them where he'd picked up Aloa but she was gambling that Kyle wouldn't know it would take the cops longer than a few hours to get the same information from the ride-share service.

Doc listened. "Yes. Uh-huh," he said. "Would you mind telling me about Ms. Snow's state of mind when she left the address?"

Aloa wished she could hear the responses on speaker, but she was afraid background noises might alert Kyle that it wasn't actually a detective who was calling.

"Uh-huh. Uh-huh," Doc said.

Hamlin shook his head, got up, and left.

"There was a note," Doc said, "but I'm afraid I can't reveal its contents." Another few moments of listening. "Yes, it appears it was written in her hand."

Aloa scribbled something on a piece of the newspaper and shoved it toward Doc.

He read the scrawled sentence and raised an eyebrow at her again. "Of course, her previous mental health issues add to the idea of suicide," he said.

Aloa nodded. *Good.*

Then: "Did she say anything about a head injury, about being hit by a small pickup truck?"

Aloa made a frantic cutting motion across her throat. She didn't want to spook Kyle.

"It's pretty much a dead end," Doc amended hastily. "Nobody got a plate number and nobody saw the driver, and of course, now that Ms. Snow is dead . . ." Doc let his voice trail off and made the OK sign at Aloa.

"Well, thank you, Mr. Williams. You've been very helpful. Sure sounds like a suicide," Doc said. "You have a nice day now." He clicked off the phone.

"Have a nice day?" Aloa said.

"Too much?"

"A little," Aloa said. "What did he say?"

Doc lifted his wineglass and Tick splashed in more red. "He was real nervous at first."

I'll bet, Aloa thought.

"He kept saying he didn't know what was wrong with you, but that you seemed out of it and were asking crazy questions. He was a little too insistent, if you know what I mean. Like he needed to convince me," Doc said. "He told me he thought you were going home, but that you must have asked the driver to take you to the headlands instead."

"That's not what Arjun said," Tick said. "He told me the fare was to the headlands. You want me to call him? I got his number."

"I believe you," Aloa said.

"He couldn't get off the phone fast enough," Doc said. "I think he's guilty."

"So do I," Aloa said, anger growing at how he'd almost caused her death—one that would have cemented the idea that she was damaged goods for the journalists who would read her obituary.

They were silent for a long moment.

"What's next, Ink?" Tick asked.

"We let him relax, get comfortable," Aloa said, "then we'll make our move."

Aloa wandered through the mansion, its rooms decorated in so many shades of white she couldn't imagine there were names for all of them. Outside, night had fallen. She folded her arms across her stomach. She wanted to be alone.

P-Mac had made a pot of spaghetti and, although she wasn't hungry, she managed to down a small bowl of it. Afterward, she'd used the owner's computer and password to go online. There, she'd found a story in the local section of the *Chronicle* about the discovery of the bodies of four homeless people. According to the article, police were mum about the investigation but interviews with people at the Jungle revealed detectives had been asking about drug use or sales by each of the victims. When the bodies' connections to the Church of the Sacrificial Lamb were exposed, Aloa knew, the story would jump to page one. It was one of the sad truths about the nation that while the murder of some pretty white girl usually landed on page one, the death of a person without a home or money merited only a few inches in the back of the paper. Unless it turned lurid, which this one would.

She hoped Keisha and her daughter would be OK and remembered what Quinn had said about her visits to the Jungle being so dangerous.

The only danger was to those who actually had to live there.

She stared out the windows on to a stone fountain and wondered if Quinn was trying to get hold of her. She was walking a little too close to the legal edge by being with Hamlin and the Brain Farm, although she consoled herself with the idea that no arrest warrants had been issued. Yet. Besides, she wasn't sure Quinn would believe her if she told him her suspicions about Kyle. Their last conversation hadn't exactly been complimentary—or conducive to sharing.

She moved through the living room, examining a large bowl of oversize glass cherries, a painting of a woman on a horse, a pillow embroidered with the word "Love."

She thought of Michael and their years together. His protectiveness. Their almost desperate sex on the couch. His abrupt disappearance from her life. She wondered what he would think if she told him about the baby they'd conceived so long ago. The one who had lived in her womb for four months, then disappeared in a wash of tissue and blood. The doctor at the clinic had called it a miscarriage, but Aloa thought that was too simple a name for something so devastating, something that also tore out a piece of her heart. One of these days, she would have to tell him. She shoved the thought from her head, although she knew it would resurface as it did sometimes when she saw a mother with her child or a pregnant woman. It wasn't a constant grief. Just one that rose up and surprised her because of how much it hurt.

On she went, moving through the foyer and into the library where rows of books filled floor-to-ceiling white shelves. Soft lighting fell from the ceiling and flames danced in the gas fireplace. She could live in this room.

She perused the shelves: classics, bestsellers, books on international art and poetry. She was reaching for a book of poems by a local writer when she heard a hiccup. She turned and saw a shadowed lounge chair facing the window. A half-empty bottle of expensive cognac sat on a table next to it.

"Who's there?" she asked.

A figure leaned forward, lamplight revealing Hamlin's face. His eyelids were at half-mast and the corners of his mouth dragged down. He lifted a tumbler filled with golden liquid in salute.

"And there she is, Lois Lane," Hamlin said. "The savior of the world."

He took a slug of cognac and flung himself back in his chair. "Who are you going to accuse next?"

"Excuse me?" Aloa said, stepping toward him.

"Well, first you said it was a drug dealer who killed Corrine and now you think it's that neurotic twerp Kyle who stabbed her? Corrine said he threw up when she killed a spider in front of him."

Was that true?

"So now I figure I'm pretty much screwed," Hamlin continued and splashed more cognac into his glass.

"You know, if you told the cops about your son, you'd be cleared."

"No," he said with a finality that let Aloa know now was not the time to push the idea.

"Did Corrine talk to you about Kyle?" Aloa asked instead.

"She didn't like him, that's for sure."

"Why did she let him stay?"

"Her husband. He was quite the despot."

Aloa moved closer, settling herself on a footstool across from him. "Tell me more."

Hamlin swirled the tumbler and took an exaggerated sniff of the cognac before gulping half of it down and beginning to speak.

"He liked to be looked up to. Had a savior complex, I think. It sure as hell was that way with Corrine."

Hamlin stared into his glass as if the story could be found there. Aloa waited.

"About fourteen years ago, Corr was caught inside a bank during a robbery. Three guys stormed in, ordered everybody on the floor, then, for some reason, they shot one of the tellers. It was a big story back East but not much about it here. The teller had a nine-month-old baby. Her husband lost a leg in Iraq."

Hamlin's eyes shined in the low light.

"And?" Aloa prompted.

"And Christian came in after it was over, wearing a suit and flashing his badge. He was supposed to interview all the customers. You know, FBI and all that."

Hamlin took another sip of his drink.

"Anyway, Corr had lost it when the gun went off. She'd pissed herself and was crying and pretty shaken up. The other agents just ignored her, but Christian went out and got her a pair of sweatpants from his car, then he drove her home and made her soup or something and that was it. They got married six months later."

Hamlin fell silent.

"I'm not sure how that makes her husband a despot."

Hamlin sighed. "Because that little bit of shame was always in the background of their marriage. It was like he never quite let her forget she was weak and that he'd saved her. And she had just enough self-hatred to believe him."

Hamlin threw back the rest of his drink.

"Then, they have the accident and she's the one driving."

"And the guilt ate her up," Aloa said.

"It hollowed her out," Hamlin said. "She was pretty messed up when I met her, but so beautiful, you know. Like this flower in the desert that's just trying to survive. I think I helped her. A little."

"But you weren't in love with her?"

He shook his head. "Too selfish, I guess."

He poured another finger of cognac and tilted the bottle in her direction. She declined.

"Did she say anything about Kyle?"

Hamlin swirled the liquid in his glass. "He was a jerk who seemed to think he was in competition with her for Christian's affection, but she couldn't get rid of him. Like I said, Christian needed to be adored."

"And you don't think Kyle would kill her? Even if, for instance, she tried to fire him?"

"Maybe if he got angry enough, but I don't think so. He'd just go behind her back like some junior high queen bee."

Which left Hamlin as the prime suspect. Did he realize that?

He looked at her through bleary eyes. "So who's your next suspect, Ms. Pulitzer Prize? Mrs. Peacock with a rope? Colonel Mustard with a revolver? Oh, I know, it's Professor Hamlin with a knife. A big, fat knife."

He lolled his head against the back of the chair. "I'm so screwed. What made me think I should trust you and why did I go along with my dad's stupid plan? If I didn't look guilty before, I sure do now."

It took Aloa a moment to connect the moniker "dad" with Tick. "Why *did* you go?"

Hamlin looked toward the ceiling and ran a hand over his scruffy beard. "He showed me the letters he'd written that my mother sent back without me knowing. Turns out, he did love me." He threw back the rest of the cognac. A tear rolled down his cheek. "That's the hell of it all, now isn't it?"

At 1:00 a.m., Aloa gave up on sleep. Each time she closed her eyes, a dizzying image rose of the sea crashing onto a fringe of rocks far below her feet. She threw off the covers, wrapped herself in a white robe embroidered with the name Whilshire House (who embroidered their house's name on robes?) and padded downstairs. She poured herself a glass of water from a pitcher in the refrigerator and headed for the library. Without her motorcycle and cello as insomnia cures, words would have to substitute.

She flipped on the lights in the library and walked the shelves, trailing a finger along the titles. Georgia O'Keeffe. Ansel Adams. Works by playwrights from England to the United States, from Colombia to Japan. Her finger stopped.

Aoi No Ue. Wasn't that the book she'd slid back into its spot at Christian Davenport's house?

Pulling the slim volume from the shelf, she settled onto a leather couch, wrapped herself in a throw, and read.

Lady Aoi was the wife of Hikaru Genji, the emperor's second son. He'd married Lady Aoi when he was twelve and she was sixteen. The difference in ages bothered her, and it stung even more when her husband began to take lovers as she grew older. When the play opens, Lady Aoi is deathly ill and believed to be possessed by a spirit—the jealousy of one of her husband's mistresses, a woman named Lady Rokujō.

Lady Rokujō had lost favor with Lady Aoi's husband and also lost face when her carriage was shoved aside on the road to make room for Lady Aoi's coach. She wanted revenge.

Priests were called, and in a ferocious fight, Lady Rokujō's spirit was finally subdued and Lady Aoi survived.

Aloa closed the book and looked out the window to a pool of light that puddled on the asphalt from a nearby streetlamp. Was there a reason this book about jealousy and revenge—one that hinted at the very thing she believed of Kyle—had been sticking out from Christian Davenport's bookcase?

She thought of the cases she'd covered. A preschool teacher who'd murdered her husband's mistress with a machete blow to the head, a restaurant owner who'd rigged his partner's car with C-4 after their business went bankrupt. The playwright was correct. Jealousy was a powerful spirit, one that could turn even an ordinary, mild-mannered person into an angry beast.

And while Kyle Williams might be mild-mannered, what he had endured as a boy made him no ordinary man.

DAY 11

Bright winter sunlight greeted Aloa as she came down the stairs at 8:00 a.m. She wore yesterday's clothes, although she'd rinsed out her underwear and dried it overnight over the shower door. At some point, she would either have to go home or buy some new clothes. She thought of her ruined leather jacket and felt the tiniest arrow of mourning once again.

"Coffee?" she said as she came into the kitchen. Her head had cleared, but her body felt like she'd been on the losing end of a roller derby game.

P-Mac cocked his head toward the coffee maker and Aloa poured herself a mug, swallowing two ibuprofen she'd retrieved from her daypack. The coffee tasted like a cross between river mud and radiator fluid. She grimaced and sat down. What she wouldn't give for her French press and a bag of good beans right now.

"When do we do the deed?" P-Mac asked.

They'd come up with a plan last night after dinner.

"At ten," Aloa said. "That's when the relief nurse comes. I saw it on the calendar. She comes in four times a week for a couple of hours so Kyle can run errands." The whiteboard in Davenport's bedroom was graffitied with appointments—a nutritionist, a masseuse, doctors, and the therapist—along with notes for shopping, extra help, pharmacy orders, outings, and equipment maintenance.

"So we tail him and see if we can get a look at his truck while you talk to Davenport?" Tick said.

"Exactly. See if there's evidence he hit me—dents, blood—and I'll find out whether Corrine was planning to fire Kyle that night," Aloa said. "With any luck we'll have both a motive and proof of the hit-and-run by this afternoon." She glanced around the kitchen. "By the way, Tick, where's your son?"

"Sleeping off a bottle of cognac," Tick answered.

"When I talked to him last night, he told me you'd kept all the letters you wrote to him," Aloa said.

"So sue me. I'm a hoarder," Tick grumped, although both he and Aloa knew it wasn't true.

"Will you get to see your grandson?" she asked. Hamlin had told Tick about the boy after he'd read Tick's letters.

"I've seen a picture of him," Tick said. "Burns showed me. Good-looking kid. Maybe someday I'll meet him." He coughed, swiped at his eyes, and stood. "Damned wind is kicking up my allergies."

"He's allergic to human feelings," P-Mac said.

"Or maybe I'm allergic to windbags." Tick stomped from the room.

Aloa watched his hunched shoulders and thin gray ponytail as he left and felt a rush of affection for him.

"Let him be, fellas," she said.

At 9:30 a.m., Aloa and the Brain Farm climbed into the Escalade, pulled out of the mansion's two-car garage, which also held a Maserati and a gorgeous BMW motorcycle, and headed for the Davenports' house. Doc parked down the hill where they could see anyone who entered or exited the house. At 9:55, a tall woman in blue scrubs knocked on the door. At 10:01, Kyle came out of the house with a bundle of reusable grocery bags under his arm.

"Got him," said Doc as they watched Kyle trudge to the top of the steep street. He looked tired, like he'd aged a decade.

Murder will do that to you.

"That's my cue," Aloa said and started to get out of the car. "Give me my phone, Tick."

"The only thing I'm giving you is a big plate of no," he said.

"What if something goes wrong? What if somebody tries to mug me while I'm waiting for the bus to take me back to your place?" She hated to play the helpless woman card, but sometimes you had no choice.

Tick rubbed his nose and looked out the window. "All right, but only for emergencies. Otherwise you keep it on airplane mode. The cops already found us once."

"Will do," Aloa said, taking the phone and shoving it into the pocket of her borrowed jeans before slipping from the car. "Now go on before you lose him."

"Stealthy as she goes, boys," P-Mac said.

It took two rounds of knocking before the nurse opened the door.

She was in her midthirties with red hair and full lips.

"I'm here to see Christian Davenport," Aloa said.

"No one was on schedule," the nurse said. She had a thick Russian accent.

"It's important," Aloa said. "I know he'll want to hear this."

"Whatever you say," the woman answered and stepped aside.

Aloa found Davenport in his chair in the study, looking into the backyard, the room filled with the notes of some country-western tune.

"Christian?" Aloa said.

He wheeled the chair around and something flickered across his face. Surprise? Annoyance? Aloa couldn't read it.

"Jesus," he said. "Kyle said you committed suicide. Right after you were here."

"He might call it suicide," Aloa said, coming into the room, "but I think a better name for it is attempted murder."

Davenport piloted the chair toward her. "What the hell are you talking about?"

"May I sit?" She wanted to be eye to eye with him.

"Help yourself."

Aloa took a chair. "Remember when I was here and you had Kyle bring me tea?"

"I remember. You came in here saying you thought Hamlin wasn't the killer and making noise about that ridiculous investigation in Afghanistan, which is not part of anything by the way, and then you got ill. You said you had an accident."

"That's not why I got sick. Kyle put something called tiger's-mouth root in the tea. It comes from China and causes dizziness, nausea, and hallucinations. He sent me to the headlands, hoping I'd jump."

"Whoa. Back up there. You're not making a whole lot of sense."

"Shall I talk more slowly? What part don't you understand?"

"The part where you accuse Kyle of trying to kill you."

"How about I lay it out." Aloa leaned forward and ticked the points off on her fingers. "You ask Kyle to bring me tea. I drink it and start to hallucinate. I'm sent off to the headlands where I almost jump. I'm dizzy and nauseous, hearing voices, and I find out there's this thing called tiger's-mouth root that fits everything I experienced, right down to the taste in the tea and the smell."

"Kyle wouldn't hurt anybody."

"He's done it before. He fed weed to his business partner's kid to get revenge."

"Where are you digging up this stuff?"

"I talked to his ex-business partner."

"Why would Kyle do something like that?"

"Because whenever Kyle gets cornered, he lashes out." Aloa rested her elbows on her knees so she was close to Davenport's face. "I'm about 99 percent sure he killed your wife and I'm also pretty positive he hit me with his truck to try to get rid of me."

Guitar and violin leaked from the speakers. The notes had a sad feel.

"Let me turn down the music," Davenport said. He moved a gloved finger and the volume decreased. "You're saying Kyle killed Corrine?"

Aloa nodded.

"And then tried to kill you? Twice?"

Another nod.

Davenport considered her. "That makes no sense. What about all the evidence that points to Hamlin? The texts, the phone records that put him in the neighborhood when Corrine died, the fact he was afraid he'd lose his teaching job. I've been on the prosecution end of plenty of investigations and the case is good. He had opportunity. And motive."

"The professor was nearby but not for the reason you think. He has an alibi. A good one."

"What is it?"

"I can't tell you, but I'm sure the cops will know it soon enough. If they try to arrest Hamlin, I can pretty much guarantee he'll talk." Aloa studied Davenport: the pale skin, the dark eyes, the wasting body. "That leaves two possibilities. Kyle or you."

"How could I stab my wife, Ms. Snow?"

"Exactly. So that leaves Kyle."

"How about you spell out this nefarious plot for me?"

"First, your neighbor sees a left-handed person knock on the door. Kyle is left-handed. Plus, he's wearing blue jeans. Hamlin doesn't own a single piece of clothing that's not black. I checked."

"That's what you're relying on?"

"Details, remember?" Aloa said. "Then, your wife opens the door, which I doubt she would do if it were a stranger, which rules out the idea of robbery—or a hit man."

Davenport's eyes narrowed. "That's not even remotely funny."

"I didn't intend it to be. According to Kyle's ex-business partner, a week before Corrine died, he told your wife about Kyle giving weed to his son and she said she was going to fire Kyle. Did Corrine talk to you about that?"

"Not that I remember."

"Well, I think she did it that night. Whether she'd planned it or whether Kyle said something that pushed her over the edge, I think she fired him. I think he left and got angrier the more he thought about it. He came back and killed her—and before you ask, Kyle's so-called alibi is for the wrong day. I checked."

Aloa let the information sink in. "He sees you as a father figure, you said so yourself. And by firing him, Corrine was cutting him off from you. He would be angry. He'd feel abandoned. He spent his formative years being abused and beaten. Who knows what he's capable of?"

"But I heard Hamlin talking . . . ," Davenport began.

"That's called confirmation bias. You wanted to believe it was Hamlin."

"The psychologist said Kyle was better."

"Looks like he or she was wrong."

"And you said he fed weed to a little kid?"

"Apparently he did."

Davenport turned his chair and moved it toward the window. Outside, sunlight dappled the vegetation and made the pool dance with a thousand diamonds.

"Would you mind opening the doors?" he asked.

Aloa came over and pushed open the French doors, and Davenport piloted the chair onto the small wooden deck. The air smelled of damp soil and fresh growth. The sun made Davenport's face seem even more pale. She could see the dark shadow of his beard. What would it be like to be unable to do even the most basic things?

"I used to come out here and watch Corrine swim," Davenport said, almost as if he were speaking to himself. "She was like a dolphin or a mermaid. She had a beautiful body. So strong. So powerful. But she never believed that about herself. She thought she was weak. And me? I was the opposite. I always thought I was strong."

Aloa waited. A gray mourning dove fluttered onto the back fence.

"But, you know, fate doesn't really care what you think of yourself," Davenport continued. "Fate does what it does. It puts you in a chair or it puts you in the ground. You can try, but there's no way to fight it, or to understand it."

"I'm not sure I believe in fate," Aloa said.

"How else to explain this whole screwed-up world? How else to explain what happened to Kyle, to Corrine, to me?"

The dove sounded its sad five-note cry once, then again. The faint sound of traffic came to Aloa's ears.

"The thing is, Kyle uses herbs, Aloa. He has a guy in Chinatown. He goes there once a month for antianxiety tinctures. And the day you were hit? He was out for a lot of the afternoon. He told me he had an eye appointment. Sonia, the nurse you met, was here. He wasn't."

Aloa could see his jaw muscle twitch.

"Why didn't I see it? Why did I let it go on? All the stuff he said about her. The way she started avoiding him. She knew he hated her. It must have been the affair. Kyle heard about it and he probably shifted his feelings about his mother to Corrine. That mom of his, and I use the term 'mom' loosely, was always bringing guys home. Then she drove off with some trucker she hardly knew and left Kyle alone, prey for that kidnapper. I can see it now, how Kyle would see Corrine as betraying me, betraying the only family he had. He was angry at his mother and jealous of the man she chose over him, and when he and Corrine argued, or if she tried to fire him, the rage against his mother kicked in. Transference."

"Like the book that was pulled out the first time I came here. *Aoi No Ue*."

"A story about the power of jealousy," Davenport said. "Why didn't I see it?"

"My dad used to say life follows its own path, like water. You can't really control it."

"So he believed in fate too?"

"In a way. He believed life was the way it was, but that we shouldn't simply surrender to it. He thought if we didn't expect too much and looked for the simple beauty of just being alive, we would be happy no matter what happened."

"An interesting guy. A biology teacher, right? Sorry, I had Kyle check you out after you came here the first time."

"He was pretty incredible."

Silence fell.

"So what do we do?" Davenport said after a time. "Do we call the detectives?" He swiveled the chair toward her.

"Not quite yet."

She wondered if the Brain Farm had found what they were looking for.

"Would you mind if I poked around? Maybe I could find the stuff he used on me," she asked.

"Do you read Chinese? I doubt if anything's labeled in English."

"You're right."

"It's probably better to let the police find it, anyway. Chain of evidence and all."

The mourning dove flew off with a whistle of its wings.

"I'd like to talk to Kyle, to see his reaction," Aloa said.

"He should be back in an hour."

"I need to get one more piece of evidence before I do."

"You remind me of her, you know. Strong and smart, but full of doubts. That's why you had your problem, wasn't it?"

"I'm sorry?"

"Starving yourself. It takes strength to do that. You have to fight against every instinct. You were down to eighty-nine pounds, if I remember right."

"How about we don't discuss body size?" Aloa said. A memory needled her brain but disappeared.

"I was just saying you have incredible discipline. I like that. It's why you're good at what you do, but discipline can also be destructive."

"I didn't ask for your psychoanalysis," Aloa said.

"Sorry. You're right. I have a tendency to do that. Psychoanalyze."

"How would Kyle know about your wife's affair? Did you tell him?"

"There weren't a lot of secrets in this house. I imagine he overheard us talking and read her texts. He liked to snoop. I caught him reading my emails a few times."

"Would he have confronted Corrine about the affair?"

"I don't think so. He's more of a sniper. Hit without being seen."

An interesting analogy.

"If Corrine fired him that night, would she have told you?"

"She probably wouldn't want to upset me any more than I already was. Remember? It was the night she was going to tell the professor to leave her alone. She was basically taking a vow of chastity for me. That was pretty heavy for both of us."

"So Hamlin never showed up?"

"If I believe what you say—that Hamlin has an alibi—then I guess he didn't."

"Was anything missing from your house after that night?"

"I'm not sure what you're getting at."

"I'm wondering where Kyle got the knife. If he brought it or if it was here. If it was something you had."

"I don't keep daggers around the house, if that's what you're asking."

"So Kyle brought the knife?"

"Apparently. He also must have taken it with him, since the murder weapon wasn't found. What are you thinking, Aloa?"

"I'm thinking I need to ask him more questions."

"Excuse me." The Russian nurse appeared on the deck. "Is time for medication."

"In a minute," Davenport said. "I'll call you when I'm ready."

"*Da.*" The nurse disappeared.

"So when will you have this evidence of yours?"

"Soon, I hope."

He looked away, then back at her. "Come back tomorrow. I'll get him ready for you. Stir up his insecurities, get him off-balance, maybe bring up some of his old memories. Open up the crack so you can break him: the way we did it in the army."

"There's no need," Aloa began.

Davenport pressed his lips into a tight line. "There's every need for me to do it, Ms. Snow. If that bastard killed Corrine, I want him so tied up in knots he won't be able to get loose. I want him to confess. I want him to pay."

Aloa opened the front door of the mansion and slipped inside, following the sound of voices into the kitchen where P-Mac was hunched over a laptop on the table.

"We got him, Ink," Tick crowed when he saw her. "The little weasel can run but he ain't going to be able to hide."

"Yup. We found something. Something the guy won't be able to explain away," P-Mac said.

Aloa pulled up a chair.

Tick dropped a sealed sandwich baggie in front of her. "Whoop, there you go," he said. Inside was a jagged rectangle of something black embedded with one half of a snap fastener.

"It's a piece of your jacket. From the sleeve," P-Mac said. "We found it wedged under the rear bumper of his truck."

"While he was grocery shopping," Tick added and beamed. "Doc followed him inside and me and P-Mac crawled around under his Toyota. We're pretty sure the leather even has your blood on it."

Aloa groaned and put her head in her hands.

"I told you not to bring up the blood," said Doc.

"It's not about the blood," Aloa said. She lifted her head to look at the men. "I asked you to look for evidence, not to take it. Remember that thing I told you about chain of evidence? If it's not there, the judge will just throw everything out."

"The hell with chains," P-Mac said. "We got something better: a video. Just in case that little lizard tried to wash his truck or something."

He turned the laptop toward Aloa and started a shaky video showing the exterior of Kyle's truck, the bumper, the wedged piece of leather, and Tick lying on the ground and removing the bloodied fabric.

"I used a roach clip. No fingerprints," Tick said proudly. "So when do we make our move on the guy?"

"It better be soon," Doc said. "I saw on Nextdoor that the cops were all over Burns's house. They were hauling stuff out."

"Does Burns know that?" Aloa asked.

"I told him last night, after you went to bed," said Tick. "But I said you were hot on the trail and everything was cool."

Aloa remembered the evening's conversation with Hamlin and doubted everything was cool. "Has anybody seen him? It's almost noon."

The men looked at each other.

"I'll go check," Tick said.

Five minutes later, Tick was back in the kitchen.

"He's gone," he said.

They stood in the garage, the Escalade and the BMW motorcycle gleaming under a row of spotlights, right next to the empty space where the Maserati had been.

"I didn't even notice it was gone," Doc said.

P-Mac walked a circle around where the sports car had rested. "We were pretty hyped up, I guess."

"What am I going to tell Barbara?" Doc said. "That was her dead husband's car."

"The bigger question," Tick said, "is where do we find Burns? If the cops get to him first . . ." He let his voice trail off.

"Maybe he's headed south, like we talked about," P-Mac said.

"He wouldn't leave the kid," Tick said.

The answer bubbled up and overflowed.

"He went to get him," Doc said.

"Son of a jackrabbit," Tick said.

"Let's get moving," said P-Mac.

"Wait," Aloa said. "Do you know where the boy lives?"

Tick threw a look at the rest of the Brain Farm. "It's possible we do."

"You have to tell me," Aloa said.

The Brain Farm scratched their heads and shuffled their feet.

"Tell me," she demanded.

"Time's a'wasting, boys," P-Mac said and threw open the side door of the Escalade while Doc climbed into the driver's seat.

"Your grandson is Burns's alibi, Tick. You have to tell me where he is," Aloa said.

Doors banged closed.

"If he takes the boy, that's kidnapping," Aloa said.

"Sorry, Ink," Tick said, climbing into the passenger seat. "I have to help him. I can't betray him again."

He slammed the door and Aloa heard the locks click. The garage door rolled upward.

She pounded on the side of the car. "Wait," she called. "You're going to make things worse."

The Escalade glided backward into the street.

"Don't be stupid," she shouted. "At least tell him to come back."

The last thing she saw was Tick mouthing a single word at her.

"Sorry," he said.

Aloa wandered through the huge house, cursing the Brain Farm for their disregard for rules, and Hamlin for making it so hard to prove him innocent.

Even if Quinn trusted her—which he didn't at the moment—she had no proof that Kyle had tried to kill her beyond a jerky, amateur video of his truck. She also had no solid evidence he'd drugged her in an attempt to stop her. Plus, there was the tricky question of what she'd say if she called Quinn and he asked if she'd been in contact with Hamlin and the Brain Farm.

Her best option, as far as she could see, was to question Kyle, record the interview using a phone app the Novo tech team had showed her, and hope Kyle stumbled. Then she could present Quinn with proof.

She looked out the bedroom window to the neighborhood below. A gardener in overalls clipped a boxwood hedge in front of a huge Spanish Colonial–style home. Next door, a Range Rover pulled out from the garage of a house that looked like a grand chateau had gone missing from the French countryside and somehow landed here. She wondered about the stories inside these houses. Did the rich suffer as much as the poor or did money buffer you from pain?

Before Aloa could get too far with her thoughts, she heard the doorbell chime. For the briefest of moments, she wondered if Quinn had discovered Hamlin's hideout; it would be very hard to explain why she was here. She considered sneaking out the back door but instead retraced her steps and peeked out one side of the window. A black Porsche SUV was parked in front of the house.

What was Michael doing here?

The doorbell chimed again and she thought about not answering. But since he owned Novo and was technically her boss on this story, it was probably better to open the door. She went downstairs.

"Aloa?" he said when he saw her.

"Good. You remember my name." She didn't know why she was being so snarky to him. "I'm sorry. I mean, come in." The ibuprofen she'd taken was wearing off and a headache threatened.

Michael was dressed in jeans and a long-sleeved T-shirt. His brown hair was tousled as if he'd been on a sailboat or gone windsurfing or done one of those sports pictured on his Instagram page, which she sometimes stalked late at night but always hated herself for doing.

"I wanted to talk to Tick," Michael said. "I heard through the grapevine the police served a search warrant on Hamlin's house. It may be time for his son to turn himself in. I know a good lawyer."

"Well, I think Hamlin is going to need one," Aloa said. "He split this morning and Tick, Doc, and P-Mac went after him. They think he's going to take his son and go into hiding."

"Tick has a grandson?" Michael said.

"Why don't I make some coffee and I'll catch you up?" she said and headed for the kitchen with Michael in her wake.

Thirty minutes later, they were outside on a flagstone terrace finishing up their coffees. The sky was blue and Aloa could smell the faint scent of salt air on the breeze.

"So it was Kyle Williams who killed Corrine Davenport," Michael said.

"I'm pretty sure," she said.

"And Hamlin is kidnapping his son right this moment?"

"Probably already done it."

"What was he thinking?"

"That he didn't want to lose his son."

The words, combined with the sight of Michael, set off a sudden memory of her long-ago child—their long-ago child—but she shoved it away. Now was not the time.

"Did you try calling them?"

"I did but they aren't answering."

"Maybe I could look for the boy. If Hamlin didn't take him, you could get the alibi and Hamlin could come back."

In addition to Novo, Michael Collins was the founder and CEO of a tech company that dealt in big data. If anybody had the resources to locate Hamlin's son, it would be Michael and his team.

"That would help."

Michael inched forward as if he might stand up. Instead, he studied Aloa.

"It feels like you've been avoiding me," he said.

"Just busy," Aloa said.

He wove his fingers into a dome, resting his elbows on his thighs. Up close, Aloa could see the flecks of gold in his brown eyes.

"I know you said you didn't want to know why I left, but there was a good reason, Aloa."

"It doesn't matter."

"Yes, it does," Michael said. "It matters to me."

"I don't need to hear it."

"I'd like to tell you, though."

Aloa heard the faint cry of a seagull in the distance. It was time to face what she hadn't wanted to face. "OK," she said.

"I left because I got a lead on Michelle's killer and I had to check it out."

Michelle, Michael's teenage sister, had disappeared on a trip to the mall, her body found two months later with a scarf wrapped tightly around her neck. A few weeks after that, police had arrived at Michael's home with a search warrant, hinting Michael's father was a suspect. Afterward, Michael's father had taken a Winchester Model 70 hunting rifle and put an end to his family and to himself. Michael never knew why he'd been spared.

"I thought your dad . . ." Aloa's voice trailed off.

"I never believed it. My father wouldn't have strangled Chelle with a scarf. He would have done it with his bare hands."

"Oh, Michael."

"Yeah, right?" He unlaced his hands and sat up straight in the chair. "Anyway, I was always looking, you know. Even when I was living with you and your family. You remember Michelle had an abortion right before she died?"

Aloa nodded.

"Well, I got a lead on a guy, somebody she was seeing secretly and who left town right after she disappeared. I heard he went to New York and I went after him. I was stupid and confronted the guy. He left and I chased him. To California, and after that to India, doing odd jobs and learning how to program so I could track him. Then he OD'd in Darjeeling and I just kept wandering. Africa, Turkey, Spain. I don't know. It was like I couldn't stop moving. Then I met my partner, Vikas, in London and we started our company and, well." He lifted his hands and let them fall.

"You could have called," Aloa said.

"I know."

"Dad wasn't the same after you left." Michael had been like a son to him.

"I'm sorry."

"I don't think sorry cuts it. He had a heart attack. Because of the stress." Even as Aloa said it, she knew, and had known for some time really, that she couldn't blame Michael for her dad's death. It had just been easier to do it all these years.

Michael stood. "You're right. I'd better go."

"No. What I said wasn't fair." She stood too.

"I have to catch a plane." Michael's eyes searched hers. "Can we talk about this when I get back?"

"Yeah, sure," Aloa said, although part of her wanted him to cancel his flight, to sit on this patio and figure out why their lives had gone the way they had.

Michael turned toward the house. "I'll have my guys find Hamlin's kid. I'll give them your number."

"OK, thanks."

He looked back over his shoulder. "I'll call you," he said, then opened his mouth as if to say more but stopped. With that, he was gone.

Aloa stayed outside a few minutes longer. For all these years she'd believed Michael had left because she wasn't enough for him, that he'd fled rather than have to stay with her. Her mother hadn't helped, with her daily reminders that Aloa was too fat or wore ugly clothes or needed to "try looking like a girl for once." Her mother's criticisms had plowed the soil for the seeds of restriction, and Michael's sudden disappearance and her father's death had fertilized her need to control what was around her. It had been easy for her sickness to bloom. Now he was saying he'd been chasing his sister's killer? How did you deal with being wrong for so many years?

She gathered up their cups, went into the house, and swallowed two more ibuprofen, washing them down with a tall glass of water. Then she tapped her phone out of airplane mode.

There were two voice mails from Erik, one from Quinn, and one from an unknown caller that had come two minutes ago. She touched the last message.

"Hey, um, this is Keisha, you know, at the Jungle." The young mother's voice was almost a whisper. "You said to call you and, um, well, that guy is back. The one who was hanging around Star's place before she got offed. And, um, well, I saw him drag Elvis out of here the night before they found his body, you know, and I didn't say anything because, well, I didn't want them to start investigating or something and take Destiny away, 'cause they would. So I was wondering if you could call? The cops, I mean. The guy is wearing jeans and a black jacket and cowboy boots and I don't know if he knows we're here but he's just waiting and staring. Like he's some vampire or something. I got a little hole in my tent and I can see him. He's over by Peacock's place. It's a red tent, and I'm, um, really afraid. Please call the police. Hurry. OK?"

It took Aloa only a second to make her decision. She tapped in Quinn's cell number.

"Where the hell are you?" he answered in greeting.

"Doesn't matter," Aloa said. "You need to get backup and go to the Jungle right now."

"Are you trying to piss me off even more?"

"No, listen. The guy with the snake boots, the guy who was at the Sacrificial Lamb church? Well, he's there right now. At the Jungle."

"How do you know? Is that where you are?"

"No, but I got a call about two minutes ago from a woman who is. I helped her out a little and gave her my card. She said the snake-boots guy was watching her. He was standing near a tent that belongs to some guy named Peacock. You need to hurry."

"You're not playing with me, are you?"

"I wouldn't do that."

"So where do I find this Peacock?"

"I don't know exactly, but I know where the woman who called lives. She's in the middle of the camp. She's got a blue tent with a green beach chair out front and probably some kid toys. She has a little girl. She's about two years old." Aloa heard the squeal of Quinn's chair and guessed Quinn was already up and heading out his office door. "She said she's too afraid to come out, but the guy with the snake boots isn't far from her. Go in by the dumpster on the east side, across from that big concrete wall. Make a right turn and then go left for a while. You'll come to an old washing machine, then go right for about fifteen yards. It's near there. You don't have much time."

"Hang on," Quinn said to her. Then: "Lighthall, you come with me; Burt, you get a couple of squad cars to meet us at the Jungle. We're picking up a suspect. No lights. No sirens."

He was walking now, his voice hitching with each stride. "So where are you? Erik called and said you ran off."

"I had some things to check out."

"You better not be with Hamlin."

"I'm not."

"But you know where he is?"

"I don't." Technically that was true.

"I'll call you later," Quinn said and disconnected.

Aloa quickly redialed Keisha's number. "Come on, come on," she muttered.

No answer.

She left a message saying help was on the way and thumbed off her phone. She wished she had a way to get to the camp, to make sure Keisha and her daughter were OK.

She'd stuffed her phone in her jeans pocket and begun pacing across the huge kitchen when an idea came.

Half a minute later she was wearing her denim jacket, her pack slung over her shoulders, and standing next to the gleaming, black-and-chrome BMW R 1200 GS motorcycle in the garage.

The more than five-hundred-pound bike was a lot heavier and more powerful than the old Honda CB-350. It was like the difference between driving a Volkswagen Beetle and a race car.

She'd found the bike's key hanging in a cupboard next to three expensive helmets, one of which fit. She'd slipped on the headgear, gave a pre-apology to Barbara's late husband, and started the bike's engine, which came alive with a throaty growl. She'd pressed the garage door opener, spent a few minutes getting acquainted with the bike, and, finally, pulled out onto the street, her fingers tight on the handgrips.

The thing was a beast, almost effortlessly powerful. The engine purred and the ride was smooth. She steered it through the city toward the Jungle, sweat dampening the T-shirt under her jacket, her eyes searching for drunken men who might stagger out in front of her and her ears listening for trucks that might not stop in time. She knew the old saying that it was good to get right back in the saddle, but this wasn't just getting back into the saddle, this was riding a whole new horse.

What kept her going were thoughts of Keisha and her daughter. Both of them were in danger, even if Snake-boots didn't realize Keisha had seen him drag off Elvis. Keisha was a mother who used drugs and, if Snake-boots was wandering the Jungle looking for people to punish, she would have stood out. The cult's members were their own judge, jury, and executioner, and she guessed they would delight in making Keisha pay for the sin of endangering her child. Aloa thought of the evil way the victims had died and felt a shiver in her belly.

She made the last turn and slipped the BMW between two parked cars a block from the homeless camp. She tore off the helmet, walked a few steps, then, thinking of little Destiny in her pink jacket, began to run.

She swerved around a tattooed man pushing a baby stroller stacked with bulging garbage bags and pounded past a Muni stop. A few yards from the tent city, a barefoot young woman with long blonde hair sat against an old storefront, oblivious to the world while she slid a needle under one of her toenails.

Such a waste, Aloa thought even as she rounded the corner to find Quinn's unmarked car just pulling into a parking spot near the huge concrete wall that bordered the Jungle. The doors opened and Quinn and Lighthall stepped out. Lighthall was a big-boned woman with broad shoulders, untrusting eyes, and an attitude that, Aloa had heard, earned her the nickname Kick-Ass Kate or Kicka for short. She wore a dark pantsuit and a duty belt with a gun at her waist.

Aloa sprinted toward them.

"Hey! You," Lighthall barked. "You stop right there."

"What the hell, Snow?" Quinn said.

Aloa skidded to a halt, ignoring both the order and the question. She pointed toward the tent city. "You have to get in there," she said. "Now."

"We're waiting for backup. They're three minutes out," Quinn said.

"But you don't understand," Aloa said. "The woman? The one with the kid? She saw Elvis kidnapped. The guy with the snake boots dragged him out."

"Jesus, Snow, you might have mentioned that a little earlier," Quinn said.

Lighthall folded her arms across her ample chest. "And just who are you?"

"A journalist. I work for Novo."

The detective turned. "Really, Quinn?"

"Relax. She's all right."

"I never met a reporter that was all right," Lighthall said, but she must have known not to push Quinn further because she pressed her lips together and gave only the slightest shake of her head.

"Listen. We have to go. Now. If he knows she's a witness, he might kill her right there." Aloa pointed to the hive of fragile shelters and broken lives that was the Jungle. "He's got a knife."

Quinn frowned. "The witness saw it?"

"No, but if he used a knife to slit his victims' throats, it makes sense he's got one now."

"How about you leave the analysis to us," Lighthall said.

Quinn turned his gaze on the camp.

"There are a lot of people in there," Lighthall warned. "We should wait for patrol."

He seemed to weigh a decision. He turned to Aloa and pointed. "Her tent is over by that pillar?"

"Close to it."

"We can't risk waiting," Quinn said. "Lighthall, you go in from the south, by that old truck. Come in slowly. We don't want to spook the guy and have all hell break loose. We want to keep this as low-key as possible."

"I know what I'm doing," Lighthall said.

"I'll come in from the north. If you see him first, keep an eye on him. Maybe he won't do anything until patrol gets here." He turned to Aloa. "Description?"

"Tall, about six feet. He's wearing jeans and a black jacket and those cowboy boots. Sunken cheeks. Dark eyes. No facial hair."

"Got it," Quinn said.

"Lighthall, you radio the cars. Tell them we're going in."

Then to Aloa: "You wait here."

"But—" Aloa said.

"But nothing," Quinn said.

212

"Yeah, don't move," Lighthall said and touched a hand to her duty weapon, reminding Aloa who had the power.

Aloa watched the two detectives head out, her nerves firing, her mind remembering the little girl who loved to dig in the dirt.

She looked at her jeans and at her Timberlands, got a pair of sunglasses and the pink beanie out of her pack, and put them on. She hoped the snake-boots guy wouldn't recognize her and that she would look like that blonde girl on the street, somebody who might come into the Jungle looking for a fix.

She glanced right and left and walked toward the camp.

A dog barked. A grimy, bone-thin man in torn pants curled motionless in the gutter. Aloa prayed he was only passed out and not dead.

She squeezed past a tent spray-painted with a swastika and entered the Jungle, the warmer weather intensifying the pungent smell of garbage and feces.

Wary eyes watched and she reminded herself not to walk with long strides as she usually did, but to play the part of a slightly dope-sick user. She hunched her shoulders and dug her hands into her pockets.

"Whatcha need, baby, 'cause I got some of it right here," called a male voice. "I got it all nice and warm here in my jeans. Come on, baby."

She ignored the crude heckler and kept moving. Her destination was a slapped-together hut made out of shopping carts and tarps. The hovel would give her a view of Keisha's tent without being seen. She hunched next to it, praying its occupant was either out of commission or not home, and pulled the beanie a little lower on her head.

A few people milled around the camp, but mostly it was peaceful. A moan came from a nearby tent, followed by a hacking cough. She let her eyes travel along the meandering path through the huts and tents and saw a dark sliver of someone leaning against a concrete freeway support about five yards from the tent where Keisha and her daughter lived. She looked more closely and could see the toe of a cowboy boot. It was him.

"Come on, Quinn," she muttered under her breath, counting the seconds in her head.

Suddenly, there was movement in the tent and a loud wail.

Snake-boots stood up straighter and stepped from behind the pillar.

Ah hell.

Snake-boots approached the tent with long strides. His mouth was set; his shoulders as taut as a bowstring. He stopped in front of the nylon shelter and gave a low whistle. The same one she'd heard outside Elvis's tent.

"Go away," Keisha called.

"I got something for you," Snake-boots said and squatted, his hands resting loose on his knees.

"I don't want nothing," Keisha said.

"Oh yeah? I saw you using yesterday. I got a nice half right here. Just think how you'll feel. Come on out. I'll give it to you," Snake-boots said.

"You go away."

"Ah, come on out. You know you want it."

"I'm staying right here."

Snake-boots stood. "Listen, bitch. You can come out easy or come out hard. Your choice."

"Oh, like the way Elvis did?"

Aloa swore under her breath.

What was Keisha doing?

Snake-boots seemed to rock back slightly at her words. "Hard it is," he said and squatted again, pulling a knife from his left boot and slowly drawing it down the fragile nylon. One long cut and then another.

Keisha screamed.

"Nobody cares, Keisha," Snake-boots said and drew another long cut in the tent. A muffled sob came from inside the tent.

Aloa was up and moving before she knew she was going to do it.

"You there, Keish?" she called, hunching with a hand across her stomach in what she hoped was a good imitation of a junkie.

Snake-boots turned. She could hear a dog bark and shouts at the far end of the camp.

Where was Quinn?

"I need something, K," Aloa said. "I need it bad. I'll pay you back."

"Go get help," Keisha shouted. "Call the cops."

Keep the ruse going. Give Quinn and Lighthall more time.

"Come on, K." Aloa moaned.

Snake-boots rose. "Get lost."

Aloa stopped and wrapped her arms more tightly across her stomach. "Hey, maybe you got something? I'm feeling bad," she said. "Real bad."

"I don't have nothing for scum like you." Snake-boots's eyes were hollow and dark. He held the blade out from his side. "Unless you want this," he said.

The sight of the knife and the knowledge of what it could do to a body sent a pulse of adrenaline through Aloa.

Flee, her heart warned her, but her brain told her to fight. The lives of a mother and her little daughter were at stake.

Aloa straightened and saw the question in Snake-boots's eyes.

"I wouldn't be so cocky if I were you," she said.

Snake-boots frowned. His fingers tightened on the knife handle. He glanced over his shoulder. Everything appeared normal. He turned back to Aloa. "And why is that, bitch?" he asked.

No sign of Quinn.

"Because you're about to get taken down," Aloa said.

"By you?" Snake-boots gave an ugly chuckle. "I'd like to see that." He took a step toward her.

A single scratched ski pole stuck out of a junk-filled shopping cart at her side and Aloa grabbed it. Her heart thudded in her chest.

"Really?" Snake-boots said.

"You'd better run. You don't have much time," Aloa said and raised the makeshift weapon, sending out a silent plea for Quinn to hurry.

"It won't take long to cut you," Snake-boots said and stepped toward her.

"And it won't take long for me to poke your eye out." Aloa held the pole like a spear.

He gave a hard laugh and tossed the knife from his right hand to his left and then back again. "Just try, sweetheart."

Aloa made as if to jab the pole at his head, but instead stabbed it toward his crotch, hitting him high in his inner thigh.

He jumped back and grabbed his leg, cursing.

Aloa stabbed again, but this time he grabbed hold of the pole handle before it hit him.

"Gotcha," he said and yanked the pole toward him, causing her to lurch forward. She caught her toe on a half-buried pipe and fell to her knees.

She let go and scrambled backward. He was only a few yards in front of her.

"Quinn," she yelled, boosting herself to her feet.

Snake-boots smiled and took a step toward her.

She saw a plastic milk crate settled next to a faded tent, grabbed it, and hurled it toward her assailant.

He batted it away and kept coming.

She picked up a lawn chair and threw it. Next was an empty forty-ounce malt liquor bottle, which she chucked at him. It passed by his head with only an inch to spare.

"You're making me mad," he said.

She saw a rusted bicycle wheel and threw it.

"That's it," he said and charged.

Later, Aloa would wonder how she'd picked the only weapon that could stop a knife-wielding man. Without thinking, she grabbed a heavy Mexican blanket from a plastic chair and with both hands heaved it like a fishing net.

Snake-boots raised an arm to ward off the covering, but it flopped over his head and draped across his knife hand.

Aloa backpedaled.

"Quinn," she yelled again.

Snake-boots cursed and flung off the blanket.

His lips curled into a snarl.

Suddenly, two arms were around his chest and Snake-boots was falling to the ground.

"Police," yelled Quinn, landing heavily on top of the suspect. "Drop the weapon."

Snake-boots grunted as he hit the dirt, then he heaved upward, lifting Quinn with him. He jerked onto his side and rolled, pinning Quinn beneath him.

Snake-boots, his arms still restrained by Quinn's grip, knocked his head backward, connecting with the detective's mouth. Blood erupted and Snake-boots scrambled out of Quinn's grasp. But the detective was quick. He thrust himself upward and tackled Snake-boots so the man fell backward.

Quinn was now on top of Snake-boots. "Drop the weapon," he said.

Snake-boots spit in his face.

Quinn pushed a hand against Snake-boots's chin so the suspect's neck arched painfully. The other hand grabbed Snake-boots's wrist and banged it against the ground.

"Drop the weapon," Quinn said.

"Go to hell," was Snake-boots's strangled reply.

Quinn's answer was to again lift the wrist of the hand that held the knife and slam it hard against the ground.

Once. Twice.

The knife fell.

Snake-boots roared, bucked, and freed one hand, then punched Quinn in the temple.

Quinn's head snapped sideways and Snake-boots threw Quinn onto his side.

The two men rolled, punching and clawing.

Aloa looked around for another weapon.

The men smashed through a small blue pup tent and tumbled into a blackened firepit. Ash flew into the air. Snake-boots grabbed a stone and raised it, but Quinn parried with a punch to Snake-boots's nose.

Snake-boots howled and Aloa felt herself being shoved aside.

"Outta my way," Lighthall said, plowing over the smashed tent, grabbing Snake-boots by the back of the jacket, and yanking.

Snake-boots fell backward, his eyes opening wide at the sight of the big, angry detective.

He scrambled to his feet just as Lighthall reached across to her duty belt, pulled out a metal cylinder, and gave a flick of her wrist. With a sound that was a cross between medieval chains and a shotgun being racked, the cylinder telescoped into a steel baton with a mean-looking knob at one end.

"Get down on the ground," Lighthall said.

Snake-boots froze.

Lighthall twitched the baton and Snake-boots must have seen something in her eyes.

He sat and put his hands up.

"Roll onto your stomach. Hands behind your back," she said.

Snake-boots complied as Quinn got slowly to his feet.

Lighthall grinned at Aloa. "And that's why they call it a sit-down stick."

She leaned down and cuffed Snake-boots's wrists. "You all right, Chief?" Lighthall asked. She pressed the baton lightly on Snake-boots's cheek to remind him to stay still.

Quinn touched his lip. It was already starting to swell. "I'm OK," he said, then caught sight of his bloodstained shirt and ash-crusted slacks. "Dammit," he said, "I just had these cleaned."

"How about you?" Lighthall tilted her head toward Aloa.

"Fine."

She leaned over the suspect. "And I don't care how you are."

"Let's get him up," Quinn said.

Lighthall hauled Snake-boots to his feet.

Quinn slapped the ash off his slacks and shook his head. "I thought I told you to stay at the car," he said to Aloa.

"I was afraid you might get lost. I couldn't just sit there."

A frightened voice came from inside the sliced tent. "Who's out there?"

"It's me, Aloa, the one you called. The police are here too." Aloa walked the few yards to Keisha's shelter. "You can come out. It's safe."

Aloa knelt and looked through the slices in the fabric. Keisha was huddled against the back wall of the tent with Destiny squeezed in her arms.

"I don't want cops," Keisha said. "Tell them to go away."

"It's OK, Keisha." Aloa glanced at Quinn. "Nobody's going to take Destiny."

He shook his head.

"Listen, there's a program I read about," Aloa said. "It's a new place. For moms with kids. Maybe you could get in."

"Is that true?" Keisha asked.

"I'll help with the paperwork if you want. We'll see what we can do."

Behind her came the sound of Lighthall's voice. "I'm going to get this scumbag into a car."

"Patrol's going to have to clear the camp for a few hours," Quinn answered. "We'll need to talk to people, look for evidence."

"I'll take care of it," Lighthall said.

Aloa leaned even closer to the tent. "It's OK to come out, Keisha," she said.

The young mother hugged her daughter tighter. "I don't want to."

"You're a good mom, Keisha," said Aloa. "I've seen it. But you need to get clean. This isn't a place to raise a smart girl like Destiny."

Destiny reached out with chubby fingers and touched Keisha's lips. "Mama?" she said.

"I know, baby," Keisha murmured.

"She needs a bed and a safe place to play and a school to go to," Aloa said. "She needs to have a chance."

Silence. Then: "You promise you'll help?"

Aloa could only imagine the number of promises that had been made to Keisha and then broken.

"I'll do whatever I can."

"I don't want to live this way anymore."

"I know you don't," Aloa said.

"Will you make sure she gets in a good place?"

"I'll find you a lawyer. He or she will make sure."

"Promise?"

"I'll do the best I can."

A few moments later, the tent door zipped open and Keisha and Destiny crawled out.

Aloa sat in the homicide detail office, waiting to give her statement. She'd ridden over on the big motorcycle, growing ever more appreciative of its smooth ride and excellent brakes. She wondered what it would be like to take it down Highway 1 at seventy miles an hour, maybe get something to eat at that café in Pescadero and listen to the fine guitarist.

She'd heard there was a goat farm outside town where you could get up close and personal with the animals and buy some good cheese. Add a nice ride back up the coast, a good bottle of wine, and someone to share it, and it would be an exceptional day. Except adding someone to the mix was the kind of thing that brought complications.

She looked at her hands. They were scratched and scraped, with half-moons of dirt under her fingernails. She thought of how close she'd come to dying, both on the cliff and in the camp, and considered what Michael had told her. How would her life have played out if Michael's sister hadn't found a secret lover? Or if Michael hadn't gone off to find her killer? And what if she hadn't made an assumption about why Michael had left?

It was no good going down that path. What was done was done. She picked a bit of mud from under her thumbnail and looked up.

Quinn was walking toward her. He'd changed shirts but his slacks were still streaked with mud. He looked tired. His top lip sported a grape-size lump.

"Can you hang for another hour? Lighthall is talking to your friend, Keisha, and I'm still in there with the guy we arrested, whose real name is Theodore Laske, by the way. One of us should be able to get your statement when we're finished. I could order a pizza if you want."

"I'm good."

"You could sit in my office. It's a little more comfortable."

"Nah. I like it here. Reminds me of the newsroom."

"Because of the smell or because only journalists and cops are stupid enough to work in a crappy office for low pay?"

"Both, I guess." Aloa gave a faint smile.

"You know what you did was dumb?"

She didn't say anything.

"But if you hadn't gotten there when you did, I'm not sure what would have happened. Lighthall said your friend got a long look at Laske when he dragged Elvis out of the Jungle. She'll be a good witness."

"Is that a thank-you?"

"I guess."

"Miss Manners would roll over in her grave."

He smiled, then grimaced, touching the lump on his lip. "You know, I'll be working late tonight, but what would you think about having dinner tomorrow?" He named a quiet bistro near Union Square, the kind of place with candlelight and waiters in long black aprons.

She thought of her empty bed and weighed his invitation against the trouble it might bring. Would he want some kind of commitment? Would he need more than she wanted to give?

"Can I let you know later?"

"Sure," he said and seemed to hesitate. Then: "Well, hang tight. Somebody will be with you soon."

Aloa watched him walk off and thought of his estranged wife.

She didn't need complications, she told herself.

Aloa had just swallowed two more ibuprofen to get rid of the headache that was either the product of her concussion or her tiredness when Lighthall showed up a little after 7:30 p.m. to take her statement.

The detective threw herself into her chair and gave Aloa a long stare. "So what's the deal?" she said. "You sleeping with Quinn?"

Every part of Aloa's body was beginning to ache. "Are you asking because you're jealous that you're not?" she said.

Aloa had come across officers like Lighthall. They were good people who'd just seen too much evil: young men with gunshot wounds to their bellies, wives with broken jawbones and black eyes, fifteen-year-olds dead of overdoses. These cops' defense against the darkness was to distrust everyone who didn't wear a shield.

"I don't like smart-asses," Lighthall said.

"And I don't like people who automatically assume women have to sleep with someone in order to get where they are." Aloa folded her arms across her chest. "I also don't think Quinn would like it if he knew you asked that question, so how about I pretend you didn't?"

Lighthall eyed her for a few long seconds. "Fair enough," she said finally and rocked forward in her chair. "Shall we get started?"

It was a small crack in the detective's armor, but it was a start.

"Let's get to it," Aloa said.

Over the next ninety minutes, Lighthall led Aloa methodically through her visit to the drug recovery meetinghouse, her encounters with Keisha and Elvis, the baggie of pills under Elvis's cot, and Aloa's first glimpse of Laske, a.k.a. Snake-boots.

Lighthall was good.

Aloa told the detective about the Sacrificial Lamb ceremony and how Snake-boots had chased her, along with how she'd figured out where Ruiz's body was located. She finished with her story of confronting Laske in the Jungle.

"Next time, you might not want to take a ski pole to a knife fight," Lighthall said.

"I'll remember that," Aloa said.

Lighthall tapped a finger on the business card Aloa had given her. "Is this a good number if I have more questions?"

"Yes. It's my cell."

"You need a lift home?"

Lighthall was offering her a ride. Apparently, she'd passed the test.

"I'm fine," Aloa said, although she didn't mention that, technically, she would be leaving on a stolen vehicle.

Aloa stood, her headache diminished enough to be tolerable. "What happened to Keisha?"

"Patrol found a little H on her so we booked her for possession—mostly so we could keep track of her," Lighthall said. "We're checking her into a locked detox facility, which she said she was OK with. The little girl's in emergency foster care. But we found an aunt in Sacramento and it looks like she might be able to take the kid for a while."

Aloa hoped things would turn out well for the little family, but knew addiction was never simple.

"You know the way out?" Lighthall asked.

"I do. See you around?"

"I'm still not a fan of reporters," Lighthall said.

"Gotcha." Aloa smiled.

She pulled on her jacket, hoisted her pack onto her shoulders, and walked out of the building into the night air. A patchwork of lights shined from the city's skyscrapers. A jetliner passed overhead. She thought she would drop off the bike, then walk home and make herself a simple dinner. It would do her good to get fresh air, to let her mind unwind before tomorrow.

She climbed astride the motorcycle, fired up the engine, and pulled into traffic. It might take a little time, but she thought she'd probably get another bike one of these days, although the BMW had spoiled her and she didn't know if could afford a more modern bike. The little Honda had been a workhorse and had opened a whole new world for her, but its brakes weren't that great and it really wasn't the kind of bike you'd want to take on a long trip.

Maybe someday.

It was a little before 9:30 p.m. when she pulled up in front of the mansion, pushed the door opener, and pulled the bike into the garage. Lights snapped on automatically and after she returned the helmet, she walked around the bike inspecting it for scratches or dings. Everything looked good.

She went outside and waited for the garage door to close. The neighborhood was so quiet it almost seemed like another world. She looked up and down the street and started walking. A few yards out, a text alert chimed and she pulled out her phone.

Something's up. Can't wait. C. Davenport.

What was he doing? Texting meant he was dictating and dictating meant Kyle might be able to hear. She swore under her breath.

Be there 20 minutes. No more texting. A. Snow.

She shoved the phone into her jacket pocket and headed back for the big bike. But before she left, she ran upstairs into the house and printed out a couple of images from the Brain Farm's video of Kyle's truck.

Just in case.

Aloa worried about parking the heavy BMW on the steep street. When something weighed almost five times what you did, it wasn't like you could muscle it around or easily maneuver at a slow speed. Just to be on the safe side, she parked it at the bottom of the hill and jogged up to Christian Davenport's house. Light shined from high windows into the small front yard. She touched the phone in her jacket pocket.

Should she have alerted Quinn?

She knew his trust in her had risen a notch with the arrest of the Sacrificial Lamb suspect, but right now, both he and Lighthall were up to their necks in the investigation. It would take hours before either one could, or would, answer their phones. She would just have to persuade Davenport to wait until tomorrow to confront Kyle. And if she couldn't, she would use the recording app both to document the interview and to use it as a weapon by threatening to send it to Quinn if Kyle got physical.

If that didn't work, there was always pepper spray. She touched the small canister she had in her pocket.

She could see the blue haze of television sets shining from windows as she hurried past. A black-and-white cat wandered among parked cars. Aloa set her phone to record, knocked, and waited. She knocked again.

Kyle's face was flushed when he finally opened the door.

"Go away," he said.

So Davenport had told him she wasn't dead.

"I'm here to see Christian."

"It's not a good time."

"He asked me to come."

"I doubt it. He's having one of his attacks. His blood pressure is up and his heart is racing. I need to take care of him or things could get bad."

Aloa wondered if he was telling the truth. It had only been twenty minutes since Davenport texted.

"Let me just talk to him for a minute," Aloa said.

The intercom crackled to life. "Let her in, Kyle."

The voice was hard-edged and filled with something.

Anger? Anxiety? Or was it fear?

Aloa stepped through the door and Kyle swore. "I'm warning you. I have to redo his catheter, and if that's not the problem, then I have to check for fecal impaction. It's what causes this to happen. I don't want you in the way."

For a moment, Aloa wondered if she should turn around.

"Kyle," Davenport roared.

Kyle shoved past her and hurried to the bedroom, where Davenport lay in the huge hospital bed, only half covered with a sheet. "I may need to redo your catheter, sir." Kyle's voice had taken on a new quality, one of submission instead of arrogance.

"The hell with my catheter," Davenport said.

"You could have a stroke or a heart attack, sir."

"Good. I hope I do."

This wasn't what Aloa had expected. "Maybe I should come back."

"No. Stay right here," Davenport barked.

Was this all to throw Kyle off-balance or was it something else?

Kyle bent and was running his fingers along the clear tubing that ran from the bag to Davenport's catheter. "Urine output is within range," he muttered. "No kinks. No constrictions."

Davenport's eyes met Aloa's. His pupils were slightly dilated, his breathing ragged and shallow.

"This isn't the time," Aloa said quietly. "Let's wait until tomorrow."

"No," said Davenport. "You need to ask him now."

Kyle rose. "Ask me what?"

"Ask where you were when Corrine died," Davenport said.

What was he doing?

Confusion washed over Kyle's face. "You know where I was."

"Do I? Because Aloa here has an interesting theory."

"Sir?" Kyle said.

"Tell him," Davenport demanded.

Aloa looked at Kyle across Davenport's bed. A tremble had started in the young man's fingers.

Start from the beginning. Try to slow this down. "Let me ask you this first," Aloa said. "Would you mind telling me about what happened to Aat's son?"

"You talked to Aat?" Kyle said.

"I did."

"He's a liar." Kyle's gaze darted to the door and back. "I don't know exactly what he told you but Sam got that cookie by himself. He'd done it once before but I caught him before he ate any of it."

"Why would Aat say you did it?"

"Because the guy always needs someone to blame for his mistakes. He blamed me for our business failing but he was the one who pushed us to get out there before we were ready. Then he needed an excuse for not moving the cookies or locking them up after I told him what happened. I would never hurt a kid. I'd never do that."

"Do you know if he told Corrine what he told me? That you tried to poison Sam?"

"Did he call her or something?" Kyle said.

"He said he came here."

"That prick," Kyle said.

"Did you get into an argument with Corrine on the night she died?"

He frowned. "No."

"Did you come back here that night? After your shift?" Aloa asked.

Kyle shook his head.

"Come on, tell her the answer," Davenport said.

"I wasn't here."

"You didn't come here around ten forty-five that night?" Aloa asked.

"No." Kyle turned. "I need to get your medication, sir."

He threw open the doors to a large cabinet to reveal shelves filled with prescription bottles, tubing, gauze, syringes, and latex gloves. "Your blood pressure is way too high."

He ticked his fingers through the supplies, finding a box and pulling a sleeve of pills from it.

"Why did you hit Ms. Snow with your truck, Kyle?" Davenport demanded.

Aloa repressed a groan. *So much for slowing things down.*

"What are you talking about?" Kyle said. He punched a pill out of the foil sleeve and carefully put the packet of medication back into its box.

He was trying too hard to look calm.

"Two days ago," Aloa said. "I was riding my motorcycle downtown and you came up behind me and hit me with your truck. You took off."

"Two days ago? I was here that afternoon," Kyle said.

"I didn't say it was in the afternoon," Aloa said.

Kyle filled a glass with water from a pitcher and came back to Davenport's side. "I just assumed, I guess." His voice shook.

Aloa slid her pack from her shoulder and pulled out the photographs.

"My friends followed you to the store and spent a little time under your truck."

Kyle ignored her and held the pill up to Davenport's mouth. "Open," he said.

"They found a piece of leather from the jacket I was wearing when you hit me," Aloa said and held up the two photos. "It was wedged under the back bumper."

"Look at what she has, Kyle," Davenport ordered.

Kyle licked his lips and shook his head almost imperceptibly.

"Look," Davenport said. Louder this time.

Kyle's gray eyes twitched toward the photos and then away.

"How do I know you didn't plant that piece of leather?" he asked.

"Because there's a video."

"That doesn't prove anything."

No need to tell him he was right.

Kyle leaned over Davenport. "Please, sir. You need your pill."

Aloa decided to press. "If the police find my blood on your truck, you're in trouble. You know that. Don't you, Kyle?"

Kyle looked as if he might be sick. He set the pill down on Davenport's bare chest and took a step back from the bed.

"Admit it, Kyle. You hit her," Davenport said.

Aloa kept her voice calm. "You wanted to stop me from finding out what actually happened to Corrine."

Kyle ran two hands through his hair. "No. That's not right. I didn't . . ." He glanced pleadingly at Aloa. "OK. I hit you but I didn't mean it. Really I didn't. I wanted to see who you were talking to, but it was foggy and that guy came off the sidewalk and you hit the brakes and I tried to stop. Really I did, but I couldn't."

A memory rose of hearing the squeal of tires on pavement before she was knocked into the air.

"When I hit you, I freaked out and left. I shouldn't have done that. I didn't mean to hurt you. Please."

He paced a few steps alongside the bed, then came back. "Don't call the police. I can't go to jail."

"It's prison, not jail, Kyle." Davenport's voice was cruel. "You should know that. Jail is where they hold you until your trial. Prison is where they beat you up and rape you, and nobody will do a thing about it."

"Oh god, I'm so sorry," Kyle said to Aloa, a low moan escaping his lips.

"First you hit her, then you poisoned her," Davenport said. "That'll be a nice long sentence, a lot of time to live behind bars. Like an animal."

"Wait. What?" Kyle stopped.

What the hell was Davenport doing?

"You don't remember?" Davenport went on. "Did you forget how you put something in that tea you made for Aloa and then sent her to the headlands hoping she would jump? That's attempted murder there."

"What? I didn't put anything in her tea." Kyle looked confused. "You were the one who told me to give her the Yan Wang tea. I would never have done it." He turned to Aloa. "It's like LSD. It's for mind expansion. He likes to use it for depression, for when the pain gets bad. I wouldn't have given that to you but he told me to."

"I did not," Davenport said.

"And you were the one who called Uber," Kyle objected. "You were the one who said where to take her, not me. I thought she was going home."

"Oh, Kyle. Such a terrible liar. What else have you lied about?" Davenport said.

"Can we talk about your visits to Chinatown, Kyle?" Aloa asked, trying to save the interview. But it was as if Aloa wasn't there.

"Did you lie about your time with Robineaux too?" Davenport asked. "You said you were too afraid to escape, but maybe you weren't. Maybe you liked it with him."

"I . . . I . . . didn't," Kyle said. "I was scared."

"When he did things to you, you wanted more, didn't you, Kyle? You deserved it, didn't you? For how bad you were. You were always a burden. A weird little kid who wet the bed and played with himself. Who wants that, Kyle? What mom wouldn't run away from that?"

Was this how Davenport broke his prisoners? The cruelty was hard to watch.

"Please. Stop," Kyle said, but Davenport kept talking.

"I took you in. I gave you everything: support, love, money. And what did you do? You turned on me. You took away what I loved."

"I didn't. What?" Kyle said.

"You killed Corrine, didn't you? She fired you and you came back and stabbed her."

"No. No," Kyle cried. "I only came back because you needed the melatonin. Remember? You called and asked me to bring it. She was alive when I was here."

"No, Kyle, I don't remember asking you to come to the house," Davenport said.

"But—" Kyle began.

"You can't prove that, can you, Kyle? Everybody knows you and Corrine didn't get along. There are people who could testify to that, and then there's your friend who told Corrine how you poisoned his kid, and that she said she was going to fire you. You snapped. You lost connection with reality. All the time we thought it was Hamlin, but it was you."

Kyle backed away, shaking his head. "No!"

Things were spinning out of control.

"Kyle, let's talk about this," Aloa said.

"Come on, Kyle," Davenport said. "Mrs. Wagner across the street saw you knock on the door. You had a knife, didn't you? And you stabbed Corrine and left her to die. You were jealous because I loved her and angry because she cheated on me. You wanted me all for yourself. Didn't you, Kyle?" His eyes narrowed. "You've always been bad, haven't you, Kyle?"

A tear slid from Kyle's eye.

"We all saw it. Even Robineaux saw it. He tried to drive the devil from you, but he couldn't. It's inside you, Kyle. You can't help yourself."

Kyle buried his face in his hands. His shoulders heaved and a tremor ran through him.

"Say you killed her, Kyle," Davenport said.

Kyle shook his head.

"Say it."

It was like watching a car crash in slow motion.

"Come on, Kyle," Davenport said. His voice was meant to cut, to wound. "You know what you did. Get it off your chest. Confess. Be a man."

Kyle looked up. His chin trembled. "But I didn't kill her," he said. "You called me and told me to bring you the melatonin because you were having trouble sleeping. You said to wear dark clothes and you got mad because you said I wore the wrong thing. You said I was stupid."

"Such a liar, Kyle," Davenport said.

"Corrine was alive. When I left, she was sitting right there." Kyle pointed a shaking finger to the chair. "She was dressed up. Like she was going somewhere. She was sitting up really straight with her hands in her lap. She was in high heels and she was wearing her hair up. She had on that watch you gave her for her birthday."

Kyle's details had a ring of truth to them.

"You're all mixed up, aren't you, Kyle?" Davenport said.

"And you were wearing the remote-control glove. Why were you wearing the glove?" Kyle asked.

"Oh, Kyle." Davenport's voice changed to one of softness and understanding. "Remember when you made it for me? Remember how proud I was of you, and you said you would always take care of me and protect me? You were a warrior then, Kyle. Remember? We talked about dignity and sacrifice. Remember the little samurai brother? Remember him, Kyle?"

Kyle didn't answer.

"His two older brothers were allowed to commit *seppuku* after they tried to assassinate their lord, and the little brother stepped up afterward and killed himself just like they did? Eight years old, Kyle, and he brought honor to his family. Think of that. Think of his strength and his loyalty. He didn't bring shame to his house like you're doing now."

"But I've done everything . . ." Kyle's voice trailed off.

"Do the right thing now, Kyle. When it matters," Davenport said.

What was happening?

Kyle walked around the bed to the window. Underwater spotlights turned the pool turquoise. His shoulders slumped. Slowly, Kyle turned.

"I didn't kill her," he said.

"Don't lie, Kyle."

Perspiration dampened Davenport's face.

"You asked me to come to the house with the melatonin. You told me to wear dark clothes and you yelled at me. You told me I was stupid and that I couldn't do anything right." He swallowed. "When I opened the door the next morning and saw Corrine and started screaming, you shouted at me to come into the room and shut up. You told me to clean you up before I called the police. You didn't want to lie in your waste."

Kyle's voice got stronger and he took a step toward the bed. "I changed you and washed you and got you dressed. I straightened the room. My hands were shaking so bad, but I did it. I put everything away. I did exactly what you said. I even moved the robot. Why was it in the kitchen, Christian?"

"I was practicing and I lost control. You know I'm not good with the glove."

"You could make the robot do anything," Kyle said. "I saw you pick a book off the shelf with it. And when I left that night, Corrine was drinking the Yan Wang tea, wasn't she? I'd forgotten, but I remember now. It was the same smell, the same color as what you told me to give Ms. Snow. And when I left, Corrine told me to take care of you. Why would she say that?"

Aloa stared at Davenport.

"You're lying, Kyle," he said. "I can tell. Remember how I can read the body? Your eyes, your posture: they're screaming deception."

Slowly, Kyle shook his head. "I can prove it," he said.

"Listen to yourself. Clawing for a way out," Davenport said.

Kyle crossed the room, opened another cabinet, and pulled out a laptop.

"What are you doing?" Davenport demanded.

"Remember the camera?" Kyle tilted his head to a small device in the corner of the room. A blue light blinked from it. "I put it there so we could monitor you if Corrine or I were upstairs, but I was so freaked out when I left that night, I went to the app on my phone and watched you. I was afraid you were going to fire me. You were so mad."

"There's a video of that evening?" Aloa said.

"There is." Kyle tapped a few keys and set the laptop on the tray in front of Davenport.

Aloa stepped to the head of the bed. The time and date in one corner of the video confirmed Kyle's claim.

An image appeared of Corrine seated in the corner of the bedroom with a cup of tea in her lap. She wore the pale-peach dress and her head hung low.

"Shut that thing down," Davenport demanded from the bed.

In the video, Davenport's voice was calm. "It's time," he said.

Corrine gave a slight nod of her head.

"Drink the tea," Davenport said from the screen.

Aloa could hear the nervous rattle of china cup against saucer as Corrine lifted the tea to her lips.

"Another sip. A good one this time."

Corrine drank.

"We had such a beautiful life together, didn't we, Corrine? Everything was good until the accident, until you did this to me. All because you weren't paying attention. You drove right through that intersection and put me in this prison to suffer, to suffer every single day." He paused. "Drink up, Corrine."

Corrine took another pull from the cup.

"I don't know how you could live with yourself, but you did. Do you know how I felt watching you swim every day when I can't even brush my teeth or blow my nose? Do you know what it felt like to have you treat me like a child? To watch you mope around because you were tired?"

"Turn it off," Davenport said from the bed.

"Watch," Kyle said.

"And then what did you do, Corrine? How did you pay me back for everything I gave you? This house? Your career? You know you wouldn't have gotten that job unless I put in a good word for you."

The video captured Corrine in profile, so Aloa couldn't see the expression on her face.

"What did you do to repay me, Corrine?" Davenport said on the video.

Corrine stared at the cup in her lap.

"I was weak. I cheated on you," she said on the tape.

"But more than that," Davenport said.

Silence.

Corrine looked up. "I fell in love."

"Yes. And what did that do?" Davenport asked.

"It hurt you."

"It humiliated me."

"Yes, that too," Corrine said softly.

She swayed slightly in her chair.

"You said you would leave him," Davenport said on the tape.

"But I didn't," Corrine said. "I went and begged him to take me back."

"So you could divorce me."

"No," she said.

"I am your husband, Corrine," he said.

"And I am a low and weak woman," she said slowly.

"But what are your roots, Corrine?" Davenport asked on the tape.

"Warrior," she said.

"And that means what?"

"Honor and loyalty."

"And were you honorable and loyal?"

Corrine's voice was so low, Aloa instinctively leaned in.

"No," she said.

"How can I believe you?" Davenport said on the recording.

"That's enough," Davenport said from the bed.

Aloa could smell his sweat, his stale breath, the sour odor of illness.

"Watch," Kyle said.

"You can believe me through a truthful act," Corrine said on the tape. She set the teacup on the floor.

"And the abdomen is the center of it, yes?" Davenport said on the video. "The mouth may lie, but the abdomen holds the truth. It's the connection between the body and the energy to act, and it's the act that shows the truth."

"Yes," Corrine said.

"If the truth is in the abdomen, then what do you have to do?"

236

"I have to open it," Corrine said. "Then you will know whether I am true in my love for you."

Omigod.

"Off. Off," Davenport shouted from his bed. Perspiration ran from his forehead into his eyes. He gave a violent shake of his head.

"Remember you are strong, not weak. Do you have it?" asked Davenport's voice from the video.

Corrine stood and went over to a cupboard. Her back was to the camera. She reached for something and seemed to hold it to her chest.

"That's good," Davenport said on the video.

Corrine swayed where she stood.

"Remember to wash your cup."

"Yes."

"You know the way?"

"I do."

"Remember, you are a warrior," Davenport said on the video.

Corrine hung her head.

"Say you love me," Davenport said on the video.

She half turned toward him. "I love you."

"Now, go."

For a moment, Corrine hesitated. Then she picked up the teacup from the floor and walked from the room.

Davenport was the monster. Not Kyle.

"Traitor," Davenport cried from the bed.

Kyle picked up the laptop. His hands shook.

"I didn't believe it at first, Christian," Kyle said. "I believed your whole story about hearing Hamlin at the house. I told myself what I saw on the video was just you disciplining Corrine like you always disciplined us."

He walked over to the cabinet and put the computer away. "Who else could it have been, I thought." His voice was low. "There was no knife and there was all that blood. I ignored what I saw."

"You saw nothing," Davenport said.

"I saw the robot in the kitchen that morning and the remote-control glove on your hand." He turned.

"I was practicing," Davenport said.

"No," Kyle said and came back to Davenport's bedside. "You convinced her to kill herself, didn't you? And then you watched her die."

Davenport turned his head toward Aloa. "Are you going to believe this nutjob?"

"I think he may be telling the truth," she said.

"And what about the blood on the gripper?" Kyle asked. "That's how you got rid of the knife, wasn't it?"

"Liar," Davenport said.

Kyle went to the corner of the room and pulled the robotic device out from behind a cluster of equipment.

It was metal, shoulder height, with an iPad, a microphone, and a gripper claw that looked like it could be used to retrieve fallen items or perhaps scratch a nose or lift a blanket. It had been hidden in plain sight behind the hoist, an extra wheelchair, and a half dozen oxygen canisters. Aloa hadn't noticed it before.

Aloa moved closer. "Blood?"

"I was so shook up at the time, I didn't even stop to think what it was," Kyle said. "I cleaned it off and Christian told me to put the thing away."

"He's trying to cover up for himself," Davenport said.

Everything was falling into place. "And it was in the kitchen the morning after Corrine died?" Aloa asked Kyle.

"Near the back door."

Aloa looked at Davenport. The veins in his neck pulsed.

"He doesn't look good," she said to Kyle.

"I'll give him his pill."

"I'll be right back," Aloa said and went into the kitchen, but not before looking back to where Corrine's body had been found. There was a clear path all the way to the kitchen door.

She could hear Davenport from the bedroom. "I don't want my damn pill. Get her out of the house, you idiot!"

Ahead of Aloa was the back door. To her left was a cupboard and to the right was a glass breakfast table with two white metal chairs. She flipped on more lights and opened the cupboard. One shelf was filled with dried goods: rice, pasta, cereal, flour. The other shelf held canned goods and jugs of spring water. Below was a vacuum, a dust pan, and a few cleaning products.

She pulled out the vacuum and looked inside the cupboard. Nothing. She opened the back door to a small cement stoop. Garden lights illuminated the foliage and the granite monolith.

Wouldn't the crime scene techs have looked here?

Nonetheless, she turned on an outside light, stepped into the yard, and pulled back the ferns that grew against the side of the house. She ran her hands over the dirt. Nothing but damp soil. She frowned and went back into the house.

The homicide detective who'd taught her about contemplating a crime scene had also taught her about search grids. She started to walk the perimeter of the kitchen.

The floor was made of beautiful old hardwood, which contrasted with the modern table. She walked toward a small window, and what she saw made her stop.

An old-fashioned floor heater was set in the wood, most likely left from when the old house was remodeled.

She knelt and looked into the heater grating.

Quickly she rose and pulled open three or four drawers until she found where the silverware was kept. She grabbed a butter knife and hurried back.

It took her only a few minutes to loosen the four screws and lift the grate.

She lay on her stomach and hung her head into the space.

There, halfway underneath the workings of the old floor furnace, was a blood-covered knife.

She rocked back up onto her hands and knees, letting the pieces fall into place in her mind.

She dusted off her hands and went back to the bedroom.

Kyle was trying to convince Davenport to take the pill, but Davenport was ordering Kyle to destroy the video.

"I found it," Aloa interrupted. "The knife was in the old floor heater."

Kyle froze, and for a moment there was no sound but Davenport's shallow breaths.

"Kyle put it there," Davenport said.

Aloa took a step toward him. "I don't think so. When I came here the first time, I saw a scrape low on the wall near where Corrine died, about ankle high. I figured something had nicked it, your wheelchair or a piece of furniture. But, just now, I saw a piece of white paint on the edge of the knife. The same color as your wall. You used the robot to move the knife to make it look like a murder, like Hamlin had done it, but you must have scraped it against the wall."

She walked to his bed. "You blamed Hamlin for Corrine's suicide. That way you could kill two birds with one stone, so to speak."

"Bitch," Davenport said.

"You watched her," Kyle said. "You watched her kill herself."

"She was a coward. She cut her throat because she couldn't stand the pain. There was no honor in her death."

Kyle's face was pale. His voice trembled. "I don't know who you are," he said.

"I am a warrior," Davenport said. "And you? You're a sneaky, bedwetting little creep who turned on the one person who treated you like a son. The father you never had."

"Stop it," Aloa said.

"I gave you everything. I took you in and taught you how to be a man and look what you did. You betrayed me."

Kyle's body slumped as if the air was leaking out of him.

"But you can make it right, Kyle. You can redeem yourself. Remember Ōta Dōkan? Remember his death poem?" Davenport said.

A shudder ran through Kyle.

"Say it," Davenport said.

"Had I not known / that I was dead / already," Kyle recited slowly, "I would have mourned / my loss of life."

"Exactly, Kyle. I'm already dead. A useless lump of bones and skin." Davenport licked away a drip of perspiration that had run down to his lip. "I used to have power. I used to make men shake when they saw me coming. Now I have nothing. No job. No purpose. No authority. All I had left was talk. All I could do was make Corrine feel bad enough to do what I should have done. To punish her for rubbing it in my face with that professor of hers. To make her pay for her sin."

His eyes blazed.

"That was my last act. I'm ready to go. Put an end to all this, Kyle. Do it now. Show your honor. Show me you're a man." He coughed and seemed to struggle a bit for air. "It's so easy, Kyle. Just pick up a pillow and hold it on my face. It's right over there."

"Kyle, don't," Aloa said.

"Press on it. Hold it there. Count sixty seconds. It won't take long, Kyle. I'm already weak. Prove you love me. Prove you deserve to be my son."

Kyle shook his head slowly. "I can't."

"Yes, you can," Davenport said. "Be who I taught you to be. Be strong. Have honor."

For a moment, Kyle didn't move.

"Kill me, Kyle," Davenport urged. His voice had gone as tight as a violin string. "Kill me right now. Just pick up the pillow."

"No, Kyle," Aloa said.

"Do it," Davenport barked.

The assistant's gaze went to the floor. "I can't," he whispered.

"Do it. I order you," Davenport shouted.

Kyle looked up. "How can I honor a man who accuses me of murder?" he asked softly. "How can I believe anything you say? You were willing to send me to prison for something I didn't do."

"A warrior serves his master," Davenport said.

"No, sir. A warrior does what's right." Kyle straightened. "You don't really care about anybody, do you? We're all nothing to you. It's all just a big ego trip, isn't it?"

"Kyle," Davenport warned.

"You played us all, just like you played that guy in Afghanistan. You had your little games, your little manipulations. You told me about it. How you wore him down by saying he was nothing and that he'd brought shame to himself and his clan. Then you told him his wife had died and his children were starving because he wasn't there to tend his field or his goats, and you left the pencil on the table, didn't you?"

Davenport shook his head.

"You hated it that he wouldn't confess. You hated it because he stood up to you." Kyle's voice quivered. "You punished him. Just like you're doing to me."

"I'm not punishing you, Kyle. I'm giving you this chance because I love you."

"No, it's because I won't take the fall for you, and if I kill you, you'll get what you want. I'll go to prison. You will have punished me too."

"He's right," Aloa said.

"Oh, such a coward," Davenport mocked. "Such a frightened little boy. You'll never be the man I am."

"That's true," Kyle said.

"You're nothing, you know. You're weak, a bug under my foot. I only tolerated you because Corrine couldn't stand you, because her seeing you every day was a reminder that, because she couldn't even bother to pay attention to the road, she'd destroyed me, that she wasn't good enough to even wipe my ass." Davenport's voice rose, the edges of his words slurring slightly. "You're a sniveling little sack of nothing, a weakling who cries the minute he's challenged. Don't think I haven't seen you out there. Sitting by the pool sobbing your little eyes out because I told you the truth. That you'll never be good enough, that you failed every test you've been given. I know exactly who you are. I know . . ."

Davenport made a choking sound. His eyes widened, and he looked frantically from Kyle to Aloa. He grimaced and choked again. He opened his mouth to speak, but no words came out. A trickle of saliva ran down his chin.

"Sir?" Kyle said.

He grunted and again tried to speak. He leaned his head back. A gurgling sound came from his mouth.

"Wa hap?" Davenport grunted. "Wa hap?" His gaze darted wildly.

"What? I don't understand," Kyle said.

Davenport opened his mouth. The left side of his face drooped.

"Oh god," Kyle said.

Aloa grabbed her phone from her pocket, shut off the recording app, and dialed.

The dispatcher's voice was calm. "9-1-1, what's your emergency?"

Aloa gave the address. "There's a man here, a quadriplegic, and I think he's having a stroke."

TWO WEEKS LATER

Aloa sat in the dusky bar, listening to the noise around her. Lawyers, their ties loosened or their high heels kicked off, leaned back in their chairs and regaled each other with stories about stupid clients and petty judges. Laughter rang out.

A covey of police officers sat around a table, their street clothes identifying them as civilians and their haircuts and demeanor letting patrons know they were anything but.

Aloa waited on a barstool, a tumbler of scotch in front of her. She wore jeans and a pale sweater left over from her days in LA. Her lips were painted dark red.

The bar's door swung open, and she could see Quinn walk in. He stood in the sliver of light that leaked from the streetlamp outside and seemed to search the room. He wore black jeans and a long-sleeved white shirt. For a moment, she simply admired the way he looked, then she raised her hand.

He saw her and came over.

She sensed his gaze flicker over her and linger on her lips.

"You look good," he said. His voice was a little husky.

"Thanks," she said and glanced away.

He settled himself on the stool next to her and cleared his throat. "What are you having?" he asked.

"Glenlivet. I developed a taste for it."

He smiled and signaled the bartender he'd have the same thing she was having.

"I saw your story," he said.

Her piece on the murder of Corrine Davenport had appeared on the Novo website this morning. It told of the collector's history of interrogations and how his career had ended on an early morning four years ago, leaving him helpless and plagued by pain and infections. Longer interviews with neighbors and Wendy Pianelli from the DA's office had fleshed out the story of his anger, of Corrine Davenport's guilt over the accident, and his manipulation of his wife. She wrote about Corrine's affair, how Davenport had set up Hamlin by sending the dummy text message to make it appear as if Hamlin had been invited to come to the house that night and instead ordering Kyle to stop by so the nosy neighbor across the street could confirm the sighting of a man at the house. She also wrote about Kyle and his devotion to the man who had saved him.

A search of journal articles in the National Library of Medicine database had led her to a medical investigation into prisoner deaths in Afghanistan, including the one involving Davenport; a second, more sophisticated toxicology report showed the presence of a hallucinogen in Corrine Davenport's system. The fingerprints on the knife also matched Corrine's. The story included quotes from those whom Davenport had helped as an FBI agent, who called Davenport a brave and honorable man who'd stepped in when they'd needed him most.

"You did good," Quinn said. "I especially liked that Machiavelli quote. The one about good men bent on doing good must know how to be bad."

"Yeah, except Davenport didn't know where good ended and bad started," Aloa said.

"It's a thin edge sometimes," Quinn said.

"Do you think Davenport will go to trial?"

"I doubt it."

The bartender slid a scotch in front of Quinn and lifted his eyebrows at Aloa.

"I'm good," she told him. Then, to Quinn: "How is he?"

"Davenport?" Quinn took a sip of his drink. "He's still in that nursing home. He still can't talk. It's all gibberish."

"Will he get any better?"

"Doctors don't know. He could be like that for the rest of his life, they said."

Aloa thought of Christian Davenport using his words as a weapon.

"The trouble is, his inability to communicate makes it hard for anybody to defend him," said Quinn, "which is why he probably won't go to trial. And even if he's convicted, where would the state put him? I doubt there's a prison that could handle his needs. If you ask me, he's in as bad a prison as there is, anyway."

Aloa twirled her tumbler of scotch between the palms of her hands. "And Kyle?"

"He got out on bail. Charged with hit-and-run driving, although your friends and their shenanigans with the evidence didn't help the case much. He's got a lawyer."

"It doesn't excuse what he did, but in a way, Kyle was a victim too," Aloa said.

"Maybe, but he could have walked away. He had a choice. Giving you that tea and letting you go off, that was reckless."

"But not provable, according to the DA. There was no toxicology report. Just my word against his."

Quinn took a sip of scotch. "Why didn't you tell me about that before?"

"I don't know. I guess because I knew you'd ask me why I drank something without asking what it was." She didn't say, however, that at the moment she'd stood on the cliff's edge, falling had felt so right.

"Lesson learned?"

"I guess."

They dropped into silence. Aloa took a pull of her scotch, appreciating its smooth flavor and hint of woodsmoke.

The veil between life and death was so fragile.

Across the bar, a waitress clunked two pitchers of beer onto the cops' table. A voice rose above the hubbub. "And there he was, this scumbag burglar with a laptop under one arm and a jewelry case under the other, coming out the front door," one of the officers said. "And I asked him what he was doing, and he said he was a method actor, and that he was going to be a burglar in a play. That it was research." The men howled and slapped palms on the table.

Quinn smiled. "You know what Lighthall said?" he asked.

Aloa shook her head.

"She said you weren't so bad for a reporter."

Aloa chuckled. "She's not so bad either."

"So what's next?" he asked.

"Well, I'm finishing up the Sacrificial Lamb piece."

There'd been two other arrests in the case.

"It's going to be posted a few days from now," Aloa said. "After that, I don't know."

"That was a gutsy thing you did out there," Quinn said. "Going after a guy with a ski pole."

"Don't forget the bicycle wheel."

He smiled and swirled the scotch in his glass.

"Remember I asked you about dinner and you said you'd decide about it later?" he asked. "It's later. How about tomorrow?"

"You mean somewhere besides here?" Aloa asked as the waitress came back into the room, holding aloft a platter that trailed the scents of tortilla chips, jalapeno peppers, and processed cheese.

"Yeah. Somewhere a bit nicer than this," he said.

"With candles and waiters in long aprons?"

"If you want."

She finished her scotch.

"Are you still married?" she asked.

He cleared his throat. "Technically, yes, but we're seeing a mediator. She's going to file next month."

Aloa hesitated, then set the tumbler on the scratched bar. She dug into her jeans pocket and laid down a twenty-dollar bill.

"Let's talk when you're technically single," she said and stood.

"Is that a promise?" he asked.

She studied him. "Maybe," she said.

The next morning, Aloa awoke to the ringing of her phone. First it was the BBC, then talk shows, and after that, a couple of political bloggers wanted to interview her about the Christian Davenport case. She talked to the guy from the BBC, did a quick interview with the bloggers, and agreed to one talk show and refused the other, referring them to Dean Potter, her editor.

Finally, she climbed out of bed, pulled on a pair of faded jeans and a long-sleeved shirt, and went into the kitchen to make coffee. Sunshine poured through her grandmother's skylights, illuminating the cracked tile countertops, the old stove, the scuffed floor.

She took her new Aldo Rossi French press from the shelf, set a kettle of water on the flame, and ground the beans. When the water was hot, she poured some into the carafe to warm it and dumped it out. She added the grounds and half the hot water for thirty seconds of what was called "bloom," then poured in the rest of the water and waited for it to steep.

The scent made her content with the world, and she debated making herself a piece of toast but decided to wait. First, she would go outside and sit in the sun. The long days of fog and her brush with death on the cliffs had made her crave warmth, blue skies, and solid ground.

She shrugged into her old wool sweater. Erik was right about its general ugliness. Maybe she would use some of the money she'd earned from the Christian Davenport story to buy herself a nice sweater and a new leather jacket. She thought about Mexico. Maybe she would go to Sayulita and swim in the warm water. Maybe she would sit in a little café and drink a margarita and watch people walk by.

She pressed the grounds, poured the coffee into a mug, and let herself out the front door.

The neighborhood was quiet. Even the monstrous home next door, which was owned by a twenty-eight-year-old and sometimes thumped with trance music, was silent. The buildings and the water and the bridge glowed in the soft light that made this place different from any other city on earth. It was the slant of the sun, the reflection of the sea, and the hills that made this a town where you could imagine dreams becoming real. Although hers were still a long way off.

She thought of Elvis and of Keisha, who'd apparently detoxed successfully and been diverted to drug court, where she would work through the steps and do community service, and if she stayed clean, her arrest would be scrubbed. Destiny was still with her aunt, but there was a possibility of reunion. It would be a long, slow climb back.

Aloa lowered herself onto the top step of the Vallejo Street steps and took a sip of her coffee. A house finch called from somewhere nearby and Aloa remembered how her father had said that a bird's song was full of trills and slides and tones that a human ear couldn't actually decipher unless we recorded the song and slowed it down. But to a bird, the melodies were as clear as if their avian brethren were shouting out their names.

It was the same way with life. Unless and until we pay attention to someone closely, we will never know who they are.

Her phone rang. It was the *Washington Post*. She let it go to voice mail. She would call back in a few minutes.

"Christ on a cracker. You pulling a Jimmy Hoffa or something, Ink?" came a raspy voice.

Aloa looked over her shoulder to see the Brain Farm cresting the hill. They were dressed in a salvaged array of vests, baggy jeans, and hats.

When they got to the steps, they bent over with their hands on their knees and gasped for air.

After they'd left the mansion in search of Hamlin, the gray-hairs had apparently gone straight to Tick's grandson's school, where Tick had somehow convinced the school secretary to call the boy to the office. The boy's eyes had widened when Tick whispered he was his long-lost grandfather, but he must have inherited Tick's improvisational DNA, because he told the school his grandpa had brought his science project from home and he needed to get it from the car.

Once settled on a curb in the parking lot, Tick had apologized for not knowing the boy existed, but said it was important to find his father. The boy told them his dad had called the night before and said he was going to a friend's cabin just outside Jackson Hole, Wyoming, to write for a while. When the boy said his father had mentioned Tick in the call, the gray-hair had to clear his throat and look away for a few seconds. They didn't tell him about the murder investigation.

Afterward, the Brain Farm had lit off after Tick's son, stopping at a casino in Reno for a burger. Once inside, they were distracted not only by the cacophony of blinking lights and winners' bells, but also by a happy hour that featured two-dollar glasses of wine and a $10.99 all-you-can-eat buffet.

They'd spent twelve hours in the casino and were back on the road when Aloa reached them and told them Hamlin was in the clear.

Aloa watched the men. "I've been around," she said in answer to their question.

"Not at Justus or at your house," Tick said and lowered himself next to Aloa with a cracking of knee joints and a whalelike expulsion of breath.

"Did you try calling?"

"We did," said Doc, who pushed past Tick to sit a couple of steps below them.

"I didn't see a message," Aloa said.

"Are you crazy?" P-Mac said. He sat down behind Aloa and stretched out flat on his back on the warm concrete, his head resting on his laced hands, his legs crossed at the ankles. "That's just what the government wants us to do."

"Yeah, we're laying a little low," Doc said.

Aloa cocked her head.

"You know where it says all-you-can-eat in casinos?" P-Mac said.

"Sure," Aloa said.

"Apparently, that means only at one sitting."

"Like they don't make enough money already," Doc grumbled.

"What happened?" Aloa asked.

"A slight run-in with security," P-Mac said.

"No sense of the injustice of poverty," Doc said.

"We loaded up on prime rib at the buffet," Tick said. "Put it in a garbage bag."

"We were going to take it to the river and share it with some of the guys we met," Doc said. "A little have for the have-nots, you know."

"But the jackboots in their security uniforms showed up, so we had to create a diversion and chuck the meat," P-Mac said. "We barely got out of there."

The men shook their heads.

"So I'm guessing you didn't climb all the way up here to tell me about Reno," Aloa said.

"Nope," Tick said. "The grandkid's having a birthday party, and I thought maybe you'd like to come."

Somehow, Tick and the Brain Farm had managed the impossible by convincing Hamlin's ex-lover that a boy needed a father—and a grandfather—in his life. In fact, a whole trio of grandfathers. Tick had done it mostly with guilt, telling her how Hamlin's inability to be a good partner had been brought on, in part, by the fact he'd believed his birth father had hated him, and so he'd walled himself off. He then wondered if she would want the same thing for her child and, as punctuation to his point, handed the ex-lover *Eternal Light*, Hamlin's book of poems that focused on his feelings of abandonment and unworthiness.

The mother had grudgingly agreed to let Hamlin visit once a week, and the birthday party was the first real test of whether this relationship would work.

Hamlin had offered to pay for food and a band.

In return, she had let Hamlin invite the boy's grandfather, Tick. Tick had then invited P-Mac and Doc, and they thought Aloa should come, too, since she'd cleared the boy's father from a murder charge.

"I bought the kid a turntable and a complete set of Dylan's studio albums, 1964 to 69. Just like I did for his dad," Tick said.

"Bought a turntable?" Doc said.

"Well, found it," Tick grumped. "I paid for the records, though."

P-Mac shoved his hat over his face against the sun and Tick pushed the porkpie hat back on his head. A container ship steamed under the bridge. Below them, seagulls circled over an overflowing trash can. A long-haired man sat on the sidewalk below them, playing a guitar. The faint notes of the song "Blackbird" reached their ears.

"So are you going to come, Ink?" Tick said.

"Sure," Aloa said and took a last pull of her coffee. "When is it?"

They told her the date and each fell quiet as the sun's warmth soaked through their skins and into their bones.

"I'm glad the fog's gone," Aloa said after a time.

"It was a helluva thing," P-Mac said.

"I think I'm going to take a trip after the next story is posted," Aloa said.

"Yeah?" Doc asked. "Where to?"

"First I was thinking about Mexico, but now I think I'll rent a motorcycle, hit Highway 1, and see where it takes me."

"There's a fine bar in Stinson Beach," P-Mac said. "Met a woman there. Didn't leave her bed for three days."

"Now that's the way to live," Doc said.

The men made sounds of contentment.

Aloa had just set her empty coffee mug next to her on the step when her phone rang.

The caller ID read "Justus."

Aloa smiled and accepted the call. "Hey, what's going on?" she said.

Gully's voice sounded as if he'd just run a great distance. "The man from above, the one I make for the breakfast?"

"Yes?" Aloa said.

"He is dead. You must to come."

Aloa gave one last glance at the bay.

"I'll be right there."

ACKNOWLEDGMENTS

The first thing an author should always do is thank their readers. Otherwise, our writings would be nothing more than a really long typing exercise. So thank you, wonderful readers, for welcoming Aloa into your hearts and minds.

I also have to thank those who made this book possible. Huge thanks to Liz Pearsons at Thomas & Mercer, whose support and enthusiasm made all the difference, and to my terrific agent, Heather Jackson, who was always there when I needed her. I couldn't have done this without either one of these smart women.

Thanks to Gracie Doyle Miller, Sarah Shaw, and the entire team at Thomas & Mercer. Their talent, care, and passion for books are inspiring. Thanks also to development editor Charlotte Herscher for pushing me to make this book better and to Shasti O'Leary Soudant for creating an absolutely stunning cover. An additional thanks to my copyeditors, Sharon Turner Mulvihill and Sarah Vostok, who saved me from the typos and factual errors that keep a writer up at night.

A big round of applause goes to my fellow writers for their wise opinions and creative minds: Kathleen Founds, Karen Joy Fowler, Elizabeth McKenzie, Liza Monroy, Micah Perks, Melissa Sanders-Self, Susan Sherman, Jill Wolfson, Wallace Baine, Jessica Breheny, John Chandler, Richard Huffman, Richard Lange, and Dan White.

I also have to send big shout-outs to retired district attorney/police homicide investigator Ron Truitt for his technical advice and insight into the world of police detectives, to Geoff Drake for all things motor-cycle, to Associated Press national reporter Martha Mendoza for her inspiration and stories, and to all the journalists out there who work hard to get it right. Also, to Tom and Mary Anne Jorde, who gave me the space to write in their beautiful home in Hawaii.

Extra thanks go out to my dad, Hank, who died last year and was among my biggest fans, and to all my family (Regina, Chris, Jack, Mary, and Garren) for their love and encouragement, and to Cody Townsend and Elyse Saugstad for reminding me you should always do what you love and everything will fall into place after that.

But most of all, I have to thank my husband, Jamie, the absolute love of my life, who is not only my sidekick on every single one of my research trips, but has always believed in me.

ABOUT THE AUTHOR

Photo © 2017 Carolyn Lagattuta

Peggy Townsend is the author of *See Her Run*, the first book in the acclaimed Aloa Snow mystery series. As an award-winning journalist whose stories have appeared in newspapers around the country, she's chased a serial killer through a graveyard at midnight and panhandled with street kids. In 2005, the USC Annenberg Institute for Justice and Journalism awarded her a Racial Justice Fellowship. Peggy is a runner, a downhill skier, and a mountain biker. She currently lives on the Central Coast of California. Follow her on Twitter @peggytownsend or on Facebook at www.facebook.com/peggytownsendbooks.